# SEAHORSE

## ***Other Boson Books by Michael Aye***

*The Reaper, The Fighting Anthonys, Book 1*

*HMS SeaWolf, The Fighting Anthonys, Book 2*

*Barracuda, The Fighting Anthonys, Book 3*

THE FIGHTING ANTHONYS
BOOK FOUR

# SEAHORSE

by

Michael Aye

BOSON BOOKS
*Raleigh*

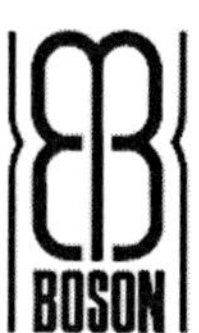

Michael Aye is a retired Naval Medical Officer. He has long been a student of early American and British Naval history. Since reading his first Kent novel, Mike has spent many hours reading the great authors of sea fiction, often while being "haze gray and underway" himself.

http://michaelaye.com

ISBN (paper): 978-0-917990-90-8
ISBN (ebook): 978-0-917990-91-5



Published by
Boson Books,
a division of C & M Online Media, Inc.
3905 Meadow Field Lane,
Raleigh, NC 27606-4470
cm@cmonline.com
http://www.bosonbooks.com

Cover art by Johannes Ewers
Graphic art by Carrie Skalla

**Author's Note**
This book is a work of fiction with a historical backdrop. I have taken liberties with historical figures, ships, and time frames to blend in with my story. Therefore, this book is not a reflection of actual historical events.

# *Dedication*

This book is dedicated to the memory of World War II hero, Master Sergeant George L. Jepson, recipient of the prestigious Silver Star Medal for "Gallantry in Action." Jepson "Jep" was First Mate aboard the P-399, *SEAHORSE,* a United States Army Air Force air sea rescue boat.

Upon reading the article, "A Thoroughbred Goes to War," featured in *Wooden Boat Magazine*, I knew the name of my next book would be *SeaHorse* and the master would be Jep Jepson. This one is for you, Master Sergeant.

## *Table of Contents*

## *Acknowledgments*

A special thanks to my friend, Joe Ragland, for the information on his ancestor, Lord Raglan. My character is based more on Joe's personality than that of Lord Raglan. I was able to gain much information for this book based on Joe's knowledge and materials. Raglan Village and Castle can still be visited today though much of the castle is in ruins.

Thanks to Carrie Skalla for allowing the continued use of her art.

In searching for a cover, the wonderful art of artist Johannes Ewers was the unanimous choice. His *Age of Sail* paintings are authentic and capture the essence of fighting ships.

As always a special thanks to my love and my life. Without her untiring devotion and editing *SeaHorse* would be nothing but a thought.

# PART I

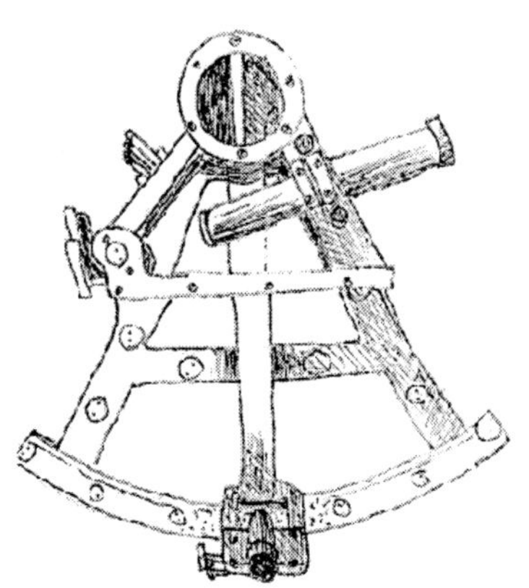

## The Forgotten Salt

I walked out of Whitehall,
Had my orders in my hand.
I saw this ragged shell,
That once had been a man.

He leaned against the building,
A timber for a leg.
He once sailed with Nelson,
Now he had to beg.

Forgotten the days of glory,
Long cast over the side.
Our country now shuns them,
Men crippled, and those who died.

I fished out a guinea,
He deserved so much more.
He said, Thank you kindly, Cap'n,
Lost me leg at Trafalgar.

Michael Aye

# *Prologue*

*"Shh... What's 'at mate?"*

*"Shut yer trap, Luke, I 'ears somthin."*

*"Awe, it's probably the master blowing 'is innards at the 'ead."*

*"Hush! I 'ears it again. It's like water lapping against the hull and loose riggings aloft."*

*"I don't see nuthin."*

*"Course you don't you bugger. The fogs to 'eavy but I 'ears it jus the same."*

*"Mr Kemp, sir."*

*"What is it, Forester?"*

*"I 'ears somthin out there sir," the seaman said, pointing into the heavy fog that filled Carlisle Bay. Even the lights from nearby Bridgetown were not visible, as the fog was so dense. "It sounds like a ship coming in, only trying to be quiet like, sir."*

*Edward Kemp was the third lieutenant aboard* HMS Prudent *of sixty-four guns. The ship had been in commission for three years now and he knew his men well. Forester was a good topman with no nonsense about him. If he was concerned enough to alert the officer of the watch, then there was something out there.*

*"Mr Richards," Kemp called to his midshipman.*

*"Aye, sir."*

*"I think the captain and first lieutenant are dining together. Would you be so kind as to relay my compliments and tell the captain we've picked up the noise of an..." Kemp thought for a moment before finishing. "...from an unidentified approaching vessel."*

*"Aye, sir," the youth replied as he hurried off to do his bidding. I didn't see any vessel, he thought, but he'd been in the Navy long enough to do as ordered without question.*

*Once sending for the captain, Kemp approached the starboard rail where Forester stood, his head cocked so he could better pick up the sounds coming from the dark. Wiping the fog from his face and beard the topman spoke, "I 'ears it regular like now, sir. No doubt it be a vessel o' some sort or tother; 'ear that," Forester spoke in a whisper. "...Voices."*

*Kemp had heard enough. Without waiting further, he called for all hands. The captain would rather him do that than jeopardize the ship.*

*"Look sir," Forester cried, alarm in his voice.*

*A red glow could be seen...growing, becoming brighter in the fog. Slowly the eerie, shadowy form began to take shape, lit up by the flames blazing aboard the approaching menace. The captain was now on deck and had witnessed the burning ship appear as a demon out of the misty fog that enshrouded the anchored ships.*

*The captain swallowed hard, suddenly nervous about the prospect of losing his ship to the approaching inferno. He turned to his first lieutenant. "Beat to quarters, Mr Duncan, and blast yonder ship to Hades where she belongs."*

*"Mr Kemp, set up the deck pumps. The fog has the ship fairly dripping but I want to be ready for every possibility."*

*"Sir." This from Forester again. "I 'ear gunfire from over at the convoy. See sir...see the flash? That be musket or pistol shots I'm thinking."*

*"I see them," Kemp replied, touching the man on the shoulder. "But I can't worry about that now. We'll check it out after we deal with this one," he said, pointing to the burning vessel.*

*Turning back toward the captain, Kemp heard Duncan say, "She's a small vessel."*

*"I could care less about her size, sir; I want the damn thing sunk," the captain retorted.*

*Kemp could now see, as the flames had increased and climbed to the vessel's mast and riggings, that it was a small ship indeed. The size of a cutter, he thought.*

*The night was suddenly shattered as* Prudent*'s guns roared out in defiance. Old the ship may be but she still spoke with authority as the ship heaved under the force of its broadside. The vessel, whatever type it had been, was nothing more now than a semi-floating wreck. The mast was by the side and sizzled as smoke and steam from its* *hot timber drifted upward. A brief gust of wind caused a torrent of sparks to fill the air then fade away into the fog.*

*Smoke from* Prudent*'s guns, mixed with that of the burning vessel, drifted across the crowded deck of the warship as men watched the last ember of the fireship succumb to the dark waters. Men coughed and rubbed their eyes, but otherwise stood silent, not fully understanding what had taken place. The fireship had had no chance.*

*"Look!" someone called out.*

*Red flares now filled the night above the anchored merchantmen that were to sail in convoy on the morrow.*

*Kemp suddenly recalled the recent conversation with Forester and quickly informed the captain of flashes of small arms fire among the merchantmen.*

*"A ruse, Lieutenant, a ruse…the fireship was nothing but a decoy, something to occupy our attention. The real target was the convoy," the captain responded.*

*"Mr Dover."*

*"Aye, Captain."*

*"Send a couple of boats with a squad of marines over to the convoy. We're probably too late to be of much help, but see what can be done."*

*"Aye, Captain."*

*BOOM!…A blinding flash and a deafening explosion filled the bay. The force of the explosion sent shockwaves across the anchorage and rocked* HMS Prudent*, throwing men against the rails and onto the deck. A few were thrown against the cannons they'd just fired. Cries of pain filled the air.*

*Lieutenant Duncan, with the help of a seaman, lifted their captain to his feet. His arm was dangling at an odd angle, obviously broken. Grimacing from the pain, the captain spoke. "A cunning soul, Mr Duncan, a cruel, devious, and cunning soul planned this. I'd not like to think what else lies in store."*

## *Chapter One*

*The closest thing to heaven is a child. The first person to ever coin that phrase must have had a child, probably a little girl,* Admiral Lord Gilbert Anthony thought as he watched his daughter not only laugh but cackle at Bart's goo-goos, funny faces, bounces and jiggles. *Damme. If I ain't laughing at him myself,* Anthony realized.

No one who knew Bart would ever picture him down on the floor playing with a baby. But it was true. This rough and weathered old salt was playing with a child, not just a child but a baby girl.

Bart had been many things to Lord Anthony over the years: trusted and loyal seaman, lifesaver, captain's cox'n, admiral's cox'n, friend, and now uncle. *Uncle Bart,* well why not. He was as close to Anthony as anybody…except Gabe…yet closer in different ways.

Watching Uncle Bart play and jostle his daughter, Anthony saw alarm quickly spread over the man's face as an unmistakable rumble came forth. When no further eruptions followed Bart smiled and said, "Sounds like a bosun's mate already, don't she?"

Anthony was beside himself with Bart's analogy and couldn't contain his laughter. Bart's big grin quickly faded and a frown suddenly took its place as Macayla Rose emitted more noises, but this time the noise was accompanied with a foul odour and substance. Bart held the child in an attempt to pass her to Anthony, who shook his head.

"Don't give her to me," he exclaimed.

"Yews her father," Bart said, his eyes watering and a green pallor spreading over his face.

"You're the one who shook her up, Uncle Bart," Anthony replied, enjoying Bart's discomfort. "You never changed a diaper?" he asked with feigned dismay.

"Yews knows I ain't, and I ain't going to start. Sides this poor child needs a woman's 'tention. Where's her mama?"

"She's out horseback riding."

"Then unless yews ready to swab decks I speck yews better find her...her nurse or somebody."

"Some uncle you turned out to be," Anthony stated as he rose from his chair.

"No worse than her daddy I'm thinking."

Anthony walked toward the long hall, leaving Bart holding Macayla still at arm's length. Looking back, he called, "Well fetch her along, Bart, let's see if we can find the nurse. Maybe she'll be able to give you instructions on how to minister to a child's needs."

"Oh, I'm sure she'd be glad to right after she teaches yew. A man ought to take care o' his own git."

***

Arm in arm Anthony walked with Lady Deborah across the flagstones in the little garden behind Deerfield manor. Her laughter had filled the air as he retold the story of Bart's ordeal when Macayla's diaper needed changing. The couple approached a small goldfish pond and sat on the little wooden bench. The sun was setting and this cast their shadows across the small pool.

Turning toward his wife, Anthony found he was still amazed at how beautiful she was. *My God,* he thought, *how blessed can a man be.* No matter how much they were together he never tired of watching her...or wanting her. She roused in him desires that were unexplainable. It was beyond sexual. He enjoyed the sound of her voice, her laughter, and her lovemaking. He enjoyed her company. She made him comfortable.

As Anthony looked back toward the big gray stone house, he realized she had made it seem like a home. Her presence had added warmth he didn't recall as a child. He quickly realized that while it was his home as a child he had few memories of it as a childhood home. He remembered fishing in the Downs off Walmer and Deal. He also remembered riding to Walmer Castle for a holiday and getting a pony one birthday. It was sad, he thought, to have so few memories attached to the family home.

Most of his memories seemed to be related to the Navy. He was a wet behind the ears midshipman who was a worldly sailor by the time he'd reached his teens. Then after one cruise his father no longer resided at Deerfield. His mother was silent when he asked about his father. She remained silent but was obviously very angry and became scornful. It hadn't been long before his sister, Becky, would write describing sudden changes in their mother's moods and personality. She related how their mother had turned to drink. The problems had increased as years went by.

Becky got married and her husband, Hugh, whose family had large holdings at Sandwich, took over things. He had hired a good overseer, employed good tenants and generally put Deerfield in good working order. *It should be his and Becky's, not mine,* Anthony thought. Something he needed to bring up later.

When he had returned home this time, Becky had tried to warn him of their mother's deterioration. However, no amount of warning could have prepared him for what he'd found. Mother, who'd always been a large woman, barely weighed ninety pounds. She called him by his father's name and cursed him for being away so much. She then surprised all by saying they would dine together that evening to celebrate his return. Anthony wasn't sure if she meant him or still had him confused with his father. Mother had rarely left her own room in the past three years. Once dressed and at the dinner table she continued to call Anthony by his father's name.

Midway through the meal she pointed toward the door, insisting it had been left open. Pigs had come in the house, and someone needed to run them out. When no one moved she began to shout and curse, "The damn pigs are now under the table."

Bart surprised everyone when he quickly rose, grabbed a broom, and made a show of running the pigs out, then slammed the door shut. This calmed Anthony's mother down and the meal was finished.

Anthony talked with the doctor, who came from Deal. The doctor explained that Anthony's mother had become demented. He related that she had lost all her mental faculties and needed to be kept sedated so as to not injure herself or discommode those around her. The doctor had told of families who could not afford the cost of medication or servants to tend to those similarly affected and they would live the rest of their lives in a place like Billingsgate. Anthony was not comfortable with the doctor's unconcerned attitude but didn't know what else to do for now. Something he'd discuss with Caleb when the opportunity next arose.

The sound of horse hooves and the creaking of the carriage wheels on the cobblestones broke Anthony's reverie. Deborah smiled and asked, "Were you thinking of some island with naked ladies?"

"Sadly no, I was thinking of mother and her madness; of how you've made this place feel like a home…oh and the thought of a naked lady did cross my mind."

"Bet it was some island girl."

"No, most definitely not."

"Who was she?"

"We'll discuss that later after dinner, after Becky and Hugh have left."

"Hummm! Are you going to try to take advantage of me tonight, sir?"

"Most assuredly, my darling."

"Tell me," Deborah asked just before they entered their home, "do you think Becky and Hugh will mind if we skip dessert?"

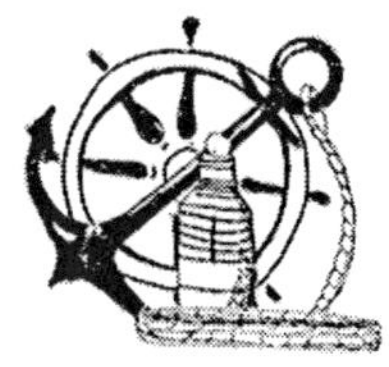

## *Chapter Two*

Gabe sat back enjoying the day. He swayed back and forth with the gentle breeze, using his father's old hammock as a swing. Lum sat in a chair next to the little rail, which surrounded the observation deck atop the house belonging to Gabe's mother. Gabe listened as Lum played the lotz and thought of his time up here with his father.

His father must have known he'd never stroll on the deck of a man o' war when he left his wife and took a mistress. That was why the observation deck had been so important. Many was the day his father, Admiral Lord James Anthony, would watch the ships in Portsmouth Harbour, Dockyard, and Spithead from this viewpoint. Spithead was probably the best-known anchorage of the British fleet. The old admiral could keep a weather eye on what the fleet was doing even if he was no longer a part of it.

Politics, his father would say, will ruin this country. It's politics that'll beach a good seaman and yet put the likes o' Lord North in power. Damn politics and politicians. Damn them all to hell, his father would say with vehemence.

*Well, I can't disagree*, Gabe thought, his mind now on the war with the Colonies. *They've buggered that up,* he thought. But if not for the war, he wouldn't be a captain and he'd not met Faith. That was the silver lining to the clouds of war. God had shown his kindness when he brought Faith into his life.

She and his mom were out shopping for a wedding dress along with Lady Deborah. When they returned, he and Gil would go to the tailor's shop for a uniform, the uniform of a British Naval captain. Gil denied it, but Gabe knew his brother had a lot to do with his rapid promotion. Not that he hadn't earned every bit of it, but Admiral Lord Gilbert Anthony had made sure Gabe's deeds were recognized, not above other officers and seaman but equally. He had not been the type of officer who took all the credit for success. No—Gil passed it around. Something Gabe wanted to do also.

"Look, Cap'n," Lum called, pointing toward the street. "Ain't that Mr Davy?"

Looking down, Gabe recognized Davy. "That's him, Lum. Go show him up."

"Aye, Cap'n," Lum replied then, headed down the steps.

It amazed Gabe how much Lum had changed over the last year or so. He still had the southern accent, so prominent in the Southern Colonies, but his speech had changed to that of a jack tar. Gone was the *naw suh* and *yas suh*.

*Lum continued as Gabe's servant more out of commitment to Faith than anything*, Gabe thought. He knew he was a free man now and as such could choose his life. Gabe would miss the man were he to leave but would never attempt to keep him against his will.

Lieutenant Davy was out of breath when he climbed the last step and walked onto the observation deck. Gabe had encouraged his officers to stop by and visit while *Merlin* was in the dockyard for refit. He visited the ship daily but while the crew was housed at the yard *Merlin's* officers had to find private lodging. While Gabe had welcomed his officers to visit, he could tell Davy's presence today was not just to socialize.

"Mr Jackson's respects, Captain. He feels we have a situation and you're needed aboard *Merlin*."

*Damn*, Gabe thought as he rose. *Can't the dockworkers do anything without my presence?*

***

"Shipworm?"

"Aye, Captain. The hull is full o' 'em. Wormy through-'n-through she be." Dover, the carpenter, was informing Gabe. "It's not uncommon for a hull to get infested with them when a ship has been in the tropics long as *Merlin's* been. Teredos loves the warm waters, they does."

Gabe had the pumps manned every morning on the cruise back to England but had thought the seams needed fixing after all the combat action *Merlin* had seen. *Not some damn worm*, he thought.

"Lucky we made it home with the bottom still in her," Dover volunteered. "Heard o' a ship one time, hull so wormy it's bottom fell out right side the dock. Woulda lost every soul aboard had they been at sea. Lost half of the crew as it was."

*Damme it he don't almost sound sorry we made it*, Gabe thought.

"Can she be repaired?" Gabe asked hopefully.

"Nay, Cap'n, old *Merlin* has done seen her day. Kindling, that's all she's good for now."

Gabe felt sick at his stomach. It was one thing to lose a ship to the elements or in battle—but to lose a ship to worms! He'd heard of shipworm but never thought it would happen to his ship. He hadn't even got his captain's uniform yet. *Would he get another ship? Would he be beached? If so for how long?* So deep in misery, it took Gabe a minute before he realized Dover had spoken again.

"What was that Dover?"

"I was just saying Cap'n that I'd demand they copper the bottom o' the next ship ye gits. That way ye ain't got to worry about worms."

*Blast you*, Gabe thought. *Any fool knew you didn't demand anything from the Admiralty. You begged for it and if enough guineas passed through enough hands you might…you just might get what you were after. Next ship…humph…next ship. I'm at the bottom of the Navy's list of captains…if I've even made it on a list yet and here's Dover saying your next ship. Hell's fire! The war would likely be over before my name comes up for a ship.*

***

"Well I guess I don't have to worry about sailing orders interfering with the wedding plans," Gabe said, trying to put a positive spin on the situation.

Lord Anthony could hear the dejection in his brother's voice as he spoke. "Aye, that's true but you'll want to be ready if a ship comes up."

Seeing the quizzical look on Gabe's face, Anthony explained, "Your record's too good to not get a ship, and with the war going on it will likely be sooner than later. Therefore, you need to keep in touch with key officers and warrants. Having a few trusted, good seamen at hand wouldn't hurt either. I'm sure they'll all be granted leave after they've been paid off. When they've spent all their prize money and back pay, have them check in with Dawkins. I know you'll keep Lum here but Alejandro, Paco, and Hawks can be put up at Deerfield. Bart and Silas are there so they can see to it they're settled in for the time being."

This took a load off Gabe's mind, as he'd been concerned about the two midshipmen and his new cox'n finding quarters. Mother's house was overcrowded with Faith, Lum, and Nanny.

"Thanks," Gabe said. "Only don't let Bart teach them too many bad habits. I don't want them completely ruined should we get back to sea."

This brought a smile to Anthony's face and with Bart's name being mentioned, he couldn't help but retell the story of Bart and Macayla's diaper. Gabe laughed until he had tears in his eyes. *Good*, Anthony thought. *The boy needs a laugh and after the wedding a ship…not too soon after but soon enough.*

The sound of a baby crying brought the men to alertness only to be relieved as Nanny rushed past them.

"Lawd, suh, that girl child of yourn sho nuff got a set of lungs. Reminds me of Missy Faith when she was jus a child. My, my where has the time done went? She's all growed up now my little child is and gonna be married. I bet dat mean old Sarah back in Beaufort would be jealous if she knowed. Well, let me hush, dat child done woke up and probably needs changing." Nanny looked directly at Lord Anthony when she said it.

Lum came to Lord Anthony's rescue seeing the worried look come across his face. "Go on with your devilment, woman. You wouldn't want it said you didn't do yo duty after Missy Faith done put confidence in you."

Nanny gave Lum a look, and then went to tend the baby but not before he gave her a slap across the rump.

"You heathen," Nanny hissed but smiled when she saw Lum turn. *It was good to be with the old coot*, she thought, knowing how much she'd missed him when they were separated.

As Nanny went to tend to Macayla, Anthony said, "Have you considered how your marriage will be received back in Georgia after the war?"

"Faith and I have discussed this at length. If we're accepted we will take over her plantation. If not we…she will sell it and settle elsewhere."

"Deborah and I have talked," Anthony said. "Unless you desire a portion of Deerfield I plan to turn it over to Becky and Hugh."

"Squire Hugh," Gabe said smiling.

"Aye, Squire Hugh."

"I have no desire for a portion of Deerfield," Gabe said, looking down at the space between his feet. "Once before Father died, I went to see Deerfield. I stopped at a tavern in Walmer, The Dolphin, and talked to the keeper. I made like I was on my way to Deal and had heard a famous admiral lived close by. The old keeper had his boy give me a tour of Deerfield. To make it look legitimate I had the boy even show me Walmer Castle. I wanted to be part of it then, to live in the big house, to be gentry and to be part of the family. When I got back to the tavern I gave the boy a few shillings and thanked the keeper for his time. As I was leaving he said, 'tell Lord Anthony old Wint said hello.' He knew who I was, that I was the bastard son. I made up my mind right then I wanted no part of Deerfield."

Trying to find words Anthony laid his hand across Gabe's shoulder and simply said, "We're brothers."

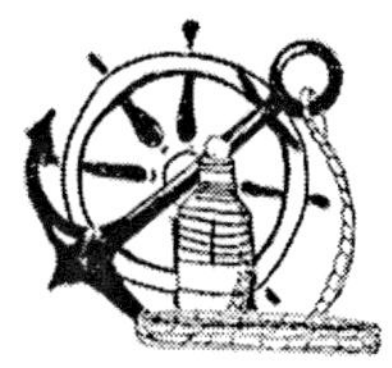

## *Chapter Three*

The skies were dark and gray as the rain poured down. To most people the general feeling would be it was here to stay.

"It will clear up by mid-afternoon," Gabe assured Faith.

"I don't know how you can be so sure," she replied, wringing her hands. "I wanted it to be a beautiful day."

"It will be," Gabe said again, trying to calm down his soon-to-be bride. "I talked to Gunnells, *Merlin's* master, and he said, 'fast as the clouds are moving this should blow over by midday'. The wedding is not till four so there is plenty of time."

Using Gunnell's name seemed to settle Faith somewhat. However, she was still as nervous as anyone Gabe had seen.

"Don't you worry none, honey, I'll have dat girl child settled down soon nuff." This from Nanny who strutted around the house. "I sho wish her mama was heah to see dat girl. Her daddy too. She's da spittin image of her mama ain't she, Lum? God rest her poor soul." Lum never had a chance to answer before Nanny left the room.

"Faith ain't the only one what got nerves," Lum said. This brought a smile from Gabe.

Gunnells's predictions were on time as usual. By noon the sky had mostly cleared with only a few remaining clouds. A coach pulled up in front of the house.

Lum, standing close to the window, looked out and informed Gabe, "Lord Anthony and Lady Deborah."

Lady Deborah and Gabe's mother, Maria, had taken over as a pair of doting stepmothers. They had teamed up and planned the entire wedding. Gabe had thought about a small wedding and a fast getaway. This was not to be. Faith would have a wedding to fit every bride's dream. Maria and Lady Deborah was firm on this.

"She's the only daughter I'm likely to have," Maria stated in a matter of fact manner. "And it's going to be done right." Knowing when to surrender Gabe let the women have their way...which they would have anyway.

When the wedding party arrived at St. Thomas a' Becket Catholic Church, a crowd had already gathered. A footman opened the coach's door and helped the ladies out. Captain Buck had been chosen to act on behalf of Faith's father and had the privilege of giving the bride away. Lord Anthony was to be Gabe's best man. Once the ladies had gone inside the church, another footman opened Lord Anthony's coach door. Stepping out Gabe was amazed at the number of coaches that were waiting in line to pull up to the entry.

Seeing Gabe fiddle with his hat, Lord Anthony couldn't help but aggravate his brother. "So now it's you with a case of nerves, is it? Well, it's not too late. The coach is there and you can haul your colors and make a clean getaway."

Gabe just glared at his brother and hissed, "Go to hell."

This brought a chuckle from Anthony. As the two made their way into the church, Gabe was surprised to see all of *Merlin's* officers, warrants, and most of her crew in attendance. So was most of *Warrior's* crew. He was further surprised to see a group of admirals. *Are they here for me, Gil, or out of respect for father*? Gabe wondered.

One of *Warrior's* lieutenants ushered Gabe to a private room. Anthony stopped and chatted with the admirals and as they turned Gabe recognized one as Dutch Moffett, former flag captain on *Warrior.*

Sitting in the private room waiting on his brother, Gabe wondered if he'd be a good husband. How would being married affect his naval career? How would Faith do with the long months, perhaps years, of separation? So many questions...no real answers. Just Faith.

The ceremony went well. All of *Merlin's* officers and midshipmen were lined up in front of the coach and formed an arch with crossed swords. This impressed Faith, and while it pleased Gabe to be so honoured, he had to duck to keep from being pierced. *Won't do to be bloodied before I've even had a honeymoon*, he thought.

The wedding reception took place at the George Inn, the only place large enough to accommodate the wedding party. Across from it was the Blue Post Inn. How many times as a midshipman had he enjoyed a wet as well as sample of some wench's charms there? *Well that was all in the past*, Gabe thought. The vicar's words were still echoing through his head: "What God has joined together, let no man put asunder."

The reception was over by midnight, which was about three hours longer than Gabe had wished it to be. Watching Faith, dancing with her, thinking of what was to be once they reached...finally reached their room and were behind closed doors caused a rush to come over Gabe.

Once when no one was close, Faith nibbled at Gabe's ear, and letting her hand slide down his front, gave a feigned look of dismay. "My aren't we a randy boy tonight?" she whispered.

"And getting more so with every minute that passes. If this thing lasts much longer we are going to slip over to the Blue Post."

"What would your mother and Lady Deborah think if we were to pull such a shenanigan?"

"Who cares?"

"I do, you lecherous heathen."

"Awh…such words from one who claims to love me, yet shows no concern for the vile, lusty humours that have consumed my very soul and desperately need to be released."

Gabe was bidding Lord Anthony farewell and reluctantly agreed to visit Deerfield after the honeymoon when he realized that Faith was not present. Seeing Gabe's look, Anthony volunteered, "Your bride made her exit after farewells to Maria and Deborah. I imagine she's waiting for you in your chambers."

Anticipation swept over Gabe, at last. After a hasty good-bye that left Anthony chuckling, Gabe fairly flew up the steps, taking them two at a time. When he reached the landing and stepped into the bedchamber, he almost fainted.

Faith was already in bed. A single candle burning on the nightstand was flickering back and forth. It gave just enough light for Gabe to see that Faith was in a pearl-colored nightgown. The gown was so transparent that as she breathed Gabe could see the rise and fall of her breasts.

"Are you out of breath because of me or from climbing the steps?"

"You."

"Are you ready for me to work on those evil humours that have attacked you so?"

"More than ready."

"Then come here my randy sailor."

***

Leaving a cloud of white dust in their wake, two coaches jolted past isolated farms, villages, and small hamlets. A couple of farmers stopped their hoeing and doffed their hats as the small caravan rushed past. At the top of a rise, the drivers of the coaches paused to let the horses blow and regain their breaths.

Gabe looked behind conscious of the fact that it had to be miserable on the driver's box of the coach behind them. He was also conscious, of the fact that he and Faith were weary travelers.

Gabe had wanted Faith to see as much of England as possible. To meet and understand the English people and know the average British subject was no different than those in the low country of South Carolina.

They had left the morning after the wedding on a tour that started in London, where he'd shown Faith all the sights, including the Admiralty. They had then traveled north along the coast to Edinburgh, Scotland. After that they turned southward to Liverpool then crossed into Wales before turning inland to Hereford. They spent a few days in Bristol before visiting Falmouth and Pendennis Castle, Plymouth, and back to Portsmouth.

They had spent two days resting at Gabe's mother's house. Nanny and Lum who had traveled in the rear coach were glad of the layover as well. Try as they might, Faith and Gabe were not able to talk Maria into visiting Deerfield even with the promise of lodging close by.

"This home belonged to your father and me," she said. "Deerfield was another distant part of his life that he tried to break away from, so why would I want to see it?"

"Because of Gil and Deborah, Mother," Gabe had said.

"They'll understand," she replied and would not discuss it further.

Now sitting atop of the little rise, the coachman called down, "A couple more small villages and we'll be there."

Faith saw the apprehension cross Gabe's face. "It will be fine. Lady Deborah told me that Gil wanted you to see what was a part of your legacy before you made up your mind about it all going to Becky's family. He wanted you to have the chance to see it first hand."

The coach started to move again, downhill this time. The horses picked up their pace as if they knew food and rest were near. As the newlyweds looked out the window they could see green pastures, cows, and a dog herding sheep as the shepherd watched from a distance. Farm wagons and carts slowed the progress of the coaches, which caused the driver to shout out curses.

"Worse than a sailor," Faith said, and then stopped Gabe from calling down the driver in regards to his language. "Probably half the fun of driving is to curse and shout at the farm workers."

"Did you do any cursing when the farmers got in your way?" Gabe asked, remembering the first day he'd met Faith.

"Damn right, if they wouldn't move," Faith exclaimed.

This caused Gabe to chuckle, then mocking Nanny he huffed up and said, "Lawd child, how you carry on so, I'll get my soap and wash yo mouth slam out. You ain't trash to be carrying on such."

The driver, hearing the laughter inside the coach thought, *Lucky sod. If I had a lamb like that I'd be laughing too…that and more.*

The road soon narrowed into a lane lined on both sides with a gray stone fence. Thick clusters of white and red roses, carnations and various colors of daisies were on either side of the entrance. No sooner had the noise of horse's hooves clattered on the cobblestone than a servant was there to assist with the horses. Another servant came to help Gabe and Faith from the coach.

Gil and Deborah appeared as if by magic and after much hugging, kissing, and small talk, Bart came out. After a few good-natured barbs at Gabe and a kiss on Faith's cheek, he took Nanny and Lum in tow so they could unpack and rest a bit.

Turning to the large two-story gray stone house, the group entered. As the door opened into a flag stone hall they were met by a butler and several maidservants. They were all trying to catch a glimpse at the old admiral's "other" son.

The group made their way into the main room where there hung above a huge fireplace a picture of Admiral Lord James Anthony. his old meerschaum pipe in one hand with the other on a ship's wheel. In the background were two ships in combat, their cannons blazing.

A servant was pouring sherry for the group. When Gabe's glass had been filled, Anthony who had watched his brother's eyes as he took in the painting said, "A toast…to father."

"To father," Gabe echoed and downed his drink in one gulp.

***

The next several days were some of the happiest Lord Anthony could remember. It was a pleasure having Gabe home…yes that was the word, *home*. Deborah and Faith had a good time spoiling Macayla. One evening Hugh and Becky came over and after a few awkward minutes Gabe and his sister acted like they'd been together all their lives. Each one of them was telling stories about "Gil" that made Deborah laugh till she cried.

After dinner that evening, Lum played the lotz and fiddle. When Macayla Rose got fussy, the women gathered together to get her ready for bed. Anthony, Gabe, Hugh, and Bart made their way down to the Dolphin to have a wet and smoke their pipes. After a round or two Bart noticed a sassy little tavern wench making eyes at him. He slipped away from the bar whispering he might be in for a bit o' mutton.

Seeing Hugh's confused look, Anthony explained Bart's meaning. "You may know about farming but you've a lot to learn about sailors."

"It appears I've been sheltered," Hugh admitted. "So I better spend some time with Bart learning more about these worldly ways of the farmers, yeomen, and serfs as I've just been made Magistrate."

"Well now," Anthony bellowed, already intoxicated. "Squire Hugh is now Hugh the Magistrate. Another round, another round for all."

## *Chapter Four*

Lord Anthony had taken the family on a day trip to Walmer Castle, which had been built by Henry VIII in 1540. It was built to counter the threat of invasion by Catholic France and Spain. It was now used as a country house for the Prince Regent.

After leaving the castle Anthony showed Lady Deborah and Faith the White Cliffs of Dover, and then they went on to Deal. "Deal," Anthony explained, "is a fishing village that lies on the English Channel. It's twenty to twenty-five miles across the channel to the Coast of France."

"Can we go there?" Faith asked.

"Not this time but hopefully we can soon. Just off the coast is what we call the Downs."

Seeing Faith's look, Gabe explained, "That's the water between the town and the sands. It's a good place for ships to anchor when there is foul weather."

"Aye," Anthony replied. Then as grave as he could be he said in a loud whisper, "It's also a place where smugglers abound carrying on their illicit trade. More than one revenue man has had his throat sliced from ear to ear."

Trying to act brave Faith said, "Well, we aren't revenooers so we haven't got anything to worry about. At least Lady Deborah and I don't."

After refreshments at the Crispen Inn the group headed home. It was just at dark when the Admiralty messenger rode up to Deerfield. Bart happened to see him arrive and escorted the messenger in the house carrying a very large envelope with the Admiralty seal on it.

Anthony and Gabe were sitting in the big room sharing a glass of wine while Deborah and Faith were off in another part of the house. Seeing the messenger, Anthony felt a sudden bout of nausea come over him. *Damme*, he thought to himself. He'd been told he'd have six months before the squadron was ready. It had only been just a week over three months. Signing for the envelope. Anthony sat down in a chair in front of the fireplace.

Breaking the seal he wondered...*Just how many times had his father done the same thing? Had he felt the anxiety and tension each time he opened the package? Was that what caused the problems between him and Mother? How would Deborah take his being recalled so soon? Would he ever be able to see little Macayla grow up? Would she know her father?*

Understanding Anthony's need to read the envelope's contents privately, Bart took the messenger in tow. "Let's have a wet to wash away the dust then a bit o' grub for yew."

Their footsteps echoed down the hall and Gabe, without being asked, lit a candle that stood on a small table next to Anthony's chair. Deborah and Faith soon returned to the room. Deborah knew something was not as it should have been upon entering.

Seeing the large envelope she cried out, "Oh no, Gil, not this soon!"

Faith went and sat on Gabe's knee as Anthony rose up to take Deborah in his arms. "I'm afraid so, darling. I've been given a new flagship and have been given command of the Windward Islands, which is headquartered in Barbados."

Deborah suddenly stood back. "Then I'm going, and if Gabe is to be a part of the squadron, Faith is coming along as well. If we can't stay in Barbados, we'll stay in Antigua." Seeing the logic in Deborah's statement, Anthony didn't argue.

Faith then spoke out, "Are you, are we going Gabe?"

"I...I don't know. I don't even have a ship."

"Well, I don't know for certain what it is," Anthony said. "But Lord Sandwich has advised you report to the port admiral in Portsmouth forthwith."

"When do you have to report to the flagship?" Deborah asked.

"By the end of the month. I am to relieve Admiral Crosby in October. It also appears we'll be transporting the new governor, a Lord Ragland."

"Humm...do you know him?" Gabe asked.

"I'm not sure but one of Lord Sandwich's cronies from the Hellfire Club was a Lord Ragland."

"And how do you know about that sex den?" Deborah asked.

"It was before your time, my dear, a long time before."

Later that night Faith snuggled so close to Gabe he could feel her chest rise and fall against his back. She then rose up and said, "You awake?"

"I am now, why?"

"Tell me about the Hellfire Club."

***

Gabe entered the George Inn and immediately recognized the admiral's aide standing just outside the closed door to one of the small private rooms. The aide, seeing Gabe in his new captain's uniform with the shiny new gold epaulet or as Bart called it "swab" setting on his right shoulder, nodded toward the bar. His way of saying, "Have a seat, I'll be with you in a minute."

Deciding not to report to Admiral Graham with the smell of alcohol on his breath, Gabe declined the drink and took a seat on one of the benches that lined the wall. He looked about the room and found it hard to believe that just over a month ago he'd shared a bed with Faith for the first time right above where he was now sitting. It would be miserable sleeping on a ship's cot again. Even one the size made for the captain's sleeping quarters.

"Captain Anthony…Captain Anthony."

Realizing he was being called, Gabe looked up just in time to see a Navy captain slam the inn door shut as he rushed out. The aide ushered Gabe into the admiral's room. Gabe immediately remembered he was one of the flag officers who had attended his wedding. He was with Admiral Moffett when Gil had paused to speak.

He had not met the admiral previously and had only spoken to a civilian superintendent when *Merlin's* hull was found to be unworthy for sea. The admiral was standing in front of an empty fireplace lighting a pipe. He was old to be a rear admiral. He was once tall but now stooped over. His bloodshot eyes had droopy bags under them. While he looked old and worn, out his voice was very firm.

"It was a nice wedding you had," the admiral said as he reached out to shake Gabe's hand. "It was also a wonderful reception. Thank you for the invitation."

Gabe swallowed hard and managed, "My pleasure sir."

He didn't remember sending an invitation. *It had to have been Gil,* he thought. He was damn glad his brother had had the wits to invite the local flag officers and dignitaries.

"Are you ready to return to sea?" Graham asked.

"Aye sir," Gabe answered.

"Good. I have a ship for you. She's the *Peregrine 36*."

"Thank you sir!" Gabe burst out, excited at the news.

The old admiral held up his hand to hush Gabe. "You may not thank me long. The *Peregrine* is an 'unhappy ship'."

Gabe felt the excitement sink.

"You lost your ship to rot. Rot made on the outside caused by shipworms. *Peregrine* is full of rot from the inside…a drunken captain who kept his whores with him at sea, a flog happy first lieutenant who let two seaman die under the lash. Half the crew has deserted and the other half has requested transfers. It's a wonder we didn't have a mutiny. I have a set of orders from the Admiralty in which I can fill in your name and the ship is yours. Or you can go home to your new bride and wait till something else becomes available."

Gabe wasn't fooled by the remark about waiting until something else was available. If he turned down the ship he'd likely be on the beach the rest of his life.

"I want her, sir."

"Good, good. I thought if you were anything like your father you would. Now about your crew. Lieutenant Jackson has been given a command. However, the rest have not been reassigned for the most part. Do you have a choice for your first lieutenant?"

Lavery's name came quickly to mind so he gave his name to the admiral. "He, Lieutenant Davy and I have been together a long time; otherwise I don't have anyone in mind."

"I know of a couple that will suit you well."

Gabe had thought he might.

"Now what about midshipmen?"

"I have two, sir."

"I have a couple of young gentlemen whom I can recommend," the admiral replied.

*This is going well*, Gabe thought.

"What about professional men, the warrants?"

"I would be happy with all of *Merlin's* sir, but I do need a surgeon."

Nodding, the admiral said, "I'll look for you a good one."

Gabe had watched the admiral's secretary make notes and was amazed at how fast his quill flew. Seeing Gabe's gaze, Graham said, "Paper and ink. It's paper and ink that keeps the Navy going."

At that time the aid returned to the room. "It's time sir."

"Yes, we can't keep anyone waiting, can we?"

Gabe knew the interview was ending so he quickly asked, "One more question. Is *Peregrine* to be part of Lord Anthony's command?"

Seeing the admiral's look Gabe continued, "I was with His Lordship when the Admiralty's messenger arrived."

"I see," Graham responded. "Did Lord Anthony promise you anything?"

"No sir."

"Good, I'm glad to hear it. We have been friends a long time, your brother and I. I never figured him or your father to be guilty of nepotism. You got your ship because Dutch Moffett said you were the best young naval officer he'd ever seen and you were the image of Lord James. To answer your question your ship will be assigned to Lord Anthony's command. Are you staying at your father's house?"

"Aye, sir."

"Very well, your orders will be sent to you directly. You may stay ashore at night until you receive further orders."

"Thank you, sir," Gabe stammered.

"Nonsense boy, I was a strutting rooster at one time myself."

## Chapter Five

The Admiralty's messenger opened the door of one of the larger private anterooms and said in a dry but polite manner, "If you would be so kind as to wait, Lord Anthony?"

Instead of sitting Anthony looked out the window. Leaves were starting to turn in the few trees visible. It'd not be long before the first frost. Now that Deborah had decided to travel to the West Indies he wouldn't miss England as much. He certainly wouldn't miss the cold. Glancing toward the sky, Anthony could see the clouds were clearing. It had rained early that morning but with the sun coming out it promised to be a warm day.

People were now filling the street and Anthony had to smile as a lady stepped around a puddle, but the two small children with her jumped into the middle and kicked water at each other. Intent upon watching the mother trying to coax the children from the puddle it took Anthony a second to realize the door had opened and he was being spoken to.

"The First Lord will see you now, My Lord." This was a different messenger. Old, gray haired, and stooped over, he had thick-rimmed glasses and a poorly fitting white powdered wig.

Following behind the ancient messenger to the First Lord's office, Anthony thought, *The war will be over before my orders can be signed*. He was finally ushered into Lord Sandwich's office where he found him pouring sherry into two glasses.

Seeing Anthony, the First Lord smiled, "Ah, Gil, won't you join us in a glass?"

The *us* meant Lord Sandwich and Lord Joseph Ragland. They had been friends since they were schoolboys together. The two had been known in their youth for not excelling in the sciences but in drink, swordplay, and general debauchery. It was said that they compiled a list of wenches they'd bedded during the week. They then presented the top ten to fellow classmates at Friday noon so that those who were boarded at the school could plan out their weekends.

The school was tucked between St. Peter's Abbey and London's best confectioners at Westminster. It was a place known for higher study, religion, and the development of future leaders.

However, the two had found it very easy to hop a fence or two, cross the grass at Green Park, cross Piccadilly and go on to Down Street. There they found cockfights and hedge taverns with brothels on the top floor. These were much more interesting to the comrades than the studies and religion at school.

The two had remained friends in adult life. Anthony had first met Lord Ragland at the infamous Hellfire Club where he had been taken as a guest. Lord Ragland had been reciting a bawdy poem that Anthony remembered to that day:

*When I first run my tongue down your smooth thigh*
*Just like a priest I kneel and bend to pray*
*And gaze with his same fervor for on high*
*My alter calls and sweet scents guide my way.*

Anthony's father had frowned upon hearing his son had visited the club. "It's a place I'd not care to have my name associated with," he said. "It's the devil's own den I'm told. A place to sow a wild seed then be away from, else you'll wind up reaping more than you sowed."

Anthony had taken his father's advice. He'd read an article that Lord Ragland had had to fight half a dozen duels for his indiscretions. He then dropped out of sight for a while, returning to his family home nestled amidst the beauty and tranquility of the Welsh borderland. Oddly enough he delved into politics and for years served as a conservative member of the Welsh Parliament. He had established ties with the Duke of Wellington and now traveled in very elite circles. In short, Lord Ragland appeared to have put his hellish days behind him.

Taking the offered glass, Anthony bowed slightly at the waist and said, "My Lord."

Lord Sandwich ignored the bow and held out his hand. "It's good to see you again," he said, vigorously shaking Anthony's hand.

"You have been a star in my crown, sir. You are also the one officer who has not failed or disappointed me. Although I should be jealous, you've made the *Gazette* so many times I'm envious."

"I've had good supporting officers, My Lord. Most of the credit for my success must be directed toward them."

"Do you hear that, Joseph?" Sandwich asked, speaking to Lord Ragland. "The man refuses to blow his own horn."

"He'd never be a politician," Ragland replied as he took the opportunity to shake Anthony's hand.

"I hope your wife and child are doing well," Sandwich spoke again.

"They're fine, My Lord."

"Good…good. Has Gabe ere…ah…recovered from his honeymoon?"

This brought a chuckle from Anthony, thinking how tired his brother appeared when he'd first arrived at Deerfield. "Sufficient enough to declare himself available to the port admiral."

"Good. He's taking a good but unhappy ship. I'm sure however that he will be able to make her into a proud ship again."

"I have every confidence, My Lord," Anthony responded.

"As have I. I have a dozen senior captains who daily beg for a ship but none more deserving than Gabe."

"Thank you for that," Anthony said.

"Now let's get down to business. You will be given command of the Windward Islands. Your senior will be Admiral Hotham, who has command of the West Indies. You will also report to Lord Ragland. He will be on hand much more than Hotham as he has been appointed as the new Governor of Barbados."

"My congratulations," Anthony said, lifting his unfinished glass in salute to Lord Ragland.

Sandwich continued, "You will be given a squadron comprised of *HMS SeaHorse*…a seventy-four, *Intrepid*…a fairly new sixty-four, two thirty-six-gun frigates…one is the *Peregrine*, which Gabe will command, and a couple of sloops plus a gun ketch to act as a tender. Gabe's old first lieutenant was given command of the ketch…*Ferret* of sixteen guns."

"Now let's talk about your mission. Your orders will be vague out of necessity. We have been given reliable information that the French will sign a treaty with the Colonies soon after the New Year. They are already building up forces to move on New York. We are also told they intend to establish bases in the West Indies and we can expect an attempt to invade several of our holdings there. As we have nothing more you will understand why your orders will be vague and open to interpretation."

"We have recently received word from Barbados of a daring attack on a convoy right under the noses of our fleet. Most of the ships carrying war supplies were either taken or destroyed without so much as a shot being fired on our behalf. We can't allow this to happen again. We already are hearing grumblings about how the war is going. It's getting more unpopular everyday."

"I have assured Lord Ragland that I put every faith and confidence in your abilities and judgment. We have to have something positive to give the public or this administration is doomed."

The stooped old messenger knocked on the door, halting the conversation. "It's time for your appointment with Lord North, sir," he informed Sandwich.

"Very well, I will be ready to depart directly." Turning back to Ragland and Anthony, Sandwich sighed, "Duty calls so I must bid you adieu. Fair winds, my friends."

## *Chapter Six*

Gabe left his meeting with the Port Admiral with a degree of excitement only to feel guilty over taking a ship so soon after he had wed. The task of taking command would cost him not only in money but time. It was the time he dreaded the most. At least he could return home to Faith in the evenings.

The Port Admiral had said the *Peregrine* was anchored off the spit just outside the harbour, further proof she was not one of Graham's favourite ships. Graham's statement about her being an unhappy ship was a discouraging hint as to the poor state of the ship's discipline and state of readiness.

The orders had been delivered to his home the same evening he had talked to Graham. Faith had stayed behind at Deerfield to help Deborah get ready for the trip to Barbados. Lum had stayed as well. But his cox'n, Paco, the midshipman Ally—as Alejandro was now being called—and Hawks had made the trip. Gabe and the three men were now in a hired cutter that was taking them from the harbour steps out to the *Peregrine*. The wind was up and the harbour had a fair chop to its waters.

The old boatman had made it plain from his look that he was aware of the *Peregrine's* reputation when he was given the ship's name he was to ferry the group to. It never ceased to amaze Gabe how quickly gossip about a ship spread. Spray from the chop dashed aboard the cutter as it plowed through the waves. Paco had wrapped Gabe's sea chest in a tarpaulin to keep off the spray.

The boatman eased the tiller over a bit to avoid a larger wave. "That be her," the boatman said, pointing to a ship.

Gabe was not happy at his first sighting of the *Peregrine.* The sails hung loosely on her yards. Stains ran down the hull where debris had been cast over the side without being washed. Ship's boats were bobbing up and down with a single rope tying them to the gangway. This made entry a dangerous proposition.

However, once he looked past the unkempt appearance, Gabe could see the makings of a fine ship. *The neglect would end today*, Gabe vowed. As the cutter came alongside Gabe was shocked at the lack of a challenge.

Paco, seeing the look of disdain on his captain's face, said, "Allow me Cap'n." He then scooted past Gabe and made his way up the gangway steps. Protocol dictated that the captain was always first out of the boat but nothing about this met Navy tradition.

Taking the opportunity Gabe gave the old boatman a handful of coins and said, "We're expecting an entire change in crew for the most part." This tip would ensure a brisk business for the boatman and his son.

"Thank ye, Cap'n. Thank ye kindly."

Gabe made his way forward but stopped suddenly. A wave had caused *Peregrine* to rise and tug at her cable. As she did so, Gabe saw that she had been coppered. *No shipworm would eat away this hull*, he thought as he moved toward the bow of the cutter.

Pausing, Gabe jammed his hat tightly on his head, and positioned his sword. Then with the next swell he grabbed a manrope in each hand…grimy, greasy manropes. He began to climb up the wooden battens to the entry port.

He could hear shouts and curses from above as Paco was giving the watch hell. It was nothing like the reception he'd gotten when he, along with Dagan, first went aboard *Merlin*. *I wish you were here Dagan*, Gabe thought. *I need you*.

Gabe was through the entry port and standing on deck before a lieutenant came running forward with a confused look, shouting out an order as he rushed to meet Gabe. Seamen rushed to form sideboys. One tripped over the tail of a rope, cursing as he hit the deck with a thud. Oddly the falling seaman's cry brought forth a sudden silence on the deck.

Looking around Gabe saw no semblance of a Navy ship. Brass had not been shined and rusty cannonballs were stacked and not placed in a brass monkey. Sails were furled loosely. Gaskets were just hanging.

"I'm Lieutenant Seymour, sir. We were not expecting you."

Gabe eyed the man coldly but didn't speak. Ally and Hawks were now aboard and stood on either side of their captain. Finally Gabe spoke.

"You're under arrest, Lieutenant, for drunkenness on duty."

"But sir, I'm not on duty."

Looking about Gabe asked, "Is there another officer aboard?"

"No sir."

"Then the charge stands."

Turning to Paco, Gabe ordered, "Have my chest brought aboard by the most sober seaman you can find."

"Aye, Cap'n," Paco replied, smiling at the cap'n's word. Well, maybe there was a sober man about but he wouldn't count on it.

Gabe made his way down the companionway toward the captain's cabin. He halted halfway down, suddenly sick to his stomach. The stench of unwashed bodies mixed with alcohol and the reek of full chamber pots filled the air. Holding his handkerchief to his nose Gabe made his way into the cabin.

Men and women's clothes were strewn everywhere, chairs were overturned. Wine bottles rolled across the deck…some empty, while others still contained fluid. Gabe would not have bet on the liquid inside the bottles being wine.

He reached the captain's desk and found it locked. The only damn thing that's as it should be. Overhead he could hear his chest being dragged across the deck. Not wanting his trunk soiled he rushed on deck.

"Don't carry it below," he gasped, taking in a breath of fresh air.

Looking at the two mids he could see a greenish pallor. They had gone below but stood outside the cabin while he looked in.

"She's about ripe I'd say, Captain," Hawks volunteered.

"Aye young sir, a bad beginning."

Ally then spoke up in his broken English. "Don't worry, Captain, we'll have this place looking ship shape pronto."

"I've no doubt, Ally."

Gabe then spoke to Paco. "Have one of the scalawags stand guard over my chest until my cabin has been cleaned."

Nodding, Paco said, "Si…aye, Cap'n." Then he went to find a burly seaman.

"Mr Ally. Mr Hawks."

"Aye, Captain," the youths said in unison.

"It's my understanding that the warrants have all transferred off the ship. I am therefore promoting both of you to lieutenant. Temporarily, mind you, but it'll go in your records."

This made the mids grin from ear to ear.

"Now, lieutenants, divide what crew we have into two groups. I want this ship scoured from top to bottom."

"Aye, Cap'n," they replied, then off they went, suddenly full of importance.

***

It was shortly before the forenoon watch that the old boatman started ferrying officers and crew out to the *Peregrine*. The first "boat ahoy" startled Gabe, as he was in deep thought about how well provisioned the ship might be and the state of inventory that was claimed on the books.

Making his way topside to see who was reporting on board, he was in time to see his new First Lieutenant Nathan Lavery coming through the entry port. Behind him were Lieutenant Davy, and two of *Merlin's* old warrants: the bosun, Mr Graf, and the gunner, Mr Druett.

"The cutter must have been crowded," Gabe said as he greeted the men. "Let's go below and I will fill you in on what so far has been a big disappointment."

After filling in his officers and warrants on the sorry state of affairs, Gabe went back to reviewing the ship's books. He now opened the "punishment" book and was horrified. Being assigned to *Peregrine* must have been hell on earth. Flogging was routinely awarded for every offense and punishment was rendered each day.

"Boat ahoy." The challenge was heard through the open skylight.

*More hands were reporting*, Gabe thought. However, Lavery would deal with it. The knock on the cabin door interrupted Gabe's review of the ship's records. Paco had been sitting just inside the cabin, acting as unofficial sentry as *Peregrine's* new detachment of marines had not yet arrived.

Gabe nodded to Paco, who opened the door. Seeing the visitor he called out, "First lieutenant, sir." Then as an after thought he added, "With another officer."

Gabe marked the page he was on by laying a quill between the pages then closed the book. Lavery stepped into the cabin, allowing the other officer to enter.

"Lieutenant Wiley, sir. Request permission to speak to the captain."

"Very well, Lieutenant Lavery, you may go."

As Lavery left, Gabe caught Paco's look…his unspoken question. "Do I stay or leave you in private?"

"You may round-up our young gentlemen, Paco, and tell them with my regrets their temporary promotions have unfortunately come to an end."

Smiling, Paco left to do his bidding.

Gabe then looked at Wiley. Other than looking apprehensive, he was turned out professionally. "Are you George Wiley, Second Lieutenant of *Peregrine*?" Gabe asked.

"I am, sir."

Gabe had noted from the records that Wiley had spoken up for several of the men who had been brought up for punishment.

"Why have you been absent from the ship?"

"I was on leave, sir."

"There was no mention of it in the ship's log." Gabe responded.

Wiley didn't look surprised but added, "I was on leave, sir. You can check with the port admiral. He will confirm it."

This was a strange answer as officers didn't check in or out with the port admiral in regards to leave.

"Are you a friend or relative of Admiral Graham?"

"Yes…ere no, but soon sir."

"Soon what?" Gabe asked.

"Admiral Graham is soon to marry my mother."

"I see," Gabe said. "What were your dealings with the admiral in regards to this ship?"

"I had asked for a transfer, sir," Wiley replied, taking a deep breath.

"Do you still desire one?"

"No sir."

"Why may I ask?"

"Admiral Graham said the ship had finally gotten a captain that knew how to run a ship and I'd be a blundering idiot not to return."

Gabe couldn't help but chuckle. "Find yourself a clean glass, Mr Wiley, and we will make a toast to a new beginning."

"A new beginning, sir, and here's to your health."

## *Chapter Seven*

Anthony and Lord Ragland had attended the Royal Theater and were discussing the play they'd seen. "You never know when we'll get the chance to see such a play," Ragland said, encouraging Anthony to go along.

Finally Anthony gave in and the two attended one of the best plays he could remember seeing. It had been put on by an Italian opera group. Not only was it good but it also was long. Lord Ragland had drunk so much wine that once the play ended and he was packed into the coach, he slumped over apparently out.

Bart climbed in a seat next to Anthony, passing him a pouch of tobacco. "Try this," he said. "Man swore it would burn slow so your pipe wouldn't get hot and it won't bite yer tongue. It doesn't smell half bad either."

Anthony had lit up his pipe and was amazed at how refreshing it was. "Not English tobacco," he said to Bart.

"Nay. Better, much better."

Then the two sat back against the seat pulling the coach blanket over them. The only light in the dark coach came from the tiny embers inside the bowls of their pipes. The coach moved along at a good clip down the largely deserted streets in the early a.m. hours. One or two other coaches rushed along trying to get home before the temperature dropped further. Small puffs of tobacco smoke escaped the coach's windows and horses hooves clapped on the cobblestone streets.

"Whoa! Whoa!" the driver shouted.

The wheels and horses were sliding on the dew-damp street. A carriage had darted out in front of the coach so the driver had to stop quickly or wreck. One of the lead horses lost its footing and fell. Bart tried to open his door but the coach in trying to stop so quickly had slid up against one of the street lamps. From up on the driver's box, you could hear curses and shouting, then a pistol shot. The shouting suddenly ceased. The three standing horses danced nervously in their harnesses.

The driver lay on the dark street groaning and gasping. The downed horse was finally able to right itself but stood wild-eyed not sure what was happening.

Several men appeared at the coach's door on Anthony's side. One of the men snatched open the door and jerked Anthony and Bart out onto the street. He had a mask over his face as did the rest of the men. However, he was the only one showing a pistol…a brace of pistols. One of them was still smoking from shooting the driver.

"Stand there," the masked man ordered. "Stand and deliver."

"Are you mad?" Anthony exclaimed. "I'm an officer in His Majesty's Navy."

This brought laughter from the highwayman. "'E said you was a lofty bugger."

"Who said that?" Anthony demanded.

"Ye jus never mind now," one of the other villains chimed in. "Ye's got a 'andsome reward on yer 'ead. We gets yer valuables and a reward. Be on wid it mate so's we can get going." This came from a man standing by the carriage.

Pulling Bart up close by his collar, the highwayman's hand went under his great cloak and whipped out a dagger and cut a fine red line across Bart's cheek.

"Now 'and it over or the next one will be 'is gullet. Quick now, your money purse, rings, and any other valuables or 'e dies."

"We're dead already," Bart spat.

"Right you are, matey," the rogue said with a laugh. Then his head exploded.

Blood, brain, and bone sprayed Bart. However, being a man of action he snatched the pistol from the dead man's belt before he hit the ground. Turning, he fired and one of the rogues hit the street, blood oozing from a hole in his chest.

The other man jumped into the carriage that had blocked their way. The driver who had been silent laid the whip to the horses and they took off. By this time Lord Ragland had descended from their coach. He calmly tucked his left arm behind his back, took aim with the pistol in his right hand, and fired. The shot echoed in the still night air and a scream was heard. The man that jumped into the carriage to make his escape now lay on the hard, cold cobblestones. The carriage with the driver dashed on into the darkness.

*Damme,* Anthony thought looking at Lord Ragland with renewed respect. *No wonder he's won so many duels. The man has ice water for nerves.*

Lord Ragland shot the first rogue in the only place he could without fear of hitting Bart...the head. A head shot from ten paces, drunk and minimal lighting. He then shot another man at thirty paces from a racing carriage.

"Well, damme," Anthony said aloud. "It was a poor showing I put on."

"At least you and Bart had your wits."

Bart was tending to the driver of their carriage. He'd been shot in the shoulder and a handkerchief was used to staunch the flow of blood. Several lights were appearing in windows along the street and a few of the more curious ventured out. A couple of watchmen were now on the scene and someone had sent for the constable. A doctor had also been sent for.

Sitting back in the coach waiting on the constable, Ragland spoke quietly to Anthony. “Do you recall the remark about a reward on your head?”

“Aye. I haven’t forgotten. I wish we’d been able to learn more. Whoever it is went out of their way to make it look like robbery rather than murder.”

“Well, it’s glad I am to be putting to sea again,” Bart chimed in.

“I agree with that,” Ragland replied. “It’ll do no harm to get out of the country for a while.”

“I wonder,” Anthony replied, deep in thought. “I wonder.”

## *Chapter Eight*

Lord Anthony looked at Bart all decked out in his new Admiral's cox'n uniform. His others had faded from being continuously washed at sea in salt water. Regardless of the new blue jacket with gilt buttons, nankeen trousers, and brass buckled shoes, Bart still looked like a rugged old salt. His hair was starting to show a little salt and pepper but that did little to disguise the fearsome appearance of the man.

"Well, Bart, you ready to go down and greet our captain?"

"Aye," the cox'n replied, "I'm ready to see yews flag flying again. It should be at the fore I'm thinking and will be before long iffen them block'eads at the Admiralty can put down their wine glasses and get out of some wenches' beds."

"Bart...you're talking about his Majesty's officers."

"More like 'is Majesty's bumpkins and that's no error."

Turning to look in the mirror, Anthony straightened the new epaulettes on his shoulders. *Would he ever see the single star replaced by two stars? Was the thought of Vice Admiral only a dream?*

"Time to go," Bart said, breaking Anthony's train of thought.

He was dining with his officers here at the George Inn. It was a chance to meet each of the captains in a neutral environment. That was a trick his father had taught him and one he'd passed on to Gabe. Tomorrow he would go aboard his new flagship for the first time. Then it would be only a matter of days before they set sail.

A knock on the door caught Anthony off guard and made him jump as he'd been reaching for the knob when the knock occurred.

"Jittery, ain't yew," Bart said.

"Hush, damn you."

"There ye go again taking out yews nerves on a poor jack tar."

Bart then opened the door to find Gabe standing there. He thumped at Gabe's shiny epaulette.

"How long you reckon that swab'll stay shiny?"

"About as long as those new buttons I say," Gabe replied. "Damn if they wouldn't make a fine target."

"We's already been a target," Bart said.

"So I've heard." Then turning to Anthony, Gabe said, "Any thoughts on who may be behind this?"

"No," Anthony answered. "I wish I did. Then we'd be on an equal footing."

Reaching into his coat pocket, Gabe took out a letter. "This arrived this morning from Dagan. Look at the date."

The letter had been written over two months ago. Dagan was fine, he'd enjoyed his visit with Uncle Andrea, and Caleb was going to marry Catherine. Then the last paragraph…the interesting part: "I feel dark days ahead. Days filled with danger for all of us." He went on to say he'd arranged passage with a merchantman and would meet the squadron in Barbados. Gabe could see the surprise on Anthony's face.

"How did he know?"

Gabe only shrugged his shoulders and shook his head.

"How does he always know?" Bart said, more a statement than a question. "He does and that's all that matters, I'm thinkin."

"You're right," Anthony replied, then reached for the door. "Let's not keep our guests waiting.

***

The evening meal progressed nicely. Lord Ragland, as the guest of honour, sat on Anthony's right with Captain Buck on the left. The rest were seated not by seniority but according to the first available chair. This was as planned.

Thomas Fletcher was in command of the sixty-four gun, *Intrepid*, which had just completed a three month overhaul. He had been in command of the ship for three years and had until recently been stationed at Gibraltar.

Francis Markham, who was a good friend and old shipmate, had just been given command of the squadron's other frigate, *Dasher*. Markham's father was a vice admiral so Anthony was sure his appointment had a lot to do with that. Not that he wasn't a good officer…he was. He and Gabe had been friends since they were mids together on *Drakkar*. He'd once been Anthony's flag lieutenant. He was a reliable man and Anthony was glad to have him.

Ambrose Taylor and Hayward Hallett, as was Jem Jackson, were lieutenants with their first commands. All three had good records as first lieutenants and had sterling recommendations. Jem Jackson was another proven commodity. Anthony was sure the ketch, *Viper*, would be well commanded. The *Alert* and *Ferret* were as new as the lieutenants who commanded them. *We'll see how they measure up*.

As the meal was finished and cigars and pipes were lit, Lord Ragland stood up. "Gentlemen, it has been a pleasant evening, but the morrow promises to be filled with government bureaucracy, so I bid you goodnight with a final toast. *To wives and sweethearts…may they never meet*."

This brought whoops and laughter, as Ragland knew it would. Soon the captains thanked their host and made their way back to their ships. Bart had ducked out earlier and made sure each of the boat crews had a wet to keep them warm. As he returned he overheard Gabe's offer for Anthony and Bart to stay at his mother's home.

"When Deborah arrives we will, but for now I'll stay here. I think I'll be safe. Bart will be here."

*That's no error*, Bart thought. *He'll be as safe as I can make him.*

***

The Admiral's barge was now in sight of *HMS Sea-Horse*...Lord Anthony's new flagship. Anthony could already see men moving about. They were dressed in navy blue and the scarlet red of the marines. Soon he'd be back in his world. Then eyeing Bart he changed his thought...*our world.*

The barge's bow hit a small rogue wave and it caused the barge to veer to larboard momentarily.

"Careful," Bart whispered, his hand on Anthony's arm for balance. "They're watching."

*That's Bart, always at my side, always looking out for me. What would he do without Bart? What would England do without all the Barts in the Navy? They were the real backbone of the fleet.*

"She flies pretty today," Bart said, pointing to Lord Anthony's flag flapping away at the mizzenmast.

The bowman stood as they were now almost alongside *SeaHorse,* his boats hook at the ready.

Tom Blood, Buck's cox'n, was at the tiller and he eased it over slightly. "Ready bowman," he bellowed. The oars were tossed and Blood removed his hat.

Anthony looked at the cox'n with a quick smile on his face. "Thank you, Blood. That was done handsomely."

Blood caught a glimpse of Bart, who nodded his approval. "Smart turnout," Bart said.

Tucking his sword behind his leg so he wouldn't trip, Anthony then waited for the swell to lift the bow of the barge. He leaped as Buck looked down anxiously waiting until he saw his admiral climbing up the side. Anthony made his way into the entry port as the marines came to attention. With a slap and click of muskets they presented arms.

Bayonets glinted in the morning sun. The morning stillness was broken with the sound of "Heart of Oak" by the drums and fifes. Buck was there smiling from ear to ear. Anthony noticed the smells first—friendly smells to a sailor—tar, oakum, paint, new canvas...the smells of a ship.

Glancing about the deck Anthony was impressed. The crew was nicely turned out. The cannons with all their tackles and gear were in perfect alignment. The decks were immaculate. The sails were tightly furled with snug gaskets. He expected nothing less and apparently neither did Buck.

"I'm impressed, Rupert," Anthony said, using Buck's given name. "It's a fine ship."

Then as they walked toward his cabin, Anthony paused here and there speaking to familiar faces. Lieutenant Lamb, now Buck's first lieutenant, the bosun, May, Marine Captain Dunlap and his second in command of the Marines, Lieutenant Bevis. Then as Anthony walked aft he stopped and turned. He recognized that face, older and more filled out and weather-beaten.

"George Jepson," he said. "Is that you?"

"Aye, My Lord."

Stepping back he eyed the man. It had been a lot of years. Jepson had just made master's mate and Anthony was a young lieutenant. He and Bart had been mates. Now here Jepson was wearing the uniform of a warrant. Not just a warrant but also the master of *HMS SeaHorse*.

"Well, damme. Where's Bart? Off loafing, no doubt." Looking toward the entry port Anthony could see Bart helping his flag lieutenant. Instantly he regretted his words.

Everett Hazard had turned into an excellent flag lieutenant, in spite of having only one arm. The other arm was lost in combat. Turning back to Jepson he shook his hand.

"Captain Buck, you have a life saver as your master. A squall would have taken me over the side but for the strong arm of your master. Yes sir, without Jepson's quick action it would have been another admiral hoisting his flag here today, for I'd be keeping company with ole Davy Jones."

"It was nothing, sir," Jepson said, uncomfortable with the attention he was being given by the admiral.

Seeing Jepson flush, Anthony changed tacks. "Now let me warn you in advance, Captain Buck. He and Bart were as close as mates could be once so I know the trouble they can get into. It's your ship mind you," Anthony continued, "but were it up to me I'd have Captain Dunlap post an extra sentry at the spirit locker."

This caused all those in hearing distance to laugh.

"Jep, you old salt." Bart had finally made his way aft and recognized his old mate. "Ye still smoking those stinking cigars?"

By way of answering, Jep just tapped his coat.

"Good…good. Let me get 'is Lordship settled in and we'll have a smoke and a wet."

Hearing this Anthony looked at Buck. "Did I not warn you?"

"Aye, My Lord, you did. It's trouble we have in the making. Maybe we should send ashore for a new master."

"Look for a good cox'n while you're at it."

Turning, Anthony ducked beneath the deck head beams. A marine sentry had already been posted. Anthony nodded to the sentry and entered the stern cabin.

"Silas and his assistant are already on board," Buck volunteered. "As is your secretary, LeMatt."

Anthony nodded as he looked about. *SeaHorse* was larger than *Warrior* had been. He had a spacious dining table. His desk and wine cabinet had been transferred as had a side cabinet.

Seeing Anthony and Buck enter the cabin, Silas waited until Anthony caught his gaze. "A glass of hock, My Lord, or maybe a cup of coffee?"

Seeing Buck smile, Anthony said, "Our flag captain would prefer a cup of your coffee, I believe."

A knock and the stamp of the marine sentry's musket made Anthony jump. He'd have Bart inform the sentry of his requirements directly.

"Flag lieutenant, suh," the marine announced.

"Yes, yes," Anthony grumbled.

Once in the cabin, Hazard said enthusiastically, "Bloke if ever there was one."

"Come on in and have a cup of coffee. I'll have Bart talk to the sergeant."

Sitting down Hazard handed several papers over to Anthony. There was also a sealed dispatch bag and several individual letters. "It appears, sir, a convoy is being put together at Plymouth and we've been given the task of escorting them to the Indies."

"Damme," Buck swore. "I was going to put *Seahorse* through her courses and see what kind of sailor she is."

The three talked on over coffee and finally the subject of the master came up.

"He and Bart were still standing under the poop deck when I came in," Hazard said. "Catching up on old times."

"I tried to find Jep when I made captain but he was away at sea," Anthony said.

"He has blue eyes."

"What was that?" Buck asked.

"His eyes," Hazard repeated. "Did you ever see such blue eyes?"

"I've seen them when they were cold blue," Anthony said. "Not a man I'd cross when he's mad. Jet black hair and blue eyes, a ladies' man till you rile him."

"I'll bet he and Bart were a handful," Buck said.

"Aye, I could tell you a few stories about them but there is not another two I'd rather have beside me when the metal is flying."

"'Cept maybe Dagan."

"Aye," Anthony agreed. "'Cept maybe Dagan."

"Well, it'll do Bart good to have an old mate around to swap sea stories with," Buck said.

"That it will, Captain, that it will," Anthony replied.

## *Chapter Nine*

A sudden gale was making life for the sailors miserable. Lord Anthony's squadron was now gathered in Hamoaze, a sheltered deep water estuary, off Plymouth. The squadron gathered here in order to escort the Plymouth convoy to the Caribbean. A pounding rain beat against the tarpaulin jackets of those officers and men whose duties kept them on deck.

Captain Buck was en route to the Port Admiral's office for a conference with the ship captains who would make up the convoy. Jepson, the master, had predicted a blow by mid-afternoon and had recommended Buck break out his foul weather jacket. Unfortunately, Buck failed to follow the master's recommendation.

*Damn Jep*, Buck thought as rain pelted his sodden uniform. *He's always right.*

Tom Blood, Buck's cox'n, had taken the master's advice and had his tarpaulin within reach when the rain started...not a cable's length from *SeaHorse*. He had offered it to his captain, who out of concern for his cox'n, or out of stubborness, had refused it. Well, they still had a long pull yet.

On board *SeaHorse*, Bart and Jep squatted in a corner under the poop just aft of the wheel and puffed on their pipes. "'E's a good sort, better 'n most yew find," Bart said, talking about Buck. "I knowed 'im when 'e was jus a lieutenant. 'E's been with 'is Lordship off 'n on ever since. We's been through some pretty tough scrapes together and 'e's always held his own. Course we's taught 'im right we did…me and 'is Lordship. Same as we did Gabe," Bart added.

Meriweather, the fourth lieutenant, had the watch. He had been tempted to order the two gossiping old salts off the deck but knew it wasn't wise to order the master to do anything. Lamb, the first lieutenant, had given a warning in regards to the admiral's cox'n. "If you don't want to spend the rest of your life on the beach, tread lightly around Bart." Well, Meriweather decided, he'd take Lamb's advice.

"Lieutenant Meriweather!" The call came just as the lieutenant passed by the poop. "Lieutenant!"

Turning, Meriweather could see it was Bart motioning for him. Not sure how to respond to an "inferior" summoning him, he paused a second, then when Bart waved again, he ducked under the edge of the poop.

"Come take a breath out of the rain," Bart said.

"I'm the duty officer."

"It's still raining."

"But I might be needed."

"They'll cry out for you. That's what you got watch standers for. 'Sides Captain Buck won't like it if the glass gets fogged up."

"But I have the duty!"

"It's still raining…it's going to fog up."

"But I'm supposed to tote the glass when I have duty."

"Well," Bart said, taking a deep breath, "keep under the poop lessen yews called and then stick it under your tarp."

"Thank you, that's a good idea."

Jep, having remained silent while Bart was talking to the lieutenant, spoke. "This will clear before the first dog watch. You can have a glass of warm brandy when you go down to eat. That'll keep the misery out of your bones."

"I'll do that."

Boat ahoy was heard, so Meriweather sighed, tucked the glass under his tarp then rushed to the entry port.

"'E 'as the makins I'm thinking," Bart said.

"Aye," Jep agreed. "At least 'e had sense enough to get out of the rain."

***

Buck was soaking wet when he returned to the flagship. He changed uniforms in preparation to report to Lord Anthony.

A gentle knock then the marine sentry called, "Flag captain, suh."

"Come in, come in."

"I guess Bart talked with the marine sergeant," Buck volunteered.

Smiling, Anthony said, "Pleasant, wasn't it?"

"Aye," Buck replied. "Bart usually gets his point across."

"How did the meeting go?" Anthony asked, knowing from past experience what the answer would be.

"Well enough for a bunch of grocery captains who whine about having no protection. Then they whine some more when told they can't sail independently and have to comply with signals and instructions."

Without asking, Silas walked into the cabin and handed Buck a glass of wine. "Another glass, My Lord?"

"No thank you, Silas. Has the weather cleared?" Anthony asked. He'd been informed by Bart that Buck had not bothered to get a tarpaulin before leaving the ship. He then was caught in the downpour in his gig.

"Aye, it's cleared."

Buck then scooted his chair a bit closer to Anthony's so he could be heard as he whispered, "Forgot my damn jacket and was too stubborn to send a young gentleman to fetch it. So there I was standing like a drowned rat. A puddle was gathering around my feet as I tried to explain sailing instructions to the convoy captains. Made a poor show of it I did."

"Well don't beat yourself up too much. There's not a sailor alive who hasn't got caught in a squall at one time or another."

Hearing voices, Lady Deborah stepped out of the sleeping quarters after making sure her husband was not involved in, as he put it, admiralty business. She and Macayla had come aboard the night before the squadron had weighed anchor at Portsmouth. Seeing Lady Deborah, Buck rose to greet her but she waved him down.

She stood behind Anthony, hands on his shoulders, and asked, "Did you invite the good captain to dine this evening?"

"I was about to, my dear." Anthony looked at Buck. "If you have no other commitment, Rupert, we would be happy to have you dine with us. I've also invited Gabe and Faith. Lord Ragland has also been invited. Once at sea we may not have a chance to do so until we reach Antigua."

"Thank you, My Lord, Lady Deborah. I'd be honoured. Will Gabe bring Lum?"

"I asked Faith to bring him along if Lum didn't mind," Deborah spoke up. "So we will see."

***

Gabe leaned against the weather rigging and adjusted his glass until the flagship came into focus. *The vessels in the convoy made an impressive sight*, he thought, with their pyramids of sail filling the early dawn sky. The sun had slowly clawed its way up until it was full on the horizon.

*No red sky this morning*, he thought, his mind on the old sailor's saying...red sky in the morning, sailor's warning; red sky at night, sailor's delight.

Last night had been a delight. He had recalled the lovemaking he and Faith had enjoyed. After he and Faith had dined aboard the flagship he had explained to his bride that there would be a slim chance of dining together again with Gil and Deborah until they reached landfall.

"So it'll just be the two of us?" Faith asked.

"No, we'll invite the ship's officers from time to time but for the most part it'll just be us," Gabe replied.

"I could get greedy very quickly," Faith said.

"I won't mind," Gabe had replied.

He had considered having Faith travel back aboard the flagship, but once Nathan Lavery, Davy, and the warrant officers had arrived, things had turned around quickly. He was glad he'd decided to keep Lieutenant Wiley. He had done a splendid job thus far and he had the respect and trust of *Peregrine's* crew...those that hadn't run.

Lum had spoken to one of the old crew in passing. The seaman replied, "Things lookin up, not a flogging in a week."

"Deck thar," called the mainmast lookout. "Strange sails off the larboard bow."

"You have a good lookout, Mr Lavery."

"Aye, Captain," the first lieutenant replied.

Unable to find the ship in his glass Gabe called to Midshipman Ally, "Signal flagship strange sail in sight."

"Aye, sir."

"Mr Lavery."

"Aye, Captain."

"Call all hands. I've a feeling about me."

"Aye, sir."

"When we are able to identify her or we have a signal from the flagship call me. I shall now go break my fast."

As Gabe ducked his head and started down the companionway, he could hear the shrill twitter of the bosun's pipes calling all hands. *That ought to wake Faith*, he thought...*the sleepyhead.*

***

Gabe had just sat down to a cup of coffee when the marine sentry knocked. "Midshipman Ally, sir."

Gabe smiled to himself. Even the marines were now calling Alejandro Ally.

"Mr Lavery's respects, sir. Flag has signaled: investigate strange sail."

"Thank you, Mr Alejandro," Gabe said, using the boy's name. It wouldn't do for the captain to use nicknames. "Now tell me, are you still satisfied with your decision to be a sailor?"

"Oh si…I mean aye sir. I would want to do nothing else."

"Very well. Now go tell the first lieutenant I will be up directly."

Gabe had yet to finish his coffee when he could feel the ship turning on a course to intercept the strange sail. Lavery was a good first lieutenant. He had taken the initiative to comply with admiral's orders. Just like Jem Jackson would have done.

Finishing his coffee, Gabe paused on his way out of the cabin to look toward his sleeping quarters. She was still asleep. *Another thing they had in common*, he thought as he left the cabin and headed on deck…*we're both hard risers.*

Before Gabe could make his way to the quarterdeck the lookout called down, "She's changed tack sir, hauling her wind I'd say."

"I'll go," Lieutenant Davy volunteered, seeing the expression that came across Gabe's face as he appeared on deck.

Within minutes Davy was back on deck. "She's a large ship, sir. The size of a large frigate, but she has hauled her wind right enough."

"That's puzzling," Gabe said. "I thought she might be a merchantman wanting to sail along with the convoy."

"That she may be," Gunnells volunteered. "There's safety in numbers."

"I don't think so," Davy spoke again. "In truth she looks like some of the Jonathan ships we've tangled with. Like a large privateer."

"Makes sense," Gabe said. "She could keep a close watch on the convoy then pounce on a straggler."

"Like in a squall," Gunnells added.

"Or at night." This from Lieutenant Wiley.

"You've got something there," Gabe acknowledged. "Mr Lavery, once we are close with the squadron make a signal to flag requesting permission to close within hailing distance."

***

The attack came suddenly and from an unexpected quarter. After two days with no sightings everyone seemed to have relaxed. The sun was going down and the sky had a reddish purple haze.

"Deck thar, signal from *Alert*...strange sail to larboard."

"Relay to flag," Gabe said, immediately a sinking feeling in his gut. "Lum!"

"Aye Cap'n."

"Escort Mrs. Anthony and Nanny below."

"Aye, Cap'n."

"What is it, Gabe?" Faith asked.

"Shh, Missy Faith," Lum said. "Mistuh Gabe got to be the cap'n of this heah ship right now. He ain't got no time foh your questions."

"Deck thar," the lookout called down again. "The ship is on a converging tack to attack *Alert*."

"Damme," Gabe said, looking at the sky. "They'll never see a signal in this light. Mr Lavery!"

"Aye, Captain."

"Fire off two red flares. That was the signal enemy in sight. Then beat to quarters."

"Aye, Captain."

"Gunfire, sir!" Lieutenant Wiley exclaimed.

"Aye. I heard it," Gabe responded.

"*Alert's* under fire," the excited lookout called down.

"You were right," Lavery said. "Privateers, by God."

"No," Gabe answered. "Davy was right."

"Flares from the flagship, sir, two white."

That meant "acknowledge." No instructions. *What instructions can she give?* Gabe thought to himself.

"Mr Gunnells, put us on a course to intercept yonder ship."

"Aye, Captain."

The gunfire was clearer now. Gabe raised his glass but could see nothing in the dying light except the flash of cannons. He shut his glass with a snap. "Mr Lavery, I'm going up for a better look."

"Aye," was all the first lieutenant had time to say. He was used to his captain doing the unexpected.

Once he made it to the mainmast lookout, he could see better.

"It be a big un, Cap'n," the lookout said as he made room for Gabe.

"Aye," Gabe snarled. "A wolf after a pup."

Ambrose Taylor, the captain of *AlertI,* was no fool. He was under full sail and zigzagging as much as he could to make it difficult for the bigger ship to bring her under good aim. The privateer was firing bow chasers.

If luck held out *Peregrine* would be able to intervene before the privateer's broadsides would be able to bear. As Gabe turned to step onto a ratline he saw something…a speck in the distance.

Stepping back up onto the platform he hissed, "Two ships! Close in company!"

He handed his glass to the lookout then cupped his hands and shouted, "Deck there! Two more sails aft. The last merchantman, she's under attack."

Gabe slid down a backstay and dropped on deck, his hands burning from his rapid descent. "Fire off several red flares and be damn quick about," he ordered.

"Mr Druett!"

"Aye, Cap'n."

"Get the bow chasers into action as soon as possible."

"Aye, Cap'n," the gunner replied then rushed off.

"What a bloody scoundrel," Lavery said. "Attacking *Alert*."

"It's a decoy I'd bet," Wiley volunteered. "Something to keep us busy. They knew we'd react to them attacking a smaller ship. Then once our attention is diverted they set the wolves loose upon the lambs."

"My thoughts exactly," Gabe said.

"Sorry sir," Wiley said. "I didn't know you were within hearing."

"I was and I agree."

BOOM!...BOOM!...the bow chasers recoiled against the tackles as they were fired.

"Damme but Druett knows his business, Captain," Lavery volunteered. "They fired quickly enough."

Smoke from the bow chasers drifted down wind, filling the air with the stench of gunpowder.

From above the lookout called down, "She's broken off, sir. The privateer 'as come about."

"Thank God," Gabe said.

Druett made his way to the quarterdeck. "I couldn't tell if we hit anything Cap'n but we gave it our best try."

*Alert* was now almost up with *Peregrine*.

"Hear that Mr Druett? They're cheering you over there. So whether you hit the whoresons or not you scared them off. I'm betting there's many a soul on yonder ship who'd stand for you a wet."

Embarrassed by the captain's praise, Druett said, "It weren't nothing Cap'n. Course if they're willing to buy, I'm willing to drink."

Standing to the side, Lieutenant Wiley heard the exchange. *This captain was different*, he thought. *The admiral was right. I'm glad I stayed*, he realized.

## *Chapter Ten*

The island of Antigua seemed to rise up over the horizon with the early dawn light. The cry of "land ho" quickened everyone's step. Even Faith had shook the cobwebs from her sleepy head and made her way topside still bundled up with a thick robe. It had been two weeks since the clash with the privateers and eight weeks since they weighed anchor at Plymouth.

The privateers' raid had been unsuccessful. *Dasher* had run down the privateers, capturing one, an old twenty-eight-gun frigate, and run off the other ship. The frigate, *HMS Lizard*, had been captured by the Colonies off Marblehead in 1776. Now she was back with the fleet—hopefully, a part of Anthony's squadron.

Antigua, Gabe had explained to Faith, was headquarters for the British Navy in the West Indies. It was here his brother and Lady Deborah had met and married. It had been a good time for him to get to know his brother as well. Deborah, he explained, held vast holdings here. This would be where she would stay with Deborah, at least until they found out how things were in Barbados.

As the island grew on the horizon Gabe realized he was glad to be back. He had missed the fellowship with the island's people who had opened their homes for all of "Lord Anthony's sailors" back in 1775. He looked forward to seeing Commodore Gardner and his wife, Greta. He smiled when he thought of Greta. How many times had she tried to play cupid for the young gentlemen and set them up with the young ladies? That was something he wouldn't share with Faith, he decided.

He'd already been given her glare when some well-endowed young lady caused his head to turn. "Get an eye-ful?" she'd asked in a most unfriendly manner. He still looked but had learned to be discreet. *If God hadn't wanted him to look upon such beauty he wouldn't have made it*, Gabe thought. However, it was a thought he kept to himself.

***

"Congratulations on a perfect landfall, Captain."

"Thank you, My Lord."

"Deck there! Ship of the line anchored off the head-land."

"That will be the flagship, no doubt," Buck said.

"Aye," Anthony replied. "It will be almost like home-coming, will it not, Captain?"

"Aye, My Lord, my mind traveled that same road. I wonder if a certain widow lady is still a widow."

This caused Anthony to chuckle. "I'm sure you'll find out, Captain, I'm sure you'll find out."

As the flagship rounded Cape Shirley, Anthony watched the men not on watch as they crowded the weather side. Some of them were clinging to the shrouds to get a better view.

"A pretty island is it not?" This coming from Lord Ragland. He had been a good traveling companion. He had dined with Anthony and Lady Deborah most evenings, along with Captain Buck. They had played cards frequently, always arguing who would have Lady Deborah as a partner. Her skill as a card player amazed Anthony.

"If we ever get short of funds," he joked, "we'll invite the gentry over so you can fleece them."

English Harbour is much hillier than I thought," Ragland said. "I'd expected it to be flat."

"Barbados will be," Anthony explained.

"There's the flagship," Bart said as he approached the group. "Gunports are open; they've a captain what cares about 'is men."

"I don't understand," Ragland said.

"It gets very hot and humid here so the tar will actually stick to your feet walking across the deck. Below decks can be unbearable. Therefore it's best for the men to rig awnings across the quarterdeck and by opening the gunports you can sometimes catch a good offshore breeze."

"I see."

"Mr Lamb." Buck called to his first lieutenant.

"Aye, Captain."

"Prepare the salute." As an afterthought he added, "Clear those idlers off the side. This is a man o' war, not some grocery barge."

Ragland nudged Anthony and smiled.

Seeing the smile Bart said, "Wonder who 'e got that from?"

No sooner had the eleven-gun salute ended when the lookout called down again, "Looks like a harbour full o' ships at anchor."

Taking his glass, Buck steadied himself and looked, calling out what he saw. "Three Frenchmen. One of the monsieurs is flying a rear admiral's flag. There's two Spaniards. The harbour is full. Lighters and other craft plying back and forth."

"Spying, damme, they know they're about to take up with the Colonies. So they're taking advantage of the neutrality to see what our strengths are, what convoys arrive, and where they go from here. They're not fooling me. Damn them I say and the Dagos with them."

Anthony had never seen Lord Ragland so exasperated.

"'E can be a fireball 'e can," Bart said, summoning up the incident. "Wonder 'e don't 'ave us loosen a broadside here and now to get it over like."

"Aye," Anthony agreed. "If we were in Barbados he might."

***

The next week was one of reunions, a quickly thrown together reception for Lord Ragland and Lord Anthony. The French Admiral Jacques de Guimond along with his Flag Captain Riguad Devereux had also been invited for the reception. The French admiral had been somewhat reserved. He was very polite and diplomatic, refusing to be drawn into discussion in regards to the war with the Colonies. His comments were, "As you know, m'sieur, we are a neutral country."

The day after the reception had taken place, Lord Anthony received a message from Lord Ragland requesting his presence. Anthony and Deborah were sitting on the veranda of the summer cottage where they had first made love. Deborah was saying the cottage was just the right size for her and Faith. There was also plenty of room for Nanny…and Lum if he chose to stay. Bart…Uncle Bart had just come to the door holding Macayla when the rider arrived.

It didn't take long for two horses to be saddled for Anthony and Bart to ride down the hill to English Harbour. Halfway down the hill Bart surprised Anthony with a sudden comment.

"Iffen we's ever beached, this wouldn't be a bad spot for it to happen."

Anthony had never really considered any life but the sea. But Bart had struck a chord. "You're right old friend. It would be easy to live out our days here."

"Like Commodore Gardner and 'is wife," Bart said.

"Aye, like Commodore Gardner."

After a pause, Bart then added, "But not yet."

"No, not yet...after the war maybe but not yet."

***

Government House stood at the top of the coast road only a hundred yards or so from where a launch was tied up, bobbing with the swell. Admiral Henry Teach was in the process of getting in a carriage for a quick trip up the hill.

A footman took Anthony's and Bart's horses while they made their way into the elegant, white building. Ground seashells crunched under their feet as they quickly walked down the path leading to the deep porch. The shade of the porch would offer relief from the sun's fierce rays.

A marine sergeant welcomed Lord Anthony but was not sure about Bart. Anthony looked at the sergeant and said, "Please find a suitable place for my cox'n to wait along with some cool refreshment."

The marine gaped, not sure how to respond. Finally he muttered, "Lord Ragland awaits you, sir," pointing to what had once been Gardner's old office. Then taking Bart in tow he made his way down a hall.

Anthony had barely the time to accept a glass of hock from one of the servants when Sir Henry showed up. Once the two admirals were seated with a glass, Lord Ragland opened a door to an adjoining room and a short, stocky individual entered. He was dressed much as a naval officer but without the apparent rank insignias.

"Gentlemen," Ragland began, "let me introduce you to Sir Victor MacNeil. He is from his Majesty's Foreign Office. He has documents with him signed by Lord North that requires us to render assistance in anyway possible."

"I will add," Lord Ragland continued, "that I have known Sir Victor for many years and have found him to be a very capable man. Sir Victor, you have the floor."

Stepping in front of the little used fireplace, Sir Victor raised his glass…after a momentary pause he said in a deep voice, “A toast gentlemen. To England…and death to the French.”

# PART II

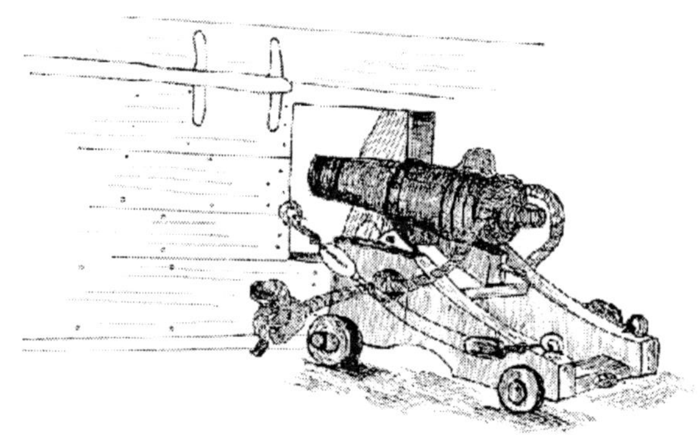

## Left Her Crying

Left her crying on the pier
When we put out to sea.
Now every night I walk these decks
Cause I can't go to sleep.

Every time I close my eyes
I can see her face.
Makes me wonder if her love
Is nothing but a waste.

My heart is so empty
When she's not around.
But if she needed help
Where would it be found?

Michael Aye

## *Chapter Eleven*

Lord Anthony lay in his cot. The only sound was the rhythmic creaking of the ropes that attached to eyebolts in the overhead. The cot seemed empty and cold in spite of the heat. It was the first night since weighing anchor in Plymouth that he had slept alone. He already missed his wife and daughter more than he ever imagined.

Bart was right. Being on the beach was not that bad. He had saved enough prize money that he should be able to retire easily. Especially when combined with Deborah's holdings. Yes, Deborah's holdings. He had not as yet considered it his as most men would have done.

The sudden shrill of a boatswain's pipes broke Anthony's thoughts. The sound of the bosun mates could be heard as they aroused the sleeping men below deck.

"All hands rouse out, rouse out you lubbers. Lash and carry."

The men below tumbled out of their hammocks quickly. The promise of being enlivened by the bosun mate's starter prevented most from being laggard. The cook lit the fires in the galley stove while the on duty watch was put to work. They rigged the pumps, and got out swabs, buckets, and holystones.

They scrubbed and washed down the deck then flogged them dry with swabs. Brick dust was used to polish the bright work. By seven o' clock, the crew was piped to a simple but filling breakfast of burgoo (coarse oatmeal) and coffee. Anthony could hear Silas scrambling around in the pantry preparing his breakfast.

"My Lord." This was from Bart. "I's let you sleep longer than be usual. Yew seemed restless like."

*I must have been*, Anthony thought, *if Bart had come in without awakening him.*

"Lord Ragland, is he awake?"

"Aye," Bart replied.

Anthony roused out of his cot and dressed quickly. He then looked at Bart and said, "Go topside and invite Buck and Lord Ragland to breakfast."

"Aye," Bart replied, easing the cabin door to as he left.

The breakfast consisted of coffee, cold cheese, pastries, and a discussion about the meeting with the foreign office agent, Sir Victor.

Sir Victor had given Sir Henry his orders recalling him to England. He alluded that it was just a normal rotation with Admiral Lord Anthony replacing him.

But in private Lord Ragland told Anthony otherwise. "British trade in the West Indies has been hit hard. To the point it's critical. Only twenty-five ships out of a convoy of sixty carrying provisions to the Caribbean arrived safely. The governor of Grenada sent a letter to Lord North stating that they would soon die of hunger if the losses were not stopped. Insurance rates have soared and the Admiralty has been bombarded with demands for protection. More than three hundred trading vessels have been captured...a good many by the daring privateer, Malachi Mundy."

Gabe had met with him, Anthony recalled, but did not mention it.

Lord Ragland continued, "Sir Henry was being recalled due to his inability to stop the losses."

Sir Victor had informed the group that it was now certain the French would enter the war...probably very soon after the New Year. He felt that Spain would soon join in as well. They had been secretly aiding the American privateer for a while now. "This has been confirmed by our agents," he stated.

Sir Victor had then pointed out the window to the harbour that spread out below them. "Do you think the eighty-gun *Sceptre* is here for her health? Where did her consorts go?" He had been speaking of the *St. Michel*, a seventy-four, and *Toulon* of fifty guns.

"They're spying," he exclaimed, "and there's not a damn thing we can do about it."

***

At Port-au-Prince, Haiti, Paul de Verge sat behind his desk drinking a glass of wine. The wine was to steady him so that he would appear outwardly calm as he spoke to the man sitting across from him.

"So you failed," he spat at the man. "You failed in the assassination attempt of Lord Anthony. You failed to capture any prizes from the convoy. You have failed me at every turn."

"Bad luck," the man across from de Verge said. "All bad luck. But we will eventually succeed in our goal."

"You have the luxury to be patient," de Verge responded. "I don't. The investors are screaming about the loss of the *Lizard*."

"They've made a fortune under my guidance," the man retorted.

Adam Montique was not a man used to being scolded like a child. He'd taken about as much as he intended from the little Frenchman that sat before him.

"I'm the one who risks his life. All you risk is a few dollars. You can tell your friends their financial resources have only been scratched by the loss of the *Lizard*. There are more than enough backers either here or on Guadalupe that are willing to undertake the cost of my enterprise.

So tell your backers Adam Montique said they can all be damned."

He then stood, and after a quick glare walked out of de Verge's office, leaving the small Frenchman grabbing for a handkerchief to wipe his brow. *Was it fear or the heat? Perhaps both*, he thought as he filled his glass.

***

Barbados was the eastern most island of the Windward Islands. Compared to Antigua it was relatively flat and somewhat diamond shaped. Barbados gained its wealth from sugarcane plantations and the export of molasses and rum. Slaves had been imported to work the fields, which were very rich.

The cry "land ho" from one of the lookouts came as the sun had begun to bear down on the ships in Anthony's squadron. Gabe paced the quarterdeck of *Peregrine*. He was in an ill humour. Like his brother he'd rested badly the previous night…the first without Faith in some months. He'd awakened to the sound of a new temporary cabin servant. It had been decided the Lum would stay in Antigua with the women…a means of protection.

The new man was not Lum and he had never acted as a captain's servant, so he had to be told what to do at every turn. Dawkins had rolled his eyes more than once, amazed over the man's continuous mistakes. However, being a landsman, he would not be missed as much as a seaman would be when taken away from his daily duties. No, none of this is what caused Gabe's mood.

It was Faith. She had been sick every morning for the last three mornings they were at Antigua. The very mention of breakfast had caused her to turn green and rush out the door. By mid-day she seemed as rosy and healthy as she'd ever been. Gabe had wanted to send for the ship's doctor but Faith had refused.

*Where the hell is Caleb?* Gabe thought, and then wondered if he'd be with Dagan in Barbados. *Would Dagan be there as he'd stated in the letter?*

Before long Ragged Point became visible...they would be in Carlisle Bay soon. To the western end of Carlisle Bay was Bridgetown. It was here that Gabe had met Caleb and that damned ape, Mr Jewels. Gabe couldn't help but chuckle thinking of the antics that blasted creature had pulled.

"What was that, Captain?"

Gabe looked to see his first lieutenant speaking.

"It was nothing, Mr Lavery. I was just recalling Caleb and his ape."

This brought a smile to Lavery's face. "Aye, Captain. I remember it well. I thought His Lordship would bust a gut with the damn monkey shrieking to high heaven as he climbed the riggings. He'd have been shot if Lord Hood had been awakened."

"Aye, those were the days, Nathan...those were the days." Glancing at his watch, Gabe said, "We've still got to pass South Point and Needham Point. I think I'll go below. Call me before we reach the bay."

"Aye, Captain."

As soon as Gabe disappeared through the companionway, Lieutenant Wiley approached Lavery. "What's this about an ape aboard Lord Anthony's ship?" Within a minute Wiley was laughing till he cried as Lavery told his story.

Word had rushed down the coast to Bridgetown that a British squadron was in the sighting. Having a wet at the Anchor and Plow, Dagan finished his drink. The tavern was one of the nicest on the island. The proprietor named his tavern to attract both the sea trade and that of the island planters. He had gotten wealthy in doing so and like many self-made men had little tolerance for lesser beings.

This morning had been particularly busy. The cook was a very smallish man, almost frail in appearance. He had been very busy when the owner arrived.

"Give me a cup of coffee now," the owner ordered.

The cook rushed to do as he was bid. Upon delivering the cup of coffee the owner drank a swallow then tossed it on the floor.

"Clean that up, you idiot, then go get me a fresh cup of coffee…hot coffee. I like it hot."

The little cook rushed back but the pot was empty and the other pot had not yet started to boil. "It will be a minute or two, sir," the cook said in a very timid voice.

"Now damn it. I want some hot coffee now or so help me I'll throw you out on your arse, you little snit."

The cook darted back into the kitchen embarrassed and mad as a hornet. He touched the coffee pot but it was not ready yet. Then he spied a bowl of jalapeno peppers he'd cut from the little vegetable garden he'd planted. He squeezed the juice of a couple into the empty coffee cup. He then filled the cup up with the still brewing coffee. He put it on a saucer and took it to the owner, who gulped it down. The man jumped up and ran to the water keg screaming profanities as his face turned red and sweat beaded up on his bald head.

The little cook slowly took off his apron, a look of satisfaction on his face. "You said you wanted it hot," he quipped as he strode out the door.

Dagan threw some coins on the table and went out after him. "That was some trick mate. What did you put in his coffee?"

"Jalapenos," the little cook said. "They're a very hot type of pepper."

"I know about them. They've been around for centuries. My name is Dagan Dupree."

"I'm Joshua Nesbit, but people call me Josh."

"Well, Josh, what are you going to do now?"

"First, I'm going to sneak into the back room," he said, pointing at the tavern. "My things are there. After that I'm not sure."

Liking the little man, Dagan asked, "Ever been aboard a man o' war?"

"No. I hired on as a cook on a merchantman once but never a warship."

"Well, come along with me and let's see if we can't find you a billet."

## *Chapter Twelve*

Commodore Lord Benjamin Hewes set sail the week after Anthony's squadron and Lord Ragland had arrived. Lord Hewes was an old gentleman who was glad to see a younger man take over as governor during these troubled times. He was to sail back to England with Admiral Teach.

Lord Anthony held a meeting for all captains, first lieutenants, and masters. He introduced Sir Victor, the foreign office agent, to his men. He explained the problem with shipping and privateers, the likelihood of France entering the war soon and the tactics he intended to deploy.

"We will take a few days to replenish our ships and then we will get down to the business at hand—winning a war for England."

After the meeting, refreshments were served, and then pipes and cigars were broken out. *New faces and old*, he thought. *How quickly they come together as comrades.* A poem he'd read came to mind.

*You laugh, you drink, you dance*
*You men who sail the sea*
*For tomorrow who's to know*
*What might assail upon thee*
*Be it gale or sword or cannon*
*A sinking ship it be*
*So live life hearty*

*You men who sail the sea*

As the meeting ended Gabe caught Anthony's eye and held back.

"So Dagan showed up?" Anthony asked.

"Aye, just like he said."

"Where is he now?"

"Having a wet with Bart and the master."

"Aye, I would expect that given the chance. Sir Victor wants to visit St. Lucia tomorrow," Anthony continued. "He has asked for two ships. More specifically he's asked for you and for the *Lizard*."

"You don't like the man do you?" Gabe asked.

"Not him as much as what he does. He's a spy…a necessary evil but an evil just the same."

After a pause, Gabe said, "The fly and the fly trap."

"My thoughts exactly," Anthony responded. He laid his hand on his brother's shoulder. "Have a care."

"I will."

"Good…now if you have no other engagements, dine with me tonight. You and Dagan."

"My pleasure, Gil. I want to tell you about my new servant."

***

The sun was hot…bright and hot as it dazzled off the glass-like surface of the Caribbean Sea, creating a harsh glare. Gabe plucked at his sweat soaked shirt. It was sodden through and through. He was thirsty as was every jack tar aboard the ship. Gabe used his hand to shield his eyes as he looked across to *Lizard* not two cables to starboard.

He wondered if her new captain was cursing the sticky deck seam that gripped at your shoes, or was he below in the shade? *He had that advantage*, Gabe thought. *If I went below I'd have to make polite conversation with Sir Victor. I wonder if yonder captain knows his ship is being used as bait.*

Richard Culzean had until recently been the first lieutenant aboard Admiral Teach's flagship. Now he was given command of a twenty-eight-gun frigate, a tribute to the departing admiral.

"A nice ship even if she is a bit old."

Gabe turned to find Dagan speaking. *He always seems to know what I'm thinking*, Gabe thought.

"It's an excellent ship for his first command."

"Well, I expect he's earned it," Dagan said. "Three years as a first lieutenant aboard a flag ship."

"Aye," Gabe answered, feeling ashamed of his retort. "At least I never had to work my way up the chain of command spending years as a first lieutenant. Thanks to Gil."

"How is the new recruit doing?" Dagan asked, speaking of the little cook, Nesbit.

"Splendid, just splendid. If only he could play the lotz or violin," Gabe replied.

"Aye," Dagan smiled. He missed Lum's musical talents as well.

"Here comes the surgeon," Dagan volunteered.

Isreal Livesey had been recommended by the Portsmouth Port admiral as a highly competent, seldom in his cups surgeon, who was also a good card and chess player. The old man was as weathered an old salt that Gabe had ever seen. His skin was like mahogany wood. He had a portly appearance with round shoulders. He also had a huge cherry-like nose and heavy jowls that looked bigger than they were because of mutton chop whiskers. His eyes drooped, not unlike one of Lord Anthony's hounds and were the saddest thing Gabe had ever seen. However, he was a jovial old soul and kept the wardroom in stitches with his jokes and tales.

A hail from the lookout made Gabe look across the way to *Lizard*. Her commission pennant, which only minutes before had hung limply, now fluttered with a small breeze. This excited the crew as they rushed to the bulwark to see. They were half naked men whose skin had lost the pale white of England and now was almost a copper or bronze color.

The calm had occurred shortly after Barbados disappeared over the horizon. Now maybe it was over. A flapping noise was heard overhead as the sails filled with the freshening wind. Then a loud snap was heard as the main sail became taut. Cheers went up from the crew.

"Mr Lavery."

"Aye, Captain."

"If you can regain control of the crew would you reset the watch?"

"Aye, Captain."

"Mr Gunnells, if you will kindly put us on a course to St. Lucia."

"Aye, sir."

"Mr Livesey."

"Yes, Captain."

"It appears your coming on deck caused the wind to return. I consider you a lucky soul. It would be my pleasure if you would dine with me tonight."

"Thank you, sir. I accept of course."

"Good," Gabe said. He then added, "With your luck I shall request you as my partner if we can talk our guest from the Foreign Office and Dagan into a hand or two."

The little surgeon clapped his hands together and smiled. "Indeed, Captain. It will certainly be my pleasure."

Gabe had known several seamen would overhear his conversation with the surgeon. It had been intended. Seamen were usually a superstitious lot. Having the captain think the surgeon was a lucky man could only help.

Gabe's cabin was cool compared to the blistering heat on deck. Sir Victor was seated next to the stern windows looking out, his mind on God knows what.

Nesbit appeared and asked, "A glass of hock for you and the gentleman, sir."

"Aye," he replied for both of them.

Seeing the little man go to retrieve the hock it was hard to imagine this mild and meek person would have the gall to pull such a stunt as he did with the tavern's owner. *I'll remember to be polite*, Gabe thought.

Gabe had just finished his hock and signing a collection of papers the purser had brought when the sentry knocked.

"Mr Ally, sir."

Once the boy was inside the cabin, Gabe could see from his excitement that something was up.

"Mr Lavery's compliments, sir, and I think I hear gunfire."

Gabe had leaned back in his chair when the sentry knocked. Now he sat upright.

"You hear gunfire!"

"Yes sir."

"Course it could be thunder."

"There's not a cloud in the sky."

"That's what the master said, Captain."

"Very well, tell the first lieutenant I will be on deck directly."

As Gabe reached for his hat, Sir Victor asked, "May I come on deck with you, Captain?"

Taken aback with Sir Victor's sudden show of manners, Gabe replied after a pause, "Of course, sir."

Seeing the captain come on deck, the helmsman whispered to the master, "Cap'n on deck."

The master then nudged the first lieutenant, who turned and reported, "Mr Ally heard the sound of gunfire, sir. Then it was heard again but so far there's too much haze to see any distance."

Seeing his captain look up, Gunnells volunteered, "The winds holding."

"There it is again," Midshipman Ally said, pointing to larboard.

"Damme, but that boy has got ears," Gunnells exclaimed.

"We will go investigate," Gabe said. "Mr Gunnells, two points to larboard if you please. Signal *Lizard* to take station to starboard, Mr Hawks."

"Aye, Captain."

"Have nets and chain slings rigged, Mr Lavery. We don't want a busted noggin from falling spars."

This caused a group of seamen to laugh. The men lay to with frenzy. The possibility of prize money was on everyone's mind.

"Gawd, Phelps! Take another turn on the tackle. That net's as loose as a Portsmouth whore's drawers."

"Buckley, lend a hand, you lubber. Haul tight now me laddies. Haul tight I say."

Graf, the bosun, was everywhere, shouting as he went. "Rose, ye little nipper, I see ya shirking." *Smack*...encouragement by way of the bosun's starter. "Now carry your load, ya laggard."

In the distance another rumble was heard, this time by all those on the quarterdeck.

"Mr Lavery, swing out the boats for towing."

From overhead the lookout called down, "Three ships...one much smaller than the other two, probably a brig."

"Who do you think they are?" This came from Sir Victor, causing a glare from the officers on the quarterdeck.

Dagan spoke up. "Who knows, but they can't all be friendly."

This caused an eruption of laughter from those gathered. Gabe gave Dagan a brief nod, thankful he'd defused any friction before it got out of hand. Sir Victor would have to learn quarterdeck etiquette.

"Beat to quarters, Mr Lavery. I fear this day is about to get hotter."

Taking his glass Gabe could see the little brig had been boarded. The deck was all but overrun by privateers.

"Your weapons, Captain." Paco, ever silent but always there, had gotten Gabe's sword and pistols. Seeing his captain look at the pistols, Paco added, "Loaded and primed, sir."

Within nine minutes *Peregrine* was cleared for action. Constant drill from the time they left Plymouth with the convoy had paid off.

"Have the guns loaded but don't run them out yet. Double shot and grape," Gabe ordered.

*Peregrine* and *Lizard* bore down on the battling ships. A ship the size of a large frigate and a brigantine had apparently captured the small brig.

"That's the same frigate we saw leaving England!" Lieutenant Wiley exclaimed. "I marked her well so I'd not forget."

"Deck there, they've seen us."

"Too late," Gabe said. "They have to fight. Mr Hawks!"

"Aye, Captain."

"Signal *Lizard* engage brigantine."

The mid ran off then halted and turned. "Aye, Captain."

"Excited that one is."

Seeing the approaching ships, the privateers made a hasty retreat back to their own ships.

Lieutenant Davy said, "Listen sir, they are cheering us on. The brig's people are cheering us on."

Suddenly the sound of a broadside vibrated across the waves. Everyone was silent as the lookout called down, "The frigate 'as fired on the brig. She be in shambles, sir."

"Damn the whoresons," Sir Victor said. "That was a hellish thing to do."

Gabe was suddenly calm, recalling something his brother had once said. "He's trying to rile you. Mad men make mistakes."

The distance was closing rapidly now. *She's larger, a forty-four at least*, Gabe thought. *We can't match her gun for gun.*

"Mr Gunnells, do you see yonder ship has her larboard gun ports open?"

"Aye, Captain, she expects us to pass that way."

"When I tell you, put your helm down. We will cross between her and the brig."

"Captain, there's precious little room."

"There's enough. Mr Davy, we will open this dance with the starboard quartet if you please. Be ready."

Lieutenant Wiley, who was to be in charge of the quarterdeck guns, looked wild-eyed at Lavery, not believing what he'd heard.

"You'll get used to it," Lavery said nonchalantly. He added, "Sails her like a yacht in the channel, don't he?"

Nearer and nearer the ships closed. The frigate's bowsprit loomed larger and larger.

"Now, Mr Gunnells, now."

*Peregrine* heeled over and men had to hold on as the deck canted. Sir Victor lost his footing but was grabbed by one of the quarterdeck gun crews.

Hanging onto a shroud, Gabe watched forward, "Wait…wait…now, Mr Gunnells, bring her up. Lively now. Mr Davy, open your ports and fire as you bear."

Gabe shouted out his orders. As *Peregrine* passed between the brig and the frigate, he saw the senseless carnage. *Peregrine* shuddered as it made its way down the side of the frigate, her guns belching fire and death as the double shotted balls and grape tore into the enemy ship.

Gabe watched with satisfaction as great pieces of the frigate's bulwark caved in. Fragments of torn planking filled the air with deadly splinters. One of the quarterdeck guns bellowed out its defiance, causing Gabe to cover his ears with his hands. They were now past the larger ship and not a single gun had fired on them, the surprise being so complete.

Shouting to be heard above the gunfire, Gabe ordered, "Cross her stern, Mr Gunnells, cross her stern."

The bang of musket fire sounded and balls thudded into the deck.

"Walk about," Gabe told Sir Victor. "No need to give the cutthroats a prime target."

Men coughed and wiped their eyes as gun smoke drifted about. Then *Peregrine* heeled again as the wheel was spun and she crossed the stern of the frigate. An explosion and screams came from forward. The frigate had its stern chasers in action and a forward gun was overturned, killing two of its crew.

Davy had the main battery firing again and again. Gun after gun fired. "That's it." He fairly leaped up and down. "That's it. Bugger them good. Put another round up her arse."

Dagan leaned over and shouted into Gabe's ear. "Boy has gone wild, worse than Caleb's ape."

Gabe burst into laughter. One of the quarterdeck gunners poked his mate and pointed at the sight of their captain laughing away in the den of battle.

"'E's 'aving a gay old time, that one is."

"Probably counting 'is prize money, I 'spect."

As *Peregrine* crossed the frigate's stern, Gabe ordered, "Cease fire…cease fire."

He then turned to Lavery, "That was well done, sir."

"Mr Gunnells."

"Aye, sir."

"Come about and lay us alongside the frigate."

"Aye, sir."

"Why?" Sir Victor asked.

Gabe held back the angry retort, realizing the man probably didn't know. "I intend to board her, sir."

Dagan again was there. "Arm yourself or go below, sir. No spectators this go around."

"Where's *Lizard*?" Gabe asked.

"She's took the brigantine, sir." This from one of the younger midshipman, Peter Chase. His little face was so smudged Gabe wanted to laugh.

"Good, young sir. Mr Hawks."

"Aye, Captain."

"Signal *Lizard*, board enemy."

"Will he know which one, sir?"

Lavery cuffed the boy a good one. "He's already took the brigantine, lad. There's only one left to board."

As *Peregrine* came about, Gunnells said, "Look there, Captain. It appears when we crossed the privateers' stern we scored a luck hit on either a rudder cable or the rudder itself."

"Damme, Gunnells!" Gabe exclaimed, taking a glass from his eye. "Bear off, bear off, signal *Lizard* to take station astern. Mr Lavery, how would you like to board yonder vessel and ask them to surrender?"

"Terms, Captain?" Lavery asked.

"Terms?" This from Sir Victor. "I'll tell you what terms: a fair trial and a swift hanging."

Gabe cleared his throat. "As we've always done, Mr Lavery. We'll sign those we can within the squadron. And we'll review the papers the captain may possess before a further decision is made. Otherwise, we'll stand off and blast them to hell. The choice is theirs."

A longboat was pulled alongside using the towing rope she'd been tied to.

"Shall I go?" Dagan whispered to Gabe.

"No, Mr Lavery has to gain the experience if he's to be ready to command at some point."

*Peregrine's* hull rose and fell with the gentle swell as the officers and crew waited for Lieutenant Lavery's return. The men remained at their battle stations…guns loaded and run out. They were ready for any signs of treachery on the privateers' part.

"Deck there," the lookout called down. "A group o' ladies, sir, 'as been brought on deck."

Everyone who had a glass trained it on the enemy ship. Six women lined the rail. Lieutenant Lavery could be seen as he went over the side and down into the waiting longboat. It was only a few minutes till Lavery climbed through *Peregrine's* entry port.

"Yonder captain is a black heart, Captain."

The group on the quarterdeck drew closer to hear Lavery's comments. "He has six women and a plantation owner aboard his ship as hostages. He says you have fifteen minutes from the time I reached this ship to set sail or he'll start hanging the hostages. One every fifteen minutes we delay. Starting with the women first. At least two of the women are related to the gentleman so he'll have to go through the misery of watching his kin hanged."

"Surely he knows we'll blast him to hell if he touches even one of the women," Sir Victor hissed.

"I said the same. The bastard only shrugged his shoulders and replied, 'They'll still be hung.'"

Looking across at the badly damaged brig, Gabe knew the privateer had the advantage. "Prepare my gig, Paco."

"It won't do," Lavery said. "Either I'm to return or it's no good. He said he didn't like to deal with more than one person at a time."

"Was anything said about the captured brigantine?"

"Not specifically but I took it he meant they sailed together."

"They'll be dead or worse if he sails off with the women aboard," Dagan said, speaking for the first time.

"I agree," Gabe answered. "Lieutenant Lavery return quickly and tell the captain to put the hostages in a longboat and he has my word of honour that when he is over the horizon we will collect the women and release the brigantine."

"Tell him," Gabe said as an afterthought, "once the brigantine is over the horizon, I will be coming after him."

As Lavery climbed down into the awaiting boat, Gabe saw Dagan following. *He needed to go to get a feel of the situation,* Gabe thought.

"Paco!"

"Aye, Cap'n."

"Take my gig over to *Lizard* and explain what has transpired. Tell Captain Culzean not to release the brigantine before my signal."

"Is it necessary, Captain?" Sir Victor asked. "Is there no other way?"

"None that I can think of," Gabe answered. "Besides I've given my word."

"No one would hold it against you," Sir Victor hissed. "You could blow them away and no one would even know you gave your word."

Gabe's sudden frown and squinted eyes frightened Sir Victor as he hissed, "They would." Sweeping his arm out and pointing to his crew. "And I would."

"They're lowering a boat, Captain." This was from Lieutenant Wiley.

*Had he heard the exchange? I don't care if he did*, Gabe realized. *Do him good to know how politicians think. Damn them all anyway.*

Gabe then put the encounter out of his mind and watched as the women were lowered into the waiting boat. No sooner had the last woman made it safely into the boat then the man was thrown over the side. He landed next to the bobbing longboat. Two of the oarsman unhooked a boat oar and held it out for the man to latch on to. The sound of laughter was heard about the privateer.

"Thinks it's funny don't they?" Gunnells said.

"Aye," Gabe replied. "They'll think it's funny when we next meet and they don't have a group of women to hide behind."

Watching the two boats, Lavery could be seen tying a rope onto the bow of the hostages' boat. He then returned to the ship trailing the rope behind them.

Once aboard he explained, "I didn't see any need to send another boat to gather them when we could just pull them over."

"Good thinking. Prepare to get us underway, Lieutenant Wiley. Mr Gunnells, lay us alongside the brig. We may still be of some use."

"Captain."

"Yes, Mr Lavery."

"As I was leaving the privateer, a man approached. He was not the ship's captain but he seemed to be in charge. He was the one who agreed to your terms. He asked me," Lavery continued, "'Who is your captain?' Seeing no reason not be honest I told him who you were. 'I thought I recognized him,' the man replied. He…ah…he then said…No offense please, Captain."

"Go on," Gabe prodded.

"He said, 'Ask the bastard how is Faith?'"

Gabe clinched his fist until the knuckles turned white. "Montique!!! It must be him."

"Aye," Dagan, who was standing close by said. "I had a feeling."

Gabe stood there staring out at the disappearing ship. Dagan laid his hand on his nephew's shoulder. "His day will come, I promise."

***

The damage to the little brig was worse than anyone imagined. One mast hung over the side causing it to list. The other mast was completely gone, leaving only a shattered stump. The rails were battered beyond recognition and huge sections of the deck planking were torn apart. Mr Livesey was being helped down onto the smaller ship. A few of the brig's crew moved around in a daze trying to comfort the few survivors. Gabe and Dagan ducked below for a quick look in the captain's tiny cabin. It was almost bare. *Not unlike Sea Wolf's*, Gabe thought.

"Not much here," Paco volunteered.

He had entered behind the two. As the three started out of the cabin, Paco stopped suddenly. Movement came from under a piece of bed linen in the corner. Gabe and Dagan stepped back as Paco took a broken chair leg and lifted the cloth.

"A dog," he exclaimed.

"A puppy," Dagan corrected.

"A damn big puppy," Gabe added.

"He's been hurt," Paco said. "Looks like somebody went after him with a blade. Do you want me to finish him, Cap'n?"

Gabe paused as if in thought. Taking a deep breath, he said, "No, there's been enough of that sort of thing already. Let's see if the surgeon can fix him up."

The puppy stared at the men, cowering until Paco reached for him. Then the dog bared his teeth and snapped at the man. Clearly startled at the dog's tenacity, Paco jumped back.

"Let me see him," Dagan said and stepped around Paco. He knelt down on his knees next to where the dog lay. He whispered softly to the dog and slowly reached out his hand. Continuing to whisper he laid the piece of linen over the dog's wound and gently picked it up.

"That's it. Now take it easy. We won't hurt you, big fellow. He's a big one all right."

"Big and tough as Sampson," Paco said.

"Why you've named him, Paco. We'll call him Sampson." Gabe said.

## Chapter Thirteen

Sir Victor went ashore at St. Lucia but was back within an hour. "We will make sail as soon as possible, Captain."

"Aye," Gabe replied. "Are we headed back to Barbados?"

"We are not. We are sailing to Antigua and there you may be relieved of my company," Sir Victor informed Gabe.

"What about *Lizard*, sir?" Gabe asked. "Does she sail in company or report back to the admiral?"

"I see no reason for her to return. She may yet prove useful."

Hearing Sir Victor's words, Gabe wasn't sure if the foreign affairs agent felt safer having two ships in company or if he was still looked upon as bait. Either way they were going to Antigua and that meant seeing Faith. *Wouldn't that make Gil envious?* Gabe thought, smiling to himself.

"Captain."

"Aye, Mr Lavery."

"I've talked to the ah…hostages, sir."

"They're no longer hostages, Mr Lavery."

"Ere, well…yes sir. At any rate Mr Houghton and his family are from Barbados. The other hostages…young ladies are from St. Johns on Antigua."

"Thank you for the clarification, Mr Lavery," Gabe said. "I'd hate to sail all the way to the Virgin Islands only to learn I was at the wrong St. Johns."

"You're welcome, Captain, though I wouldn't mind a little more time at sea to get to know a couple of them better. I don't know if you've noticed, Captain, but a couple of them are lookers."

"Humph!" Gabe responded.

The young ladies were certainly attractive even in their torn and ragged attire. The dresses the girls wore were all in a state of ill repair. Some were torn so that most of a leg was visible or the top buttons were gone so more of their chest was open showing more than considerable cleavage. All of this caused Gabe to rethink his previous thought. Maybe it's this attire that made them more attractive.

Dagan, who had sided up to Gabe, touched his shoulder and motioned to the waist of the ship. One of the young ladies sat on a hatch cover. Standing over her Lieutenant Davy could be seen in conversation with her. However, standing over her as he was he had a full view of her healthy chest.

"Bring back memories of our days back in Antigua?" Dagan asked.

"Was I so obvious?" Gabe asked.

"Like Squire Hugh's dog pointing pheasant."

"Why didn't somebody say something?" Gabe asked.

"Cause they were all looking too."

"I see," Gabe said, joking with his uncle. "I guess that included you as well."

"Me especially," Dagan replied with a chuckle.

"Well, let's get ready to weigh anchor," Gabe said, turning to give orders to the first lieutenant. Then as an afterthought he turned and called out, "Mr Davy!"

"Aye, Captain."

"Please attend to your duties, sir, before you go blind."

"Right away, sir," the young lieutenant replied and dashed off, leaving the young lady to puzzle over the comment…go blind?"

The evening air was much cooler as *Peregrine* and *Lizard* sailed northward to Antigua. Seeing his captain glance aloft at the sails the quartermaster volunteered, "Winds steady and holding, sir."

"Thank you, Yates."

"Captain, it's a beautiful evening."

"Aye, that it is, Mr Houghton," Gabe replied to the planter they'd rescued. "Few things can match the beauty of the sun going over the horizon at sea"

"I agree, Captain, especially after what we've just gone through. When we were taken aboard that privateer I just knew my time was up. I also knew a fate worse than death awaited my wife, daughter, and the other young ladies. If it wasn't for the ship's captain…he tried to behave as a gentleman but the other man…he was cruel."

"Aye," Gabe answered. "I know the man. He is evil…a devious, evil man. He's been a foe for some time now but I've yet to get the upper hand."

"Well keep your pistols loaded and primed, Captain. Loaded and primed."

"I will, sir," Gabe replied. He asked the planter if he and his family would care to dine with him that evening.

"My pleasure, sir," Houghton said. He then looked at his watch. "I will see to my wife and thank you for the invitation."

***

Nesbit rushed around making sure everything was as it should be. This was the first time the captain had entertained since he'd taken over the duties of captain's servant, or as he liked to say, captain's steward. Nesbit had recruited the "cleaner" of the ship's cooks to assist him tonight. Since the sea was calm, he'd set out candles and instead of the usual sea service he'd set out the captain's best china and crystal.

They had all sat down at the table and a glass of claret had been poured. Some of the young ladies appeared giggly over being served the beverage. *Most immature*, Nesbit thought.

A bowl of potato soup was then served after the drink had been poured. Nesbit made his way back towards the pantry when a crash was heard. He quickly rushed inside the pantry where he let go a string of profanities. They filled the air along with the sound of pots and pans hitting the deck in addition to a series of growls and barking. Gabe jumped up and made it to the door in time to see Samson win a tug of war over the roast mutton with Nesbit.

Sitting on the deck, Nesbit looked up at Gabe and said, "The main course has just been changed from roast mutton to boiled beef." He then gave a sigh and continued, "Samson, it appears, is a most disagreeable dining partner. It does seem, however, that his wounds no longer inhibit his appetite."

***

It was just after dawn that the island of Antigua broke the horizon. The air was already humid and Gunnells, the master, promised it would be much worse by midday. Soon word would spread the length and breath of the island that two warships were in the offering. Gabe had made his pre-dawn visit to the quarterdeck but now decided to go back down and have a cup of coffee.

His cabin had been turned over to the Houghton family and the four other girls so he'd have to walk quietly in order not to awaken everyone. He'd not slept well last evening partly because he was not in his quarters and partly because Faith had been on his mind. He'd find a reason to spend at least one night in port.

Sir Victor was on deck when Gabe returned. He walked over to him and held out his hand. "Captain, I want to thank you for being such a splendid host. I was very impressed on how you handled yourself against the privateer. It will go in my report."

"Thank you, sir," Gabe managed. He was at a loss for words with the sudden politeness from the foreign office agent.

"Tell Lord Anthony he may be hearing from me soon."

"I will, sir," Gabe answered, not sure if this would be considered good or bad news for the squadron.

"No flagship," Lavery reported seeing Gabe back on deck.

*That means the commodore at the dockyard will be the senior officer present*, Gabe thought. *This means if I don't bother him he'll likely not bother me.*

"Paco!"

"Aye Captain."

"Have my gig ready so that I may go ashore once we drop anchor. You may ask Sir Victor if he would care to be rowed ashore with us."

"Aye, Cap'n."

"Mr Lavery!"

"Aye, Captain."

"Make sure the young ladies are properly delivered to their families. As I'm going ashore I'm afraid you will have to remain aboard. However, I believe Lieutenant Davy and Mr Ally would not mind the inconvenience of acting as escorts until the ladies are reunited with their families."

As Dagan prepared to go ashore, Gabe noticed he had Samson in tow. Seeing Gabe's look Dagan explained, "Ship is no place for this beast. He'll be more at home with the women."

Nodding his agreement, Gabe added, "Nesbit will be relieved."

This caused Dagan to chuckle.

***

Lady Deborah's cottage had a deep wraparound porch that provided a relief from the blazing sun. A new room was being added on the left side. This surprised Gabe. If more room was needed why didn't she just move into her main house?

"I'll tell you why," Dagan said. "You can see the harbour from here, plus this was her and Gil's love nest."

Feeling dense, Gabe acknowledged Dagan's wisdom. Faith was on the porch with Lady Deborah, who watched as Macayla rolled over in a small playpen Lum had made. Seeing the approaching men, Faith rushed out to her man. After a passionate greeting, Faith gave Dagan a hug while Gabe did the same with Deborah. Watching Faith hug Dagan, Gabe could see a difference in her. The color was back in her face and it had a glow, so to speak. Maybe the island is good for her. *Has she put on weight?* he wondered. She didn't seem to be as skinny as when he left for Barbados.

Hearing the door creak Gabe turned to see Lum grinning from ear to ear. "Lawd Gawd Almighty," he said. "The captain done come home. Nanny…Nanny!"

"Hush you old goat. You wake dat baby and it won't mattah none whose heah, her Ladyship's gonna wallop you a goodun."

Hearing a yelp, Faith asked, "What's that?"

Paco was still in the saddle holding Samson. Dagan took him from Paco and set him on the ground. Faith leaned over to pet the dog and received a sloppy kiss from a big wet tongue.

"Kisses better than some I know," Faith declared, causing everyone to laugh.

"Why he's so ugly he's pretty," Deborah said.

"He's not ugly, he's a handsome fellow," Faith said. Then she asked, "Where did you find this brute?"

"We'll discuss that later," Gabe said.

As Faith turned and went back on the porch, Samson followed. When she sat down in one of the rocking chairs Samson nudged her hand with his flat nose until she started scratching his head.

"He's such a loving dog," Faith said.

Paco sitting close by said, "If you say so, Miss, but I'm not sure Nesbit would agree."

This prompted the question, "Who is Nesbit?"

So Gabe told the story about the roast mutton, causing everyone to laugh…except Macayla, who slept the peaceful sleep of a child.

## *Chapter Fourteen*

Bart made his way into the admiral's cabin and announced, "*Peregrine* and *Lizard* are entering the bay."

"Good," Anthony replied. "Have Buck signal for captain to repair on board. Better still I'll come on deck.

"Everette," Anthony said, still speaking to the flag lieutenant, "put these papers away for now. The damn ink bottle won't dry up before we return."

"Aye, My Lord."

*Some things never change*, Everette thought. *His Lordship could ignore a gale overhead but let Gabe's ship be sighted and he'd rush on deck. I wish I had someone who cared*, the lieutenant thought…then realized he did. Otherwise he'd be on the beach and not serving as flag lieutenant.

"They're a pretty sight," Buck said speaking of the two frigates.

"They sure are, Captain," Lieutenant Lamb replied, envy in his voice. "It's what any officer would want, a fast frigate."

"On independent duty," Anthony said, joining the conversation. "No frigate captain I know wants to be tied to the Admiral's coattails."

"So you recall those days of freedom as well, My Lord," Buck replied.

"As you do, Captain," Anthony answered. "We've shared enough of them."

*I wish I could have been part of it,* Lamb thought as he moved away to give the captain and admiral privacy.

***

Silas had poured hock for the group gathered in the stateroom. Gabe and Culzean made their reports, each acknowledging the other's actions.

"Did Sir Victor say what if anything he learned in St. Lucia?"

"No, sir," Gabe replied. "I got the feeling he didn't learn anything valuable as he was not ashore more than an hour before we sailed for Antigua. Once there he left the ship and thanked us for our assistance."

"Well, saving the Houghtons and the other girls means the battle with the privateer was not a total loss."

"Aye," Buck said. "I know it was a hard choice for you to make, Gabe, but I for one feel you made the right one. The rogue is a heartless one and he'd have hung the lot of them."

"I agree," Anthony added. "You made the right choice. Well, that's all gentlemen, unless you have more to add."

"I…ah…have one more thing, sir," Gabe said, his mind suddenly on his last night in Antigua lying next to Faith, feeling her warm body next to his.

"Bart, I know you are in the pantry sampling the hock, so you and Silas come on out here and bring the hock along with your glasses."

Anthony and Buck looked quizzically at Dagan, who just shrugged. Gabe filled each of the glasses with hock then said, "I wanted all of you here for this announcement."

He then looked at Anthony and said, "You're going to be an uncle, sir."

"I…I'm to be an uncle. That means you will be a father, you old scalawag. That is news."

Buck clapped Gabe a good one on the back and shook his hand. "I didn't know you had it in you, boy."

After a good hour the little gathering broke up. Cigars were put out and empty bottles disposed of. Culzean and Gabe made it back to their ships.

"That was some surprise," Bart said to Silas.

"Aye," Silas replied. "It's going to be more a surprise when "is Lordship finds out all 'is 'ock be gone."

***

The gentleman pushed open the door of the Bull's Head Tavern. Without a word he took a table behind a noisy group of naval officers. Looking toward the bar he could see more Navy officers interspersed with the scarlet uniforms of the army stationed in Barbados.

The room was busy, as he knew it would be. The aroma of coffee mingled with the odour of rum. A cook fire sizzled as a whole pig was being turned over on a spit. The stranger's blue coat, white shirt, and waistcoat along with his tanned face gave anyone looking the appearance of a merchant sea captain. This was as the stranger wanted.

The fact was he'd been rowed ashore. He then waited for the *MaryAnn,* a small merchantman, to enter the harbour before he showed himself. Not only his appearance but also the timing had to be right as well. The man ordered his meal. After that he watched as a group of officers started to play cards.

Several onlookers gathered round the table so he joined the group. It wasn't long before one of the officers had lost all his money then bowed out. Seizing the opportunity the stranger asked if he might join and was readily allowed. Playing badly the stranger gradually worked the conversation around to who was the flag officer here now.

"Was it the same as last year?"

"No, it is Admiral Lord Anthony."

"I've heard of a Captain Anthony," the man said. "But surely it can't be the same man. He was way too young."

"Probably his brother," one of the group replied. "The lucky sod. Admiral for a brother and as beautiful a wife as any man could hope for."

"I'll bet he's home every night," the man said nonchalantly. "If I had as beautiful a wife I'd be home taking care of business."

"No," another one said. "He'd like to I'm sure but she's on Antigua with His Lordship's wife. They have a plantation there."

Standing at the bar, an old salt stood waiting on his mate to join him for a wet. He'd been half listening to the young officers playing cards. This last bit of conversation disturbed him. He ambled over to the table and not too gently said, "Ye need to keep a bridle on your tongue, Meriweather."

The young officer, who was not used to being scolded in such a way, wheeled around ready to fight until he saw who'd been speaking. He'd been told more than once the master was a hellish, rough customer. Not only that, he'd seen the admiral talking to him like a mate.

Finally, Meriweather managed, "Don't be so upset, Jep. Everybody knows where His Lordship's family lives."

"Now they do," the master replied to Meriweather.

Turning to the stranger, Jep asked, "What's it to you where His Lordship's family is?"

"Why it was nothing," the stranger said. "I didn't even ask. All I said was if I had a beautiful wife I'd be home with her."

"It was him," the stranger continued, pointing to Meriweather, "what said the rest. Ask the others here."

"I heard what was said," Jep replied. "There's those whose mouth runs away with them but there's them that pry for such as well."

Jep now had his hand on his pistol, his other on Meriweather's shoulder. "What's your name, mister?"

"Miller," the man said. "John Miller. I came in with the *MaryAnn*."

"You better had," Jep said. "If I find out different I'll come looking."

Miller hastily gathered the few coins in front of him and rushed out of the tavern. Once outside he smiled to himself. He'd gotten all the information he needed. He then stole a horse that was tied in front of another tavern and rode down the road a few miles.

There a longboat with its crew waited. Dismounting, he swatted the horse on the rump and it took off back toward Bridgetown.

As he stepped into the boat the man at the tiller asked, "Did ye get what ye come for, Mr Montique?"

"I did, Amos, I did."

***

The following weeks were filled with exhausting patrols always in pairs or groups of three. The monotony of the patrols was broken up occasionally by a reception or somebody's birthday ball. Not unlike Antigua, when a young lady or gentleman turned sixteen, everybody was invited. By the time a girl reached twenty-one people began to wonder why she wasn't already married.

Lord Ragland would host a large reception should a dignitary stop by the island. The largest reception had been given by Mr Houghton in honour of *Peregrine* and *Lizard* coming to his family's rescue. It was followed up three months later with his daughter's eighteenth birthday party. While all the young gentlemen were enamored by the young lady, Christina, Houghton's daughter only had eyes for Lieutenant Davy.

"Make you jealous?" asked Francis Markham, Gabe's friend and fellow captain.

"No," Gabe replied. "Not jealous…just envious." It had been months since Gabe had had the brief visit to Antigua.

"I remember when we used to woo them," Markham continued.

"I hear that you've been keeping company with a young lady yourself," Gabe said.

"Polite company so far. She is Lord Ragland's niece."

*That explained the polite company remark*, Gabe thought.

"I'd keep it polite old friend," Gabe said. "You never tally with the feelings of a politician's family."

"Not only that," Markham responded in a whisper. "I hear he's killed a dozen men in duels."

"Only six," a voice from behind said.

This startled the two men who turned to find Lord Anthony behind them.

Red faced at being overheard, Markham stammered, "My apologies, My Lord."

"Nonsense, my boy. No apology necessary. However, make sure your back is to the wall and not an open doorway if you're saying something you don't want overheard."

"Good advice, My Lord, I will always remember it," a relieved Markham replied.

"I noticed a deck of cards on a table in a room we just passed. Would you mind following me?"

As they made their way into the room the deck of cards was still on the table.

"We have been called upon to escort a convoy to St. Augustine," Anthony informed the two.

"*Intrepid, Lizard*, and *Alert* are going to act as escort. I want one of you to follow at a distance."

"Do you have word of an impending attack?" Gabe asked.

"No," Anthony replied. "But this will be the last convoy of the season. It's now or the privateers will have to wait until next year to try their luck. I think someone will chance it."

Seeing Hazard, Anthony called to his flag lieutenant. "What will it be, high or low card that will escort the convoy?"

"Low card will escort the convoy, My Lord. An ace counts as eleven."

"There you go, gentlemen," Anthony said. "Now draw."

Gabe and Markham each drew their card.

"Captain Markham, show your card." It was the queen of hearts.

"Captain Anthony, let's see your card." It was the two of diamonds.

"Well, old boy," Gabe said with a smile. "It appears you will have a bit of time to keep polite company with…ah…I don't recall her name."

"That's because I didn't give it," Markham replied sarcastically. Then remembering the admiral was standing there he followed up in a softer voice. "It's Molly, sir, Miss Molly Ann."

***

A brisk, easterly wind brought *Peregrine* surging through the warm Caribbean waters. The convoy had left early the previous day. The rumour had been spread that *Peregrine* was carrying dispatches for Lord Ragland to Grenada. Once out of sight of land, Gabe was to come about and overhaul the slower convoy.

Gabe rested his glass on a shroud but nothing showed on the horizon. He was agitated. He'd been that way since he'd been summoned to the flagship the night before sailing. Lord Anthony, Gil, had told him about Jepson's conversation with Meriweather and the man called Miller.

"The merchantman was gone the next day so we couldn't confirm if the man was who he claimed to be or not. However, speaking as your admiral, it would do no harm in stopping at Antigua on your return trip. Lord Ragland, as has Mr Houghton, offered lodging for our wives during the holidays. If Faith is able to travel we will accept his hospitality."

Dagan eased up to Gabe. He didn't say a word. Sometimes just being close was worth more than words. That was what Gabe needed now.

Paco saw his captain and Dagan standing by the weather rail. He was troubled, Paco knew, but did not know the cause. Paco's life had been much improved since coming aboard as cox'n. He'd never known such comfort and stability. *Carried me right into his home,* Paco thought. Well, he'd face ole Diablo himself if he had to. Men like the captain didn't come around often.

Seeing Alejandro, Paco spoke to him in Spanish. He was the only one on board who still used the youth's full name and had not shortened it to Ally. "What do you think little one? Will you stay in St. Augustine with your papa or sail away with el capitaine?"

"I will stay with the captain of course."

"Good," Paco replied. "It is as it should be."

"Land ho!"

"Where away?" Lavery called.

"Off the larboard beam," the lookout responded.

Gunnells looked up from his chart and said, "That ought to be the Bahamas."

Gabe nodded but said nothing.

"I'd have thought the privateers would have struck by now," Lieutenant Wiley volunteered.

"I'm not surprised," Gabe responded. "They don't have to travel as far if they wait until we're closer."

"Aye," Lavery joined in. "I recall Governor Tonyn telling of a convoy being taken right at the entrance of the St. Augustine bay."

"Well, one way or another," Gunnells said, joining in the conversation. "They don't have long to make up their minds or we'll be headed back."

*"I hope so,"* Gabe said to himself.

***

"Captain...Captain...It's almost dawn, sir."

Gabe stretched, yawned, and sat up. He could hear Nesbit rattling around in the pantry getting his breakfast together. Pulling on the seaman's slops he wore at sea, he reached for his boot. In doing so the tiny leather patch he wore around his neck fell forward. He touched it and put it back inside his shirt.

"Faith, Faith, I won't be long," he said under his breath. The leather pouch used to hold a large red ruby. Faith had the ruby now but he wore the pouch as a symbol of an empty heart when they were not together. Gabe ran his hand through his hair and found it damp. His entire body was damp. Was it sweat or fear? He got his other boot on and tugged on his coat.

Dagan entered the cabin just as Gabe sat at his table. Nesbit had a cup of coffee waiting and poured another when he saw Dagan.

Eyeing Dagan, Gabe said, "Today's the day."

"Aye," Dagan replied. "I feel it."

A red haze filled the sky as *Peregrine* pushed northward. The sea was lively and spray came over the fo'c'sle as the bow dipped into a trough and then plowed through a wave.

"Good morning, Mr Lavery, Mr Gunnells."

"Morning, Captain," the two replied in unison.

"We have a strong wind, Mr Gunnells."

"Aye, Captain. East by sou-east she be and lively at that."

"I don't like the look of the sky," Gabe said.

"Me neither, Captain, but the barometer is holding steady."

As the sun rose the sky got redder. *The ship is strangely silent today*, Gabe thought. Not the usual jabber as men started their day. *Maybe they feel it too*, Gabe thought.

Once again it was Ally, the one with the good ears, who volunteered, "Gunfire, sir. I hear gunfire."

"Is the damn lookout asleep?" Gabe snapped, instantly regretting his behavior.

Lavery took the hint and called up to the lookout.

"I's can't see a thing, sir, sun is blazing down so."

Dagan started toward the shrouds but Lieutenant Davy beat him. "I'll go, Dagan," he said.

Dagan handed him a glass and said, "Shade the lens with your hand."

Upon hearing Dagan's advice, Lieutenant Davy fairly flew up to the mainmast lookout. "It's the convoy all right," Davy shouted down. "It's being attacked from all quarters."

"Took advantage of the early morning sun," Gunnells volunteered.

"Aye," Gabe acknowledged. "Set all sail, Mr Lavery, then beat to quarters. Let's hope we are not too late to be of assistance. Let's get out of the way, Dagan," he said as he headed for the companionway.

Entering the cabin, Nesbit said, "I took the liberty of adding a bit to the coffee."

Taking the cup Gabe could taste the unmistakable taste of brandy. Nesbit offered Dagan a cup as Gabe said, "He's been talking to Silas I see."

## Chapter Fifteen

A knock at the door and the sentry announced, "Midshipman Hawks, zur."

Hawks entered the cabin to find Gabe sitting at his table, coffee cup in his hand, legs stretched out and crossed. He was talking to Dagan as if it was Sunday make and mend. *Damme if he ain't a cool one*, Hawks thought.

"Yes, Mr Hawks, did you come down to get out of the sun or do you have a message for me?"

"No, sir…I mean yes, sir. First Lieutenant's compliments, sir, and we have identified six privateers."

"I see," Gabe answered, his legs still stretched out and cup in hand.

"Does the first lieutenant require me on deck?" Gabe asked, toying with the young gentleman.

Hawk appeared to be deep in thought then answered, "He didn't say anything about you coming on deck, sir. He only said that there are six privateers."

"Was there any mention as to size or guns?" Gabe asked.

"No, sir, only Lieutenant Davy said the one was the big bastard we tangled with recently."

"Ahem! Tell the first lieutenant I'll be on deck directly."

"Aye, Captain."

Once the boy was out the door Gabe turned to Dagan. "So it's Montique."

"It's his ship at least," Dagan replied.

Once on deck the gunfire was plainly heard and the ships could be seen from the deck.

"Looks like *Intrepid* has her hands full."

"Aye," Lavery replied. "*Lizard* and *Alert* are under heavy attack as well. Odds are definitely in the rogue's favour at this point."

"How much longer before we can engage?"

"Another quarter hour at least," Gunnells answered his captain.

"Call for the gunner."

"Aye," Lieutenant Lavery answered and the call for Druett went up.

When the gunner arrived Gabe said, "The master has said it'd be fifteen minutes before we are in range. With you sighting the bow chasers I'm betting ten. Pick out your closest target and fire when ready."

The burly gunner knuckled his forehead in salute and said, "I'll see's you win that bet, Captain."

Hearing the distant boom of the guns, Gabe could see the big privateer firing at *Intrepid*. The sixty-four was holding its own…for now. But how long before *Lizard* or *Alert* was taken? At any time another ship could join in the battle against either of them. Gabe could see Lavery looking at his watch.

*Anxious to join the battle*, Gabe thought.

Paco was now on deck with his sword and pistols. Gabe tucked the pistols in his waistband and held up his arms for Paco to put on his sword belt.

Hearing Dagan chuckle, Gabe asked, "Something funny?"

"Aye," Dagan answered. "I recalled His Lordship when he was a captain jamming his pistols home and accidentally cocking one. Bart told him to be careful like or

Lady Deborah would never forgive him if he shot off his wedding tackle."

"I remember," Gabe said, laughing.

"'Ear that bucko," a topman said to his mate. "Way the cap'n's carrying on you'd think we was going to watch a parade. He's a cool un, that one is."

The crash of the larboard bow chaser caused the crew to let go with a cheer. The other gun crews were wrapping neckerchiefs around their ears, knowing it wouldn't be long now and they'd be in action. Another crash forward as the starboard bow chaser went off.

"Just short," the lookout called down. Then added, "But they know we's here."

"Mr Gunnells!"

"Aye, Captain."

"Set your course to bear down on those two attacking *Alert*. Hawks!"

"Yes sir."

"Run tell Druett I want a steady barrage on those ships attacking *Alert*."

"Aye, Captain."

"The big privateer has broken off from *Intrepid*," Dagan said.

Taking a moment to look through his glass, Gabe said, "I see."

"They should have gone after the supply ships," Gunnells said. "Half could have played cat and mouse with the escorts while the others boarded and put prize crews aboard the merchantmen."

"I'm damn glad you aren't in command of the rogues," Gabe said. Then he continued, "No, that way they'd get a few but, if they could cripple *Intrepid* and take *Lizard* and *Alert*, they could have the whole convoy."

"Aye, you are right," Gunnells replied.

A ripple of bright orange flames erupted from the large privateer. Balls landed just short of *Peregrine*.

"A narrow miss," Gunnells grunted, wiping spray from his face to the snicker of the helmsman.

Seeing the privateer's full press of sails, Gabe ordered, "Let her fall off two points, Mr Gunnells."

Gabe then cupped his hands and shouted to Lieutenant Davy down in the waist. "On the up roll, Lieutenant Davy. As you bear! Fire!"

From bow to stern, *Peregrine's* guns fired, reloaded, and fired again, smoke drifting windward as flames belched from the gun ports. The gun captains yelling encouragement and instructions, the trucks squealed as the gun crews heaved with all their might to reload as fast as possible. Through the smoke, the privateer's captain altered course and fired a haphazard broadside.

Ragged the broadside may have been but nevertheless just as deadly. Gabe gritted his teeth as the deck shook violently when the enemy's balls slammed into the ship. Eyeing the privateer it appeared to Gabe he was trying to change course and give his guns on the larboard side, the least damaged side, a chance to fire.

"Alter course to larboard," Gabe said sharply.

"Checkmate, you rogue," Gabe exclaimed as the privateer's captain tried to change course to edge around him so that he could bring his guns to bear.

"She's in stays…she's in stays," Gunnells shouted as he hopped up and down.

Again *Peregrine's* guns fired. Gabe felt the deck shaking as her guns recoiled. A loud crash was heard on the privateer as the mainmast came down. The ship slewed to starboard and Wiley said, "Her wheel's shot away."

From forward a cheer had risen. Druett had maintained his barrage as ordered and the privateer on the larboard quarter of *Alert* was breaking off.

"Sir!" Wiley exclaimed. "Look, sir."

A white flag went up what was left of the enemy ship's mizzenmast. The sound of cannons was heard only after

*Peregrine's* hull bucked sharply. The forward mast spar dangled to starboard and lengths of rope, tackle, and cordage fell. Some of the heavy pieces cut through the spread nets, narrowly missing a gun crew.

Another of the privateers had made its way through the gun smoke, filling the gap between *Peregrine* and the open waters.

"Damme," Gabe bellowed. "Mr Davy to the starboard."

Gabe heard the sound of the marines firing from the main tops. He could also make out the bangs from the swivels, all of which was quickly drowned out by the deafening roar of *Peregrine's* starboard broadside.

Walking around so as to not make himself an easy target, Gabe saw waterspouts bracketing *Lizard* on both sides. Musket balls thudded into the planking on the quarterdeck. A cry at the wheel and one of the helmsman was hit in the throat. He tried to call out but only made a gurgling sound. Gunnells quickly took his place at the wheel only to snatch his hand away as if stung by a wasp. He changed hands holding onto the wheel until another helmsman was called. Stepping over his downed mate, his face was a ghastly green but he took over for the master without a word.

"Go below," Gabe ordered.

But Gunnells replied, "Begging the captain's pardon there will be time enough for that later."

Dagan took his neckerchief and tied off the wound as well as he could. All around the den of battle raged on. Every gun that could bear was being fired. The red sky was gone, darkened by the gray haze of battle smoke. *Peregrine's* confined world was filled with the thundering hell of cannons blazing, earsplitting screams from the wounded that caused a shiver to run down the spine, and streams of curses as the gun captains yelled at the battle-crazed gun crews.

There was the bitter taste of spent gunpowder as cannons roared…then silence. The guns had ceased firing. *Had he given the word*, Gabe wondered. The last ship was now ablaze. *Intrepid* had sunk one and captured another. *Lizard* had fought off one of its opponents. It now drifted low down in the water. The other had tried to escape but was stopped by *Peregrine*. *Alert* was still grappled to one but the British flag flew over the vessel. The other privateer still flew the white flag and like its sister ship drifted without steerage. A cheer went up on *Alert*, causing a chain reaction to each of the other ships.

"Silence," Lavery snapped, but he was unheard. Feeling a hand on his arm, he turned to find his captain.

"Let them cheer," Gabe said. "They deserve it." Then turning he called, "Mr Gunnells!"

"Aye, Captain."

"Have one of your mates lay us alongside yonder privateer. I intend to board her and I don't feel like climbing down into my gig."

"Aye," Gunnells replied. "Alongside we'll be."

"Mr Lavery, round up the warrants and let's have a damage report. Once we have everything under control, pipe up spirits."

Hearing this, the men began cheering again.

***

The deck of the privateer was in complete shambles. As Gabe, Dagan, and a boarding party crossed over, they found carnage and destruction everywhere they looked. A lieutenant led Gabe to the ship's captain, who was slumped against the bulwark. Gabe could instantly see the man was in a bad way.

"Do you not have a surgeon?" he asked.

The wounded captain said, "A surgeon is for the living, not for the dead. I fear, Captain, I will soon be with the latter."

Looking to the young officer, the privateer's captain said, "My sword, Jean."

Gabe felt strangely emotional looking down at the dying captain. He took a deep breath and said, "I could never take it sir. You fought a most honourable battle."

"It was not so when we last met. But rest assured, monsieur, it was not of my making. I don't want to die dishonourably so I tell you, Capitaine, it was Montique. He is the son of Satan. He is at this moment on a small merchantman sailing to Antigua." The captain started coughing then died.

The young lieutenant wiped tears from his eyes and said, "He was my father."

Gabe straightened up and looked at the captain's son. "Your father died with honour. Put his sword in a place of honour."

"Oui, monsieur, but I'm afraid I will not find such a place. We fight under a Letter of Marque but it's my understanding the British do not accept this."

"This time we will if you will give me your parole...on your father's honour."

"I give it, monsieur."

"Good. Do you think you can get this ship seaworthy?"

"Oui."

"Then I bid you good-by, sir."

Once back on the deck of *Peregrine*, Gabe ordered the helmsman to lie alongside *Intrepid*.

"Paco!"

"Aye."

"Prepare my gig."

Gabe then turned to Dagan, "You heard."

"I heard," Dagan answered. "But first things first. He's got a full day's head start. You could rip the sticks out of *Peregrine* and still never catch him. Lum is there. He knows Montique. He'll protect Faith."

"Aye," Gabe answered in a dejected manner. "You're right."

*I wish I felt that way*, Dagan thought.

***

Captain Thomas Fletcher stood at the entry port when Gabe was piped aboard *Intrepid*. The two had only met a few times but Fletcher had been told he was more than capable and had earned his captaincy…unlike some. He'd also been told the admiral was very fond of his young brother. It was this that made Fletcher keep silent when Gabe apologized for being presumptuous in accepting the privateer's parole.

Gabe had said that with the convoy scattered, the escort ships being in a bad way, and *Peregrine* sailing under independent orders from the admiral, he didn't think Fletcher would want his resources to be further stretched by having to watch over a bunch of prisoners. "That ship is nothing more than a leaky old tube that may founder at any minute," Gabe had added. This part had been true.

Fletcher still felt the need to assert himself as the senior officer while trying not to offend Gabe so as to have the admiral look upon him in a bad light.

"I quite agree with your thinking, Captain Anthony, but in the future discuss such matters with me before giving your word."

"Naturally sir," Gabe said, trying to sound contrite. "It was your reputation I was thinking of when I acted so. I didn't want it said one of Admiral Anthony's captains allowed a convoy to be lost while he played shepherd over a bunch of prisoners."

"You again are correct, Captain. Now I must attend gathering the convoy," Fletcher said. "So I'll see you to the side."

*I bet you will*, Gabe thought. *We saved your arse and you know it.* Gabe then thought, *No. Gil saved your arse. He was the suspicious one. He was the one that planned it all. Damme*, Gabe thought again, *but Gil was a smart one. Humph! That's why he's flying an admiral flag.*

## Chapter Sixteen

Adam Montique, alias John Miller, sat in the stern sheets of the brig's boat as it headed for the dock. He'd taken transportation on the little brig, *Hope*, when it sailed from San Juan. He'd also brought along two of his handy-men…men that would slit their mother's throat for a few shillings. He'd promised them the freedom to have their way with Faith. She had shunned all of his advances back in Beaufort. In fact it was because of her…her and that damnable British bastard she married that caused him to flee for his life.

She had cost him a fortune. He'd had a good system set up. He would raid British ships and sell the contents to the Colonies. Then he would raid the Colonial ships and sell his gains to the British. It had been easy.

Montique had befriended that fool, Commodore Gardner. Gardner awarded him contracts that allowed him to be privy to information regarding convoy sailing times, when they were expected and their strengths. He'd then have privateers ready and waiting. He'd done the same with a Colonial agent.

Montique had amassed a fortune. Now it was gone, all gone because of Faith. *I should have sold her with the other young girls we captured*, he thought. *She wouldn't be so uppity in some Dey's harem.*

"We're here, sir, at the landing," the boat's cox'n said, breaking Montique's reverie.

"Yes, thank you," Montique said, the perfect gentleman, placing a few coins in the sailor's hand.

Climbing out he didn't even acknowledge his handymen. They would meet up the hill out of sight of the brig's crew. He didn't want anybody to be able to tie him to the rogues. Once up the hill he gave each man a few coins with specific instructions in regards to seeking directions. The story was they had sailed with Captain Anthony in the past and desired to sign on again. Nothing was to be mentioned about the women at all.

***

Lady Deborah got in the carriage and took Macayla Rose. Nanny then climbed in. Her abundant weight caused the carriage to lean and its springs to groan as she struggled aboard. Nanny had spent more and more time helping with Macayla.

When Deborah protested about Nanny doing so much the old black woman replied, "Shucks, honey, it ain't no bother. I's jus practicing up foh when Missy Faith's little one comes along. Now she was a handful sho nuff…Missy Faith was. So I don't 'spect dis little girl gonna be much trouble."

Deborah had stopped protesting and was actually grateful for Nanny's help. Lum watched as the carriage headed off to English Harbour. He was glad to see them go for a while. They were adding on a small room to accommodate the little one when it came. However, Lum was limited as to when he could work.

Just that morning, Nanny had rushed out the door all flustered. "Hush up wid dat hammering, you old coot. You going to wake dat child and when she's fussy cause she didn't get her nap you gonna be rocking her."

*Humph*! Lum thought. *At the rate this room is going Missy Faith's baby will done be here and it still won't be built.* Fetching his carpenter's box, Lum started up the ladder to work on the rafters for the new room when suddenly the ladder started to slide backwards. Looking down Lum could see Samson had the bottom step in his mouth and was tugging on it.

"Get, get, you ole hound."

But still Samson tugged and growled. As he did so, slobber drooled from his mouth.

"Get, I say," Lum shouted but to no avail. He climbed down the ladder only to have Samson run off. No sooner had Lum turned and got halfway back up than Samson was back.

He barked a time or two then started tugging at the ladder again. This time, however, he pulled so hard it slipped away from the boards it was leaning against. After bouncing a couple of times, it hit the ground hard. Lum was not injured but the fall had scattered his tools and nails all over the ground.

"You blasted hound," Lum bellowed. "I ought to bust you with this hammer."

This set Samson to barking loudly as he danced back and forth with his tail wagging.

Faith ran out and cried, "What's happening?"

"This heah beast is what happened," Lum said, telling Faith about Samson's actions.

"He's just trying to play," she said as she scratched his head. "Poor baby. I bet you scared him with that old hammer, Lum."

"Scared him!" Lum exclaimed. "It was me falling off that there ladder. I was the one what was scared."

Faith knelt beside the dog, her pregnant belly protruding, and Samson licked her face.

"Come on baby," Faith whispered as she took a piece of twine and tied Samson to a nearby palm tree.

*Baby*, Lum thought. *We could hitch him up to the carriage if the horse ever went lame.*

Back inside the house, Faith looked in the mirror. Her breasts were getting heavy and her dress top felt very tight. Nanny had said to rub them with the coconut butter she had made.

"You don't want no purple stretch marks, child. You keep 'em rubbed now like Nanny says."

Lum had been working on the roof a good thirty minutes when he saw riders coming. There was something familiar about the way one man sat his saddle. It suddenly dawned on him. Mastuh Montique.

Lum leapt off the house. "Missy Faith! Missy Faith, get yoh gun, hurry now." He raced on back to his quarters to get his pistol.

Faith had just got her pistol loaded as Gabe had taught her when the front door of the cottage was flung open. Holding the pistol at her side, tucked into the folds of her dress, she tried to remain calm.

"Uncle Adam," she said, trembling with fear, not believing that he'd dare to appear so boldly. "And what do I owe this visit?"

Montique took off his cocked hat and threw it across the room toward a side table. "'Tis no concern why I'm here, only that I'm here."

The two cutthroats with Montique eye'd Faith hungrily. "She's carrying 'is kid," one of the men said. "Yew ever laid open a gut what was with child?" he asked his cohort.

"Nay, but that'll come later…after I's tasted this mutton's ware."

"Uncle Adam!" Faith exclaimed. "You can't mean you'd let them…have me."

"You had your choice once, lass. But you chose that admiral's bastard."

"But you're my uncle!" she cried.

"We could have moved away. But it's of no consequence. You made your bed. Now it's time to lie in it."

"You should leave," Faith said, suddenly resolved that if she must die she'd take one of the sods with her.

"You tire of our company already?" Montique asked. "You haven't even offered us refreshments. Has she men?"

"I'll get my refreshment in a minute," one of the men said, smiling. His teeth were almost black.

"Go to hell," Faith spat, wondering where Lum was.

"Soon as we've finished with you we'll go, whether that means to hell…who knows. But you'll be beyond caring."

"Are you gentlemen ready for this little piece of dessert?" Montique asked.

Without answering the two stepped forward. Faith cried out. Samson hearing his mistress's cries lunged several times before snapping the twine that had him tethered. He bounded for the house.

Lum had been standing just behind the door listening and praying the group would leave. When Faith cried out he knew there was no reason to wait any longer. With a pistol in his hand and a tomahawk in his belt he snatched opened the door. Without taking time to aim he just pointed his pistol and fired. A hole appeared dead center of the closest man's chest.

Lum dropped his smoking pistol and snatched up the tomahawk. Just as he went to throw it the second rogue acted very quickly and shot at Lum. The ball hit Lum just as he threw the tomahawk. Instead of hitting Montique in the head as Lum hoped, the razor sharp axe cut into his enemy's shoulder. A red spot showed where the tomahawk cut through the coat and shirt but didn't cause any significant injury.

Faith, acting quickly, raised her pistol and shot the man who had shot Lum. Doing as Gabe had instructed her she jammed the barrel into the man's stomach and pulled the trigger.

"Who you going to gut now?" she spat.

Montique, seeing Lum leaning against the wall bleeding from a shoulder wound, said, "Well, it's the white man's killing nigger. You've breathed your last, you uppity bastard."

Montique made a point of taking aim. Just as he pulled the trigger Faith hit him with her fist, screaming, "No!"

The ball grazed Lum's scalp, rendering him unconscious. Furious at Faith, Montique grabbed her arm and slung her against a chair toppling it over. He jerked her up by her hair and slammed his fist into her stomach then backhanded her.

CRASH!!! The front door splintered.

CRASH!!! This time the busted door flew open. Montique never knew what happened. Samson's one hundred twenty-five pounds crashed against the man at full speed. All Montique saw was the red eyes and black face of hell as the mastiff's jaws closed around his throat and ripped it open. Shaking the downed man from side to side the dog held on to his prey until the body went limp. Dropping the dead man, Samson went over and whimpering licked at Faith's battered face but she remained unconscious.

Lum, still dazed and hurting, but conscious, raised himself up. He took a picture of water and poured some over his face and head. This helped clear some of the cobwebs. As soon as he was able to focus, he saw Samson standing over Faith bathing her with his tongue.

As he moved toward the injured woman, the dog growled. It was then that Lum realized the black around the dog's mouth was blood. He then saw a foot and following the direction he saw Montique with his neck ripped open. His head was lying on the floor at an odd angle. Samson had come to Faith's rescue. Turning back to

Faith, he took a step and the dog growled...a menacing growl.

"Easy boy...easy now. You know ole Lum. Easy now."

The growling stopped but the bristles on Samson's back were still up.

"Easy boy. Let me see to Missy Faith, easy now."

Lum slowly moved toward Faith, letting the big dog smell his hand. Lum was finally beside Faith. "She's hurt bad," he said to Samson, who took a step back. Samson's big old droopy eyes looked like he was crying.

Moving a chair out of the way, Lum reached under Faith to pick her up and quickly withdrew his wet hand...blood.

He slowly lifted her dress and cried out, "Oh my God, oh God." His fear was realized. "How's my missy going to stand this? Oh God, please be with my Missy."

Glad that she was unconscious, Lum quickly undressed and cleaned up Faith, disposing of the bloody garments. Hearing a noise outside, Lum ran outside and flagged down the passerby.

"Please sir, go fetch the doctor and Lady Deborah. Hurry, sir, please hurry."

The rider, hearing the anguish in Lum's voice, took off at a gallop. Back inside Lum changed the cloth he'd placed on Faith's forehead, replacing it with a fresh cool one. When Faith spoke Lum jumped, not expecting it.

"Yes, Missy?"

"The baby, Lum..." tears coming from her eyes. "The baby is gone."

Lum's voice quivered, "Yes, Missy...this one's gone."

"Where's Montique?"

"Samson took care of him."

Hearing his name, Samson, who was lying at the foot of the bed, whined.

"Good boy," Faith whispered as she again fell unconscious.

## *Chapter Seventeen*

Faith had been seen by the doctor and given an anodyne. The doctor was tending to Lum's wounds when Commodore Gardner arrived. He had rushed to the scene, not only as a concerned friend but also in his capacity as Chief Magistrate, a position he had been appointed to when the new governor had arrived.

Gardner took notes as Lum told his story. "A clear cut case," he said when Lum finished his story. "But tell me, what do we do with that dog? He's a man killer now."

Stupefied by Gardner's comments, Lum spoke boldly. "Unless you wants another killin I 'spect that dog better be left alone."

"Ahem..." Gardner sputtered. "Well I guess it won't hurt to see how he behaves."

Men hired by Gardner hauled off the dead bodies while Nanny supervised cleaning the front room. As Lum's shoulder was bandaged and he couldn't finish his carpenter work, a man was fetched from the dockyard to lend a hand. A new door was hung to replace the one Samson busted.

The anodyne made up of extractum thebaicum and laudanum was given to Faith every eight hours for two full days. When the sun rose on the third day she refused the mixture. Nanny was sitting by Faith's bed when she awoke.

"My baby's gone, Nanny," Faith said with a tremor in her voice.

Taking a washcloth from a pan of water, Nanny squeezed the excess water out and wiped Faith's face. "Yes, child, I know. The Lawd done called that baby home. I dreamed just last night that baby was up in heaven. It was in yoh mama's arms and she had the prettiest smile on her face as she rocked her grandbaby."

"Oh Nanny, do you think so?"

"I sho do child. You know Nanny don't lie nary a bit. Now you lay back and rest a bit moh whilst I go fix you a little something to eat."

As Nanny went to walk away, Faith grabbed her arm. "What is it, child?" Nanny asked, seeing a frightened look on the girl's face.

"Uncle Adam...did...did they get him?"

Not wanting to go through the gory details, Nanny just nodded and said, "Yes, child, they got that heathen and I 'spect his soul is roasting in torment bout now."

"Good," Faith said. "That's where he needs to be."

Nanny turned to go when Faith called again. "Nanny, what about Gabe?"

"I don't know about that, child. He'll be home befoh long though. Don't you fret."

"He'll be mad," Faith cried, tears streaming down her face. "I lost his baby."

"Nonsense, child. Gabe will be mad sho nuff but it'll be at that evil man, Montique. If he wasn't already dead I 'spect Gabe would hunt him down and poke that old long sword he carries clean through him. Now you hush while I go to the kitchen."

Nanny eased the bedroom door to as she stepped out of the room and found Lady Deborah standing there.

"What a wonderful woman you are," Deborah said. "That was such a perfect answer you gave Faith about her mama rocking her grandchild."

"That wasn't no story," Nanny replied. "That was the truth. I could see it just as plain as day. It were the Lawd's way of letting old Nanny know that child was being taken care of." Nanny made a couple steps toward the kitchen then stopped and spoke once more. "You know, Lady Deborah, the closest thing to heaven is a child."

Deborah found herself standing staring at the black woman who was finally making her way to the kitchen. Awed by Nanny's words, she thought, *how lucky Faith was to have such a servant...no Nanny was much more than a servant or even a friend. She was more like a mother.*

***

*Peregrine's* sails began to take shape through the midday sun as people on the island of Antigua watched her approach. She was not a stranger but not so familiar that she was instantly recognized. Ships of war were common to English Harbour, so the trick was not to sight the ship but to identify it first. Old salts gathered under the thatched awning of a small tavern and spent their time trying to be the first to correctly identify each ship. The results usually meant a free wet and bragging rights till the next ship approached.

Antigua being a small island, word had quickly spread about the assault and shootings that took place at Lady Deborah's cottage. Therefore, when *Peregrine* was sighted, haste was made to spread the word. Because of this Commodore Gardner was waiting when Gabe's gig reached land.

Sitting in his coach, Gardner quickly explained the events. Faith was safe and gaining strength. Lum was recovering well and Samson had left Faith's side only to answer nature's call. After Gardner had finished his narrative, Gabe looked at Dagan.

"You knew didn't you…about the dog, I mean? You knew he'd protect Faith."

"I had the feeling," Dagan answered. "I didn't know to what extreme but I had the feeling."

"Gabe," Gardner spoke once more to the boy who had turned into a man before his eyes. "Faith is worried about you blaming her for the loss of the child."

Gabe went to protest but Gardner held up his hand to halt him. "I…we know different. However, you have to reassure Faith."

Gabe nodded his understanding and the rest of the carriage ride was in silence until they pulled up to the cottage.

"One more thing, Gabe," Gardner said. "*Viper* was in port a few days back. I sent a message to Lord Anthony about the situation when she sailed. I hope you didn't mind."

"No sir," Gabe replied.

He was now anxious about facing Faith. *If only I'd been here*, he thought feeling guilty.

Dagan seemed to read his thoughts. "You couldn't have known, Gabe. Now clear your mind and let's go see your wife."

***

A faint cool breeze rustled through the palms overhead. Gabe reached for the bottle of wine in the wicker basket. The cork made a tiny pop as it came out. Faith giggled at the sound. After filling the glasses, Gabe replaced the bottle and lay by Faith at the edge of a small fresh water pool located at the back of Lady Deborah's plantation. They had driven the carriage down in the late afternoon and now the faint light of a new moon shone down into the glade and reflected off the pool's surface. A bird called from somewhere deeper in the trees.

Faith had kicked off her shoes and dangled her legs into the water. Gabe sat on the blanket at the edge of the pool his arm around his wife. It had been a week since he'd returned to Antigua and his wife.

There had been a tearful period but Faith seemed to be putting it behind her. Samson…that dog was forever at her side and now lay with his eyes on the picnic basket. Faith had given the beast every scrap that was left. Yet he lay watching to see if another morsel magically appeared. The big brute had made Gabe step lightly a time or two the first day until Faith soothed him. Now Samson seemed to accept Gabe. And to show his appreciation he gave Gabe a sloppy lick when they'd sat down to eat. Either that or he was seeing how Gabe tasted if there wasn't enough food.

Gabe wasn't quite sure but Faith had clapped her hands, and exclaimed, "Oh look, Gabe, he likes you."

Gabe smiled, wiped his face, and said, "But how…as friend or food?"

This caused Faith to laugh and Samson to jump about and bark. This was the first time she had laughed since he arrived in Antigua. He was glad he'd taken Lady Deborah's advice about the two of them getting away together.

"Gabe, can you swim?" Faith asked.

"Of course," he replied.

"Lum said some sailors can't," Faith continued.

"Well, this one can."

"Good. Let's go swimming."

With that she stood and pulled her gown over her head. The reflection of Faith's gorgeous breasts and naked body there in the moonlight was more than he could stand.

"Lord Almighty," Gabe muttered.

Tossing her wineglass aside, Faith yelled, "Close your mouth and come on," as she dove into the clear spring fed pool.

Gabe downed his glass of wine and removed his clothes. "You look like one of the Greek goddesses I read about," he exclaimed as he looked upon his wife standing waist deep in the moonlit pool. *Damme, if I'm not a lucky man*, he thought as he jumped into the cool water. When he surfaced the water, he walked up to Faith.

She put her arms around his neck and pulled him to her so that he could feel her breasts against his chest as their lips met in a long, loving, and passionate kiss.

"I love you, Gabe."

"And I love you."

"We'll have another child, won't we, Gabe?"

"Aye, my love…in time, as God wills."

Taking Gabe's hand, Faith climbed out of the little pool of water and lay down on the blanket. Gabe sat beside her. He rested on one elbow and held her hand. He leaned over to kiss Faith and she put her arms around his neck and drew him to her. She ran her hand through his hair and with a finger traced the furrow where a bullet had once grazed his scalp, leaving a strip of gray hair.

"Hold me, Gabe. Hold me for a while."

The two lay there for a long while, in one another's arms. It was a loving, healing time.

Slap…"Damn mosquitoes everywhere." Samson rose up as Gabe laughed. "What a way to end a romantic evening," he chuckled. "Hurry now. Let's get dressed."

## *Chapter Eighteen*

Once *Intrepid*, *Dasher*, and *Alert* returned from convoy duty, Lord Anthony decided it was time for the flagship to do its share of the patrol work. With the holidays approaching the likelihood of meeting any privateer or Colonial ship was remote. However, *SeaHorse's* hands had been in port long enough.

"There are only so many exercises we can do in port," Buck had stated, the key being "in port."

*Lizard* still had need of repairs so she needed to stay in port until the repairs could be finished. Anthony made Fletcher acting commodore until his return and assigned *Dasher* and *Ferret* to patrol with the flagship. *Viper* would act as dispatch vessel. Lord Ragland had bid Anthony fair sailing and again extended the invitation to bring Lady Deborah back for the holidays.

"Houghton will be more than happy to accommodate Captain Anthony and his wife," Ragland said. "It will give us all a time of togetherness at Christmas."

*Lord Ragland could be most persuasive,* Anthony thought. Seeing Bart, Anthony said, "Are you ready to get to sea, old friend?"

"Aye," Bart replied. "I feels the need of a bit of space and some fresh air."

"You'd find enough fresh air on the island," Anthony declared, "if you'd stay out of those smoky, old taverns. Between the rum and wenches you've probably spent half the prize money you got saved."

"Nay," Bart exclaimed, using his thumb and finger like a measure. "Only a wee bit."

"Then what are you doing?" Anthony asked.

"Adding to me retirement. Aye! Jep, he's got a good head for cards. So with me as 'is partner we's relieved some of these planters of a purse or two."

Suddenly concerned, Anthony questioned, "Not too large a purse I hope?"

"Nay, we ain't taken control like of nary a plantation but they's a few who might be a bit short when it's time to visit some trollop on Saturday night."

"Well, their wives might appreciate that," Anthony said, a smile on his face.

"Aye," Bart replied. "But the trollops don't."

"How do you know that?" Anthony asked.

"Cause they done said so. One done offered old Jep a sample of 'er wares to not play."

Finding this interesting, Anthony asked, "Did Jep take her up on the deal?"

"Nay. 'E said she wasn't worth the money 'e'd lose and were no use to have two people upset."

"Two?" Anthony asked. "How'd he figure two?"

"The planter when he wouldn't play cards with him no more," Bart said. "And Jep's little doxy who'd lose her money if he took the other's preposition."

"You mean proposition."

"That's what I said. Anyway, Jep said the percentage just didn't add up. Yew know what they say," Bart added. "Ye can't please everyone."

Hearing a chuckle behind him, Lord Anthony turned to find his flag lieutenant.

"I didn't mean to eavesdrop," Hazard said.

"Nonsense. On an open deck how can you not overhear?" Anthony replied.

Seeing a leather pouch tucked under Hazard's arm, Anthony sighed and said, "You've got work for me, don't you Everette?"

"Yes sir."

"Well, put it on my desk and see if you can talk Silas into getting us a cool beverage. I'll go below once we're underway."

"Aye, My Lord. Jepson says we're in for a midday squall and it's approaching that time now."

"Well, Jepson ought to know," Anthony said, looking at the cloudless sky. Then turning to Bart, he continued, "I'd not bet against him."

This caused Bart to laugh at the private joke.

Standing by the wheel, the quartermaster watched the men laughing. *Lucky sod,* he thought to himself. *All that Bart has to do is stand around with 'is Lordship whilst the rest of us 'as to work for a living. Not even the officers ask 'is comings and goings. Pet, that's what 'e is…admiral's pet. Still what I wouldn't give to be in 'is shoes.*

***

The squall came and went just as Jepson had predicted. The squadron made a show of heading toward Grenada then changed tack and headed due east.

"No need to let the spies know exactly where or which direction we're headed," Anthony said to Buck and the master.

"Before dusk puts us on a course nor-northwest, I want to look in at Martinique. I want to see if the French admiral we met at Antigua is there. I also want to see what kind of ships may be anchored."

"You think France will side with the Americans?" Buck asked.

"Sir Victor does," Anthony replied. "He said in his letter to me that the French at St. Lucia are building up their war supplies and improving the island's defences. His agent said it was more obvious at Martinique. We need to be ready."

Buck looked skeptical at this remark. "With one seventy-four, sixty-four and a few frigates? We could be standing with our cannons loaded and run out and still not make a good show. France has increased her fleet while most of ours has been laid up to rot."

Anthony couldn't help but smile. Buck could get worked up quickly.

"Silas," Anthony shouted to his servant, who was standing by the lee rail. "Hurry with a cool glass. I fear the flag captain is about to have apoplexy."

"Aye, My Lord. Lime juice or something with more substance?"

"Substance I think," Anthony replied.

Not slowing down, Buck defended his ranting. "The West Indies would fall like dominoes if the French invaded. Then the damn dagos would be in for their pound of flesh. Lord North and Lord Sandwich had better be listening to the likes of Sir Victor. I don't like the sod but he knows his business."

"Why don't you write the First Lord and extend him an invitation to visit his Majesty's possessions in the West Indies?" Anthony teased.

Taking a deep breath, Buck said, "That do about as much good as inviting a whore to a wedding."

***

The following morning, Buck was standing on the quarterdeck talking to *SeaHorse's* master when Anthony came on topside.

"Captain Buck, Mr Jepson," Anthony said in greeting the men.

"Jepson has just pointed out St. Lucia," Buck said, pointing off to larboard.

"Do you know much about the island, Mr Jepson?"

"Aye, My Lord. I was telling Captain Buck that yonder harbour is Gros Ilot. With its location at the northern tip of the island, one could watch the coming and goings at the French depot at Fort Royal on Martinique."

"An answer to a riddle, Mr Jepson."

"How so, My Lord?"

"When Sir Victor wanted to know if the French were increasing their defences he had Gabe...Captain Anthony carry him to St. Lucia. Your knowledge of the island explains how his man knew so much."

"Well, if the French do side with the Colonies I expect Martinique will be the most important base for them on this side of the world," Jepson remarked.

"I read," Buck said, "that during the Seven Year War that almost fourteen hundred English merchantmen were taken in the West Indies, and the principle ports for the rogues was Fort Royal on Martinique."

"Aye," Jepson replied. "And it don't take much to imagine a few privateers' systems depend upon it now. That and Havana."

"Those are my thoughts as well," Anthony said. "That's why we'll take a look see."

"Keep the monseers on their toes," Buck commented. "Let them know we got our eye on them."

"Exactly," Anthony remarked. "Put a person who can record in the tops with the lookout captain. I think I shall invite you, the master, a couple of lieutenants, and a few midshipmen to dine tonight. I shall leave it at your discretion as to which lieutenants and midshipmen will be invited."

"Thank you, My Lord. Duty permitting we shall be glad to accept," Buck said. Then he continued, "Is there a hint as to what the main course will be?"

Anthony paused as if in thought, then replied, "I have not yet consulted with Silas. However, knowing Jep and his relationship with Bart, I bet he'd have the information before I do."

"My Lord," Jepson said, turning a little flushed. "You give me too much credit."

"I doubt that," Anthony said. "You didn't get to be a master by being dull."

He turned to go below, and then added, "I'll bet that's something a planter or two back on Barbados has learned."

Hearing Jepson mutter something Buck waited until Anthony was through the companionway and out of ear-shot before asking, "What was that, Jep?"

Looking around before he answered, Jepson finally replied, "What I said was Bart ought to keep his trap shut."

Buck couldn't help but chuckle. "Let me tell you something you probably already know, Mr Jepson. Between Lord Anthony and Bart there are no secrets."

"Aye," Jepson replied. "I never figured there was. I just don't want the word to get out about our whist playing. It could affect our winnings you know."

*Damme*, Buck thought. *But ain't he a cool one.*

***

The meal that evening was a pleasant affair. The junior midshipman stumbled through the simple toast to King and country in his haste to get at the meal. Neal, the second lieutenant, was a very educated man and impressed Anthony in his grasp of how important the West Indies were in regards to commerce.

"Do you feel the Spanish will follow suit and aid the Colonies if France does, Mr Neal?" Anthony asked.

Neal paused to gather his thoughts and form his reply. "I do, sir. They would have very little to lose by not doing so and considerable to gain. They have always opposed us when they could. While they and the French are officially neutral they openly allow freedom for Colonial ships and privateers to come and go. Therefore, I feel they've already decided."

Taking a drink from his glass, Neal continued, "Besides, Captain Buck says they will, so I consider his professional opinion to be gospel."

"Here, here," the surgeon applauded. "A man who knows where his bread can be buttered."

This brought laughter from the rest of the group...except the midshipmen who barely paused from their eating. They paused only long enough to make sure they weren't being addressed.

Anthony then turned to Lieutenant Johns and asked, "What did you find interesting about the ships that were sighted at Martinique today?"

"First, My Lord, was the number. You always expect a few but not the number we counted today. The other thing is outside the half dozen warships, the ships were deep water merchantman. Not island traders and the likes. That tells you they are stocking up. Taking it all into consideration I would have to say they were gearing up for war."

"I concur with your observations, Lieutenant. Now let's see what the old salt says. Mister Jepson."

"It's as evident to me as it is to the rest of you, sir. France is ready to go to war along side of the Colonies. What is also obvious is the strategic importance of these islands. I know it, you know it, My Lord. Sir Victor knows it but it's the politicians that have their heads in the sand. I already feel we've lost the Colonies. Lord North hasn't taken it seriously enough. The home folks don't want the war and so it's left up to sods like us...begging your pardon, My Lord."

When Anthony nodded Jepson continued, “It’s up to the likes of us to overcome the shortcomings of the politicians. They speak of guts and glory. As you know, My Lord, and as these officers will soon learn,” Jepson continued, nodding toward the young lieutenants and the midshipmen, “it’s our guts they’re talking about.”

The table was silent when Jepson finished. The young officers were thinking about the master’s words and realizing the truth in them.

Anthony broke the silence. “A toast, gentlemen…to those that go down on the sea in a ship.”

## Chapter Nineteen

HMS *SeaHorse* and her consorts arrived in Antigua to find a large welcoming party. Lady Deborah was there with little Macayla, who was turning into a set-in-her-ways little lady. Her mother said she was only showing her family traits…those on her father's side. Gabe was there with Faith, who showed little of the tragedy that had recently befallen her. Commodore Gardner was there with his wife, Greta.

The carriages and footmen crowded the landing so there was little to gather once the boats from the ships landed. Lord Anthony and Captain Buck was in the admiral's barge with Bart at the helm, smiling from ear to ear once the welcoming party had been spied. Captain Francis Markham, commanding *Dasher*, was next. He and Gabe had been friends since they were both midshipmen.

Commodore Gardner had arranged for a luncheon at the inn. It was here Captain Buck renewed an old acquaintance. She was the widow of a wealthy plantation owner. She and Buck had enjoyed each other's company when he'd been the first lieutenant on *Drakkar* a few years back. *A few more wrinkles in the face caused by the tropical sun but otherwise she had changed very little*, Buck thought. She was alone and glad to accept Buck's invitation to join the others for the luncheon.

Watching Buck and the widow, Lady Deborah leaned over and whispered to Anthony, "Want to bet Captain Buck makes his apologies and leaves early?"

"It's hard for us simple sailors not to fall into the clutches of you wily women, so I'd not bet," Anthony replied. All the time he was thinking, *Damn you Gardner, it's been months since I was alone with my wife and you had to arrange a luncheon. Why couldn't it have been dinner…tomorrow?*

Reading his thoughts, Deborah whispered, "Soon my love…soon."

Glancing up from the table, Anthony saw Bart and Dagan walk through a doorway into another room. *They'll have a wet and bring each other up to date on the happenings since they last talked*, Anthony thought. *What would England do without the likes of them…them and men like the master, George Jepson?*

***

The ride up to the cottage never ceased to amaze Anthony. The peaceful tranquility of the island as viewed from the hilltop. He remembered the first time he and Bart had ridden up this road. How the sea and the sky almost merged. The small island in the distance now covered in clouds…Potters Cay. The rustle as a gentle breeze blew the palm trees. This…this was home. Would the peaceful existence be shattered by French or Spanish cannons?

"I pray not."

"What was that dear?" Deborah asked.

"Just thinking aloud," Anthony said, not wanting to worry his wife.

Taking his arm, Deborah pulled her man closer. Something was on his mind. Something to do with the war and something he didn't want her to fret over. Snuggled close to her husband, Deborah too remembered the first time he'd come up this hill to visit. She also remembered the days Gabe lay wounded and racked with fever in one of the cottage's small bedrooms.

She remembered the letters Anthony had written to the families of fallen sailors. *Damn this war*, she thought. *It had taken so much out of this man she loved. Hadn't he already done enough? How often must he risk his life? Well, tonight she'd take his mind away from it all. As Bart says "and that's no error."*

***

Bart and Dagan were at a table when Jep walked up with a fresh round of ale. Sitting down he nodded toward the door at the man who had just entered.

"Sir Victor," Bart hissed. "We's can't get rid of 'is kind cans we?"

"Aye," Jep said. "Wonder what's up this time?"

"I'm sure we'll know soon enough," Dagan said with a sinking feeling in the pit of his stomach.

"Maybe 'e'll pick another ship to ferry 'is arse here and yon," Bart said.

"No," Dagan answered. "It will be Gabe. He's seen him in action. He knows that he's a capable man."

"Maybe His Lordship won't let *Peregrine* go," Jepson said. "He'd be in a fix if the French attacked and we was short a ship."

"Nay," Bart replied. "Me admiral loves 'is brother like 'e were 'is son. But he'd allow Sir Victor to use Gabe. 'E 'as a letter from the admiralty making it clear we's to offer every assistance possible. Them's the words best as I can recall."

"Well let's hope the frogs stay at home," Jepson said.

"Aye," his mates replied in unison.

Recognizing the group at the table, Sir Victor made his way over to them. "Greetings gentlemen."

"They ain't no gentlemens at this table," Bart snorted, only to feel a nudge in his ribs by Jepson.

"And to you sir," Dagan said as he rose. "Would you care to have a glass of ale?" This was said in the face of a glare from Bart.

"No, thank you. I was seeking directions to Lord Anthony's lodging. I understand it's not close enough to walk, that one would need a horse."

"'E ain't there," Bart said with an edge still in his voice. "'E won't be back till tonight. Yew jus tell us uns where you are staying and we'll see 'is Lordship gets the word."

Sir Victor listened and seemed to contemplate on Bart's words. "You seem most disagreeable today, sir. I've done nothing to offend you, have I?"

"Your being here offends me," Bart said.

Jepson's jaw dropped upon hearing Bart's words. Dagan cleared his throat and went to speak. He too was surprised at Bart's animosity.

"Keep yer trap closed for a bit," Bart said upon Dagan's attempt to intervene. Bart then turned back to Sir Victor and said, "I got nothing 'gainst yew personal like. It's jus when you come around it puts 'is Lordship in a spot. That I's don't like. So let me jus tell yew there's nobody what means more to me than 'is Lordship…'is Lordship and 'is family. So I's plainly telling yew…government man or not…yew cause 'urt to come to 'is Lordship, I'll be out to do some 'urting me self."

Sir Victor stood there. He'd never been talked to in such a way. Why, he could have the man flogged for insubordination. But no…he might be killed, but the man would never be flogged. *Loyalty…I've never seen such loyalty*, Sir Victor realized. This man had threatened him out of loyalty. Sir Victor took a deep breath, not quite trusting his emotions.

After a lengthy pause, he looked at Bart and said, "I commend you sir. That was well spoken. I only wish I had someone who cared as much for me. However, you may rest assured that whether you like it or not, I do what I do for England...all of England. We sometimes lose sight of our actions, how we treat those around us, feeling the end justifies the means. I apologize for my abruptness at times. I shall endeavor to not endanger your admiral or any of his officers and men anymore than I would myself. However, I must always consider the lives of many against the lives of a few, including my own life. So let me say, I could be more of a gentleman in how I go about my work but it is work that must be done."

Upon hearing Sir Victor's words, Bart held out his hand. "Maybe I was a bit too 'asty."

"Nonsense," Sir Victor declared, meaning it. "Let me buy a round and you let His Lordship know I'd like to see him upon the morrow if it's convenient."

"Aye, we'll do that," Dagan said quickly and watched the man as he departed.

"'E ain't such a bad bloke once you get to know 'im is 'e," Bart said.

"It's a wonder he didn't put a sword through your gullet," Jepson said. "You had me worried there for a minute."

"Aye," Dagan said, seeing a side of Bart he'd not seen nor wanted to see again.

***

The next day Bart was standing under the poop when Lieutenant Hazard escorted Sir Victor to the gangway. Seeing Bart, Sir Victor smiled and waved. Bart returned the wave.

When Hazard came back toward Bart he said with a frown, "His Lordship wishes to speak to you."

Anthony saw his cox'n enter the cabin and called, "Bart!"

"Aye."

"What's this I hear of you calling out Sir Victor," Anthony growled.

"I didn't call 'im out," Bart replied. "Not regular like anyway. I jus told 'im I would."

"Aye, I heard all about it," Anthony answered. "Said he admired you more than anybody he'd ever met," Anthony continued.

"Silas!"

"Aye, My Lord."

"Let's have a glass of hock."

"At once, My Lord." Then he went to get a bottle out of the bilges. The fresh supply was dwindling fast.

Anthony then turned back to Bart. "I'm honoured by your loyalty and friendship. But, Bart, that man is a King's officer."

"I know," Bart answered..."but 'e'd still be called out."

Anthony opened his mouth to speak then closed it. *That damn Bart, he got the last word in again.*

## *Chapter Twenty*

Sir Victor sat at a round table next to a window. The shutters were open, allowing a small zephyr to enter the dark tavern. Looking out the window the dockyard could be seen. A ship was being unloaded so that it could enter the dock for repairs. It was not one of Lord Anthony's ships. It was likely one that had been caught up in a squall and needed repairs before it could continue on.

There was no sign of battle so it had to be weather, Sir Victor concluded. A waiter brought his tankard of ale over with a promise that his meal would soon follow. Once the waiter was gone, Sir Victor turned back to look out the window. The breeze had picked up a bit and the smell of tar, turpentine, and cordage mingled with the distinct smell of the sea.

The waiter and a servant girl were now at the table. "I think you'll find the mutton very tasty," the waiter volunteered. He turned and took a bowl of green peas and one of boiled squash from the girl. She then hurried off and quickly returned with a loaf of fresh baked bread, butter and a jar of lime marmalade.

Bowing as he backed away, the waiter said, "Just sing out if I can bring you anything else, sir."

Sir Victor nodded his thanks, as he'd just placed a piece of warm buttered bread in his mouth.

Outside the window the sound from a party of seamen could be heard as they walked across the ground oyster and seashells that lined the path, making a crunching sound with every step. The men made a colorful group as each seemed to be dressed differently. Some wore broad striped trousers while others wore plain sailcloth. One had a fancy red waistcoat while the others wore ordinary blue jackets. All wore hats set at a jaunty angle with various colored handkerchiefs tied about their necks with pigtails hanging down.

There was something about these men that made Sir Victor think of the fiercely loyal Bart and Jepson. These were sailors off a warship. They had that certain air about them. *No wonder England ruled the sea*, Sir Victor thought.

After finishing his meal, Sir Victor made his way to the waterfront. Lord Anthony had promised a boat to pick him up about three o'clock. The squadron was to sail on the evening tide. Once they reached Barbados, Sir Victor would then take passage to Halifax. He'd asked for Captain Anthony but now was reluctant to separate the young captain from his bride after her recent ordeal.

However, duty and needs of the King came before personal life. Captain Anthony understood that. The boat was waiting with Captain Buck's cox'n, Tom Blood, at the tiller.

"A fine day is it not?" Sir Victor observed speaking to Blood.

"Aye, sir," Blood replied. "The breeze has cooled things off a might so it's not too hot even for the middle of the afternoon. Lots better than the cold and rain back in Portsmouth."

"Aye," Sir Victor said, using the Navy lingo, "much preferable."

***

Lord Anthony, Lady Deborah and Macayla were already aboard *SeaHorse* when Sir Victor arrived. Buck greeted the Foreign Service gentleman as he made his way through the entry port. A petty officer quickly hoisted Sir Victor's trunk aboard while Sir Victor and the captain were talking.

"His Lordship has extended an invitation to join him once you're settled in," Buck said.

"Thank you, Captain," Sir Victor replied. "But would I be in the way if I remained topside until we're underway."

"No, you'd not be in the way," Buck responded. "And you're welcome to watch from the advantage of the quarterdeck."

"Thank you kindly, Captain."

Sir Victor had already learned one didn't enter upon the quarterdeck without an invitation, so he felt privileged. What he did know was Captain Buck was just trying to give his admiral a little more time alone till Lady Deborah and the child were settled in.

"Mr Jepson," Buck called to the master.

"Aye, Captain."

"Would you say the tide has freshened so that we may get underway?"

"I would say so," Jep replied.

Buck then called the midshipman in charge of signals. "Make signal, Mr Lewis. Prepare to weigh anchor."

"Aye, sir," the youth acknowledged as he ran to carry out his task.

"Mr Lamb."

"Aye, Captain," the first lieutenant answered.

"You may get us underway."

"Aye, sir," Lamb replied and then started barking out orders.

Pipes shrilled and the decks came alive as men ran to their stations, urged by shouts and curses from petty officers, each wanting their division to beat the others.

"Move you slack-arsed landsman. There's not a proper seaman in the lot of ye."

"Move ya bloody whoreson," the bosun yelled. "Evans, how long you been aboard this ship?"

A yelp of pain as the bosun's ratten hurried along a laggard.

"Stand by the capstan."

Jepson crossed to Buck's side and said, "We'll have rain before Barbados, possibly a squall."

Buck only nodded as he called out, "Mr Johns, a shanty if you please."

"Aye, Captain," the lieutenant replied, and then called for the fiddler.

The sound of the fiddle filled the air as Decker, *Sea-Horse's* bosun, roared out, "Now me little sweethearts. Let's show the buggers on the hill what a sight it be to watch a man-o-war get underway."

Looking, Sir Victor could indeed see a group of people had gathered to see the squadron weigh anchor and set sail. *How many of them are spies?* Sir Victor's suspicious mind wondered.

"Anchors hove short," Lamb reported to Buck, who only nodded.

Lamb lifted his speaking trumpet and ordered, "Loose head sails."

Jepson had made his way back to the big double wheel, watching. His eyes were on the canvas sails that were flapping and cracking as they filled with the wind.

"Be ready," he warned the helmsman.

"Lay a course to take us from the harbour and to Barbados," Buck ordered the master.

As the sails filled and the ship began to move, Lamb lifted his trumpet again, "Loose topsails." Like thunder the great sails billowed out.

"Anchors aweigh, sir," Meriweather cried out from the fo'c'sle.

Clank, clank, clank. The sound was coming from the capstan as it pulled the hidden anchor from its depths.

"Get the courses on her?" Lamb asked Buck somewhat timidly.

"Aye," Buck replied not wanting to embarrass the first lieutenant. *He knows what to do*, Buck thought, *so why does he always ask…a quiet conversation for later.*

"Mr Lamb."

"Aye, Captain."

"Let's have the topgallants on her once we clear the harbour."

"Aye, sir."

The anchor was now clear of the water and Decker could once again be heard from near the capstan. "Carter, you grog faced villain, heave."

The men put their backs into it and with a final heave the anchor dangled like a great pendant just below the cathead. "Heave, you blood bullocks." And the anchor was catted home.

Sir Victor watched from his vantage point on the quarterdeck as the people on the hill got smaller and finally vanished. He sat there a while longer, wondering how many times ships such as this weighed anchor leaving loved ones behind, often never to be heard from again. *Damme, but I'm getting soft*, he thought. But still he looked at those who chose the sea in a new light.

For the remainder of the afternoon, *SeaHorse* and her consorts drove steadily through the warm Caribbean Sea, but overhead the sky was changing. Dark clouds now blotted out the sun and the seas had picked up as the wind increased. Feeling the increase in the sea, Lord Anthony came on deck as Jepson was telling Buck it wouldn't hurt to put another helmsman on the wheel.

"I feel we'll have to reduce sail," Buck said, seeing his admiral.

Anthony nodded in acknowledgment, the wind already making it difficult to speak.

The squall came ten minutes later. It was accompanied with a heavy rain as black clouds filled the horizon. Looking aft, Anthony could see the rest of the ships in his squadron.

"They are all on station," Buck shouted. "For now."

"How's our heading?" Buck asked Jepson.

"Fine so far, winds steady sou-sou-east, but the barometer is on the rise."

To mark the master's words, the wind shifted causing the wet sails to flap.

"Mr Lamb," Buck called.

"Aye, sir."

"Man the braces. If the wind continues we'll be taken aback."

"Aye, sir."

The bosun had no sooner piped all hands and the yards were braced around when the perverse wind shifted back to the southwest creating another evolution. Looking aft once more Anthony was alarmed to find the sky was so thick and dark that he couldn't see anything beyond a cable's length.

Sir Victor was feeling the effects of the weather as well. He turned to go below only to stagger as the ship crashed through a rogue wave. He caught hold of a ratline to keep from falling onto the heaving deck. As he righted himself, a gust of wind plucked his hat from his head. Tom Blood, standing next to his captain, saw the hat in the air and gave a leap, catching it just before it flew over the side.

"Damme, what a catch," Buck said, patting his cox'n on the shoulder.

"Thank you, thank you kindly," Sir Victor said, wiping the wet cocked hat with his handkerchief. "It's a new one. I should have known better than to wear it on deck."

Blood offering his arm for Sir Victor to steady himself said, "I always look to the captain. If his noggin is covered I wears me hat. Otherwise I don't."

"I'll take your advice," Sir Victor said as he made it through the companionway.

Bart had made his way topside with Anthony's tarpaulin. The wind roared and the rain now came down in torrents.

Smiling at Jepson, Bart said, "Looks like we're in for a deyluge."

Anthony, finally getting his coat buttoned up, asked, "Pray tell, where you got that idea?"

"From seeing all the water what's running down the scuppers, that's where."

Bart was right. Water flooded over the scuppers and at times was sloshing over the coamings and down through the hatches to the decks below.

*SeaHorse* drove through the gale. The sails had now been reduced to foresail and topsails. Once the sails were set the men were sent below unless they had the watch. They were tired and wet but at least they were out of the wind.

The officers stood on the quarterdeck as the thunder rolled through the sky and streaks of lightning pierced the dark clouds, darting in every direction.

Buck turned to Anthony and said, "There is no need for you to remain on deck, My Lord. I'm sure Lady Deborah is at her wits end with the gale. You should go below. We will call you if we need you."

"Aye, Rupert. I think I will."

Anthony made his way down the quarterdeck ladder and steadied himself by holding onto a shroud as the ship was rolled by a huge wave. Still holding onto the shroud, Anthony put his other hand on a cannon as he righted himself, drenched to the bone. At this moment a tremendous noise was heard aloft and a shock was felt throughout the ship.

Lightning had struck the ship at the main top and ran down the wet lines in every direction, leaving a trail of smoke drifting off the lines. A loud shriek was heard as those on the quarterdeck could see Lord Anthony being shocked with the lightning running from the shrouds through His Lordship and into the heavy metal cannon. Without thinking, Jepson jumped from the quarterdeck and hit Lord Anthony squarely, knocking him loose from the line he'd been gripping.

A trembling sensation shook the ship and cries of alarm was heard as the topmast exploded from the continuous bolt after bolt of lightning hitting it, showering the deck with splinters and debris. Smoke filled the main decks and seamen came rushing up through the hatches, fear on their faces.

Silas and Lady Deborah rushed out through the companionway only to come to a sudden stop as they saw Lord Anthony lying on the deck. Smoke was coming from his hair and the soles of his boots. One sole had curled away at the seams. Jepson rose from the deck, bruised with blood dripping from his broken nose. Bart knelt down and picked up his admiral and carried him to the bed in his cabin while Buck sent for the surgeon.

Lady Deborah wiped the tears from her eyes and was led by Silas back to the cabin. Lieutenant Hazard made his way from the wardroom into the admiral's cabin just as Bart laid Anthony down on his cot. Hazard took Lady Deborah's hand at the point and Silas went to help Bart undress Anthony. Little Macayla slept the innocent sleep of a child.

On deck, the sun reappeared as the clouds and the rain went away. But still a cloud hung over *HMS SeaHorse* as the ship sailed on toward Barbados.

## *Chapter Twenty-one*

With a warm fresh breeze Lord Anthony's squadron made good time heading to Barbados. The crew now over the shock of being hit by lightning went about their duties in a relieved if not cheerful manner.

"It was on a whaler," Decker was saying. "A bolt hit the mainmast and traveled the length of the ship—down every shroud and backstay from stem to stern. Every line was scorched. The ringbolts were seared, leaving charred marks in the deck. The lookout in the crosstrees lived but was never the same again. Burnt the hair slam offen his head. No eyebrows either. Always seem to be staring off into the distance, he did."

Lieutenant Johns had the watch. It was make and mend; otherwise he'd have busted up the group. He didn't know if Decker's story was true or not but he was sure every man jack would tell the story again, adding to what happened to the admiral. Seamen were a superstitious lot and if Lord Anthony pulled through this they'd say he was lightning proof.

As soon as the seas had calmed down, Buck had signaled *Peregrine* to close with the flag and captain to repair on board. Dagan must have known something was amiss as he accompanied Gabe after the ships had hove to. Gabe made it quickly to his brother's side after a brief conversation with Captain Buck, who briefly explained what happened.

The ship's surgeon was about to perform a bloodletting to relieve the vapours that the lightning had caused. Seeing the man's instruments Dagan said, "No," in a very firm voice.

"Now see here man." The surgeon started to protest the intrusion, but as the surgeon looked into Dagan's cold black eyes, the objection died without completion.

The sleeping quarters were very dark so Dagan opened the gallery windows and skylight. Almost like a miracle, once the light filled the cabin Anthony stirred. A groan, then a stretching and with that he opened his eyes.

Looking about him, Anthony spoke, "My head feels like it's been hit by a broadside."

Unable to control her emotions, Lady Deborah burst out in tears but a smile was on her face. Bending over she showered Anthony with one kiss after another. "My darling, we were worried so."

"What…what happened?" Anthony asked.

Bart explained how lightning had hit the fore-topmast, a long continuous bolt that traveled the entire ship.

"Was anyone hurt?" was Anthony's first question.

"Only you, My Lord." This from Captain Buck, who had entered and had his hand on Gabe's back.

Dagan turned to leave the now cramped sleeping quarters. In doing so he came eye to eye with Gabe. He still had a concerned look.

"He'll live," Dagan whispered as he made his way out of the cabin.

Seeing Dagan depart, Bart followed. Once on deck Bart offered Dagan a clay pipe and tobacco as he dug out his own pipe. Seeing the two light up, Lieutenant Johns started to protest but remembering previous warnings from Captain Buck, closed his trap. After all it was make and mend.

***

Bart entered Lord Anthony's cabin wiping his face with his handkerchief. "We're just past South Point," he said, informing Anthony as to their position.

"If you will be so kind," Anthony said, speaking to Hazard, his flag lieutenant. "Give my compliments to the flag captain and let him know I'd like to speak with him as soon as convenient."

"Aye, My Lord." Hazard answered and made his way to the quarterdeck.

Soon the marine sentry stamped the deck with his musket and announced, "Flag captain, suh."

"Carlisle Bay is in sight," Buck said upon entering. That was Buck's way of informing Anthony the visit would have to be brief.

Coming to the point, Anthony said, "About Jepson, how is he doing?"

"He's doing well, My Lord. You know his kind. Tough as English oak."

"Aye," Anthony said. "I would like to do something for him but I confess I don't know what to do."

"I'm not sure he expects anything," Buck replied.

"I know, but for his quick thinking I could have been fried to a crisp."

A knock at the door and once again the marine sentry stamped his musket and announced, "Midshipman of the watch, suh."

"Lieutenant Lamb's compliments, sir," the midshipman said, addressing Captain Buck. "We're entering the bay, sir."

"Very well," Buck replied. "I'll be up directly." Turning to Anthony, Buck said,"Nervous."

"The lad?" Anthony questioned.

"No, Lieutenant Lamb. He knows what to do but is hesitant to act without my approval," Buck said in disgust. "Gawd help the ship if I fall."

"Maybe you should take him aside," Anthony said. Then as an afterthought, he added, "Maybe you should become suddenly ill the next time we weigh anchor. He'll then have to sink or swim."

"And if he sinks?" Buck questioned.

"Then he doesn't need to be the first lieutenant," Anthony replied in a matter-of-fact way. "We can't let one person endanger the entire ship."

"Aye, you're right, My Lord. I may have Jepson speak with him."

"Not a bad idea," Anthony replied. "Now be on deck with you. I'll come up directly."

***

Sir Victor was on deck when Anthony appeared.

"My Lord," he said. "It's good to see you doing so well."

"Thank you," Anthony replied. "It appears we are approaching the anchorage."

Taking a deep breath, Sir Victor said, "I can smell the shore."

As they looked towards the shore the beach and palm trees were clearly visible. The sea had turned to a pale green as the water shallowed.

"Eight fathoms," someone forward cried out.

Seeing the questioning look on Sir Victor's face, Anthony explained, "They're checking the depth."

Nodding his understanding, Sir Victor replied, "It wouldn't do to run aground, would it?" Glancing about the ship he spoke again, "The men seem to have gotten cleaned up."

Anthony saw that most of the crew had freshly shaven faces. Their hair was pulled back into neatly tied queues, most with black ribbon but blue and red was also noted. Clean trousers and shirts had been adorned.

"The lure of Bridgetown," Anthony said by way of explanation. "Local rum by the barrel and willing trollops. A sailor's dream, sir."

A midshipman approached Anthony. "Yes?" Anthony asked, not waiting for the youth to beg his pardon.

"Captain's compliments, sir, and we're about to begin the salute."

"Thank you, young sir."

Then turning to Sir Victor, Anthony said, "I shall go to my cabin and make preparations for going ashore."

"And I as well," Sir Victor replied.

Before returning to his cabin Anthony turned once more to Sir Victor, "When do you anticipate leaving for Halifax?"

After a pause, Sir Victor replied, "I will have to talk to Lord Ragland first to be for sure but I'd not think it would be till after Christmas...possibly after the first of the New Year."

Once back in his cabin, Anthony could see that Lady Deborah had Silas and the lone servant girl busy. It amazed him how much it took for women to make themselves presentable. She had four trunks with her and would have had double that had he not brought up the lack of space. Of course, one was for Macayla...or so Deborah said.

"Surely you don't need all that," he said.

"Surely you don't want me dressed like some tavern wench."

Trying to be coy, Anthony had responded, "Well, there's some what'll turn a head."

"Yes, I've seen your head turn enough to know," she chided. "Don't think I've forgotten how your eyes bugged out at some of Greta's parties."

"I only look at what's being presented," Anthony said in defence. "The more that's shown, the more I look. Seems like I recall that certain green dress you wore…now that one near took my breath away."

"Gown…it was a gown. It was meant to get your blood running."

"Damme, if it didn't do its job too," Anthony replied. He then put his arms around his wife and pulled her to him. "Maybe it's time for a little more thunder and lightning."

"Hush," she hissed. "The servant will hear you." But a smile filled her face. "Who knows what might take place tonight."

"A date it is, madam," Anthony said as he took a step back and gave an exaggerated bow.

Standing over next to the pantry, Silas shook his head. *Teeched! Damned if that lightning bolt didn't fry something in His Lordship's head. Wonder iffen 'is lightning rod is still working proper like*, Silas thought to himself with a smirk on his face.

## Chapter Twenty-two

The dancers whirled about on the highly polished dance floor. Young men, some wealthy planter's sons, others wearing the distinctive dress uniform of either the Navy or the Army mingled about. They were each trying to catch some girl's eye with their dress and swagger. The young women were dressed in brightly colored gowns of various descriptions, designed to show off each young lady's attributes.

Lord Anthony and Lady Deborah were taking a breather and enjoying a cool glass of Sangria. Gabe approached them and accepted a glass from a passing servant.

"Faith looks beautiful tonight," Deborah volunteered.

"Aye," Gabe responded, proud of his wife. "She seems to be enjoying herself. She has promised at least one dance to every officer aboard *Peregrine*."

"It's good she can enjoy herself," Anthony replied. "This is what she needs to put her recent ordeal behind her."

"Here comes Lord Ragland," Gabe spoke quietly. "I see he has our Foreign Service gentleman with him."

"Aye," Anthony replied. He didn't know why but he always had bad feelings when Sir Victor was around. He was a genuine fellow and well mannered so Anthony could only sum up his feelings with one word…spy.

"Greetings Gil," Lord Ragland said, using Anthony's given name. He then turned to Deborah, bowed and said, "My lady you look positively radiant tonight."

Anthony agreed wholeheartedly and could not wait till the evening was over and he was alone with his wife.

Wiping his face with a lace handkerchief, Ragland volunteered, "It's hellish hot tonight."

Even with the great French windows opened wide to allow what wind there was to sweep through the governor's house, the heat was still intense. The faces of the dancers were all red and gleamed with sweat. Collars had been pulled loose and were damp with perspiration. The amount of spirits that had been consumed was also taking its toll. The glowing chandelier that hung from the high ceiling flickered as a pleasant, cooling breeze found its way through the open windows.

"Thank the Lord for that," Deborah said. "I felt like I was about to melt."

Once the dance was over, black red-liveried menservants circulated through the crowd, offering trays of cool beverages. The orchestra made up of free black men laid down their instruments, sweating from the last number, which had been a tune played at a fast tempo.

Faith made her way across the dance floor and after a whisper in Deborah's ear the ladies excused themselves.

"Ladies always excuse themselves in pairs," Sir Victor exclaimed. "If men were to do that it would soon be rumoured they were sodomites."

Drink was definitely making itself evident. His speech was somewhat slurred and his statement while true was not the gentlemanly thing to mention at such a gathering. Across the dance floor Gabe spied Lieutenant Davy. He was in conversation with a young lady of twenty or so years.

She had sun-streaked blond hair that hung down in curls to either side of her ears. Her gown was a pink silk. She carried a green embroidered fan that she flicked about as she talked. A strand of pearls hung around her neck and fell between two creamy white breasts that were pushed up by a tight corset. In spite of the West Indies heat and humidity the girl was stunning...absolutely stunning. Not a drop of perspiration was seen.

"I see Lieutenant Davy is fairly intrigued."

"Aye," Anthony responded to Gabe's remark.

"Young love," Ragland volunteered.

"Quim...not love. Quim is what's on that boy's mind," Sir Victor said with a belch.

"Ahem...she has breeding and wealth," Ragland said, overlooking Sir Victor's drunken state.

"Matters little when she's in heat," Sir Victor spoke again. "They all act the same when they're in heat. It matters little who they arc, street strumpet or Queen of Sheba."

Realizing things were about to become embarrassing, Anthony caught the eye of his flag lieutenant and motioned him over.

"Mr Hazard, Sir Victor is feeling the ill effects of the heat. Would you be so kind as to escort him back to his quarters and assist him in his preparations to retire for the evening?"

"My pleasure, My Lord," said Hazard, who clearly didn't relish the idea of dealing with a drunk.

"Thank you, sir," Lord Ragland said. "I don't know what has come over our friend. Most unbecoming I declare."

"We have all had moments we'd rather forget," Anthony said, not wanting to make more of the situation than it warranted. Turning back he was just in time to see Lieutenant Davy and the young lady disappear through the open doorway. *Taking a breather*, he thought...*I hope.*

Lieutenant Davy was living a dream. He'd never been so close to such a beautiful creature. His heart pounded as hand in hand they walked through the garden to a small bench that sat under a gazebo. As the two sat down fireflies winked and inside the orchestra started to play again. Davy leaned over and kissed Annabelle. Her perfume mingled with the scent of flowers that filled the little garden. As their lips met, Annabelle took Davy's hand and brought it against her chest.

"I love you," she whispered as once again her lips sought and found his.

Davy's hand was now resting upon the softness of her breast. *I think I'm in heaven*, he thought as he cupped her breast while her hand drifted down to below his waist…to his erect manhood.

"You whore! You bitch of a whore."

Not believing his ears, Davy opened his eyes to find an irate young man staring down upon the two as they sat on the bench.

Annabelle glared at the man shouting down obscenities. "You cad," she spat back in a raging fury.

Davy, now raging himself, rose abruptly and said, "Apologize, sir. I demand it."

"Demand it? I couldn't give a tinker's damn what you or this whore demand."

Without thinking, Davy slapped the lout. The sound echoed in the night and it became deathly still.

"That's enough." This came from Marine Lieutenant Baugean.

Davy, seething with anger, again demanded, "You'll apologize to the lady, sir."

"I've never apologized in my life and I'll never apologize for speaking the truth."

"Liar!" Annabelle screamed.

The music had stopped and hearing the commotion outside the dancers walked out onto the terrace.

Still feeling the sting on his face from Davy's slap, the man said, "You'll answer to me for that, sir."

Gabe, Lord Anthony, and Lord Ragland had just made it through the door when the man made his remark.

"Leave this house now, young sir!" Lord Ragland roared.

"I had that in mind, sir," the man said bowing. "I find the company insufferable."

Davy took a step forward, determined to defend Annabelle's honour.

"And you, sir," the man smirked, "are a fool to defend what Annabelle doesn't possess." Still touching his face the man continued, "Nevertheless you've marked me so I will have satisfaction."

Turning to Baugean, Davy said, "I'll need a second."

Baugean came to attention, clicked his heels together, and gave a slight bow.

"Good," the man said. "My second will be contacting you upon the morrow to make the arrangements." The man then turned to Lord Ragland. "I apologize for spoiling your ball, sir. However, the fault was not mine."

***

Lord Anthony sat in a cushioned leather chair discussing the previous evening's events with Governor Lord Ragland. "Annabelle's father, Sir William Bolton, is the second richest plantation owner on the island. Jonathan Penn, the young man who demanded satisfaction from your lieutenant, is a bit of a hothead. He is given to drink, gambling, and the weekly visit to Peg's place for a romp. Jonathan's father…ere stepfather, is Mr Winston Penn. He's the wealthiest man on the island. They moved here from the Colonies back in 1758. He did not like the view the Puritans took when he married a woman with a child. He has succeeded where others failed and has bought a couple of plantations thereby adding to his original holdings. He is a hands-on type of gentleman and meets with his foreman and overseers daily."

"You've discovered all this in the few months you've been here? It's incredible," Anthony said.

Smiling, Lord Ragland responded, "The favourite pastime on an island such as Barbados is gossip. Lend a willing ear and you'd be surprised what you'll hear."

Seeing Lord Ragland's glass was empty, a manservant poured more lime juice from a pewter pitcher. There was obviously ice still in the container as the outside was beaded with condensation. Once his and Lord Anthony's glasses were refilled, Lord Ragland continued.

"The rumour is Sir William is in debt to Mr Penn. It is also rumoured that for all his money, the one thing Mr Penn doesn't have is a title. A marriage would produce…hopefully produce grandchildren that would be titled. If an arrangement were to be made so that Jonathan and Annabelle married, it is hinted that all debts would be forgiven."

"I see," Anthony said.

"Looking at the prospects on the island," Ragland continued, "Annabelle had probably resolved herself to the fact that she would eventually become Mrs. Penn. Though I'm told she has never relished the idea. They have been seen together for the last several months at all the socials and parties but anyone paying attention could tell she doesn't love the lout. Then here comes the dashing young, heroic Navy lieutenant. He has tales of foreign lands. He's fought battles on the high seas. To her way of thinking, he is a regular Romeo. Compared to Lieutenant Davy, Jonathan is nothing but a rich, spoiled bully of a boy."

"I tell you this," Ragland said, downing his glass of juice. "This little incident has caused a rift among the locals. Sir William, by all rights, should call out Jonathan for the remarks said to his daughter. If this were to happen

I'm sure Mr Penn would make the boy apologize pleading drunkenness. However, with a third party involved and it being someone who's attracted the attention of Annabelle, I don't think Winston will intervene. I understand the seconds have met and the duel is scheduled."

"Aye," Anthony replied. "It is to be conducted at sunrise tomorrow morning. There is a hill between here and the Penn plantation. The parties will meet there."

"Is there nothing you can do?" Ragland asked.

"No. If it were two of my officers I would intervene," Anthony said. "However, if I put Lieutenant Davy under arrest and restricted him to the ship, I'd lose a good officer. He's already told Gabe…Captain Anthony he'd resign his commission if need be. Besides, if he didn't show up, he'd be branded a coward throughout the West Indies."

Sighing, Lord Ragland stood up and walked to a window and peered out. "Well, Lieutenant Davy will get no thanks from Sir William if he does defend his daughter's honour. He needs Winston Penn's money."

"Maybe he should talk to Lieutenant Davy," Anthony responded. "With the prize money Lieutenant Davy has tucked away over the years and it drawing three percent annually, he could possibly buy his own plantation."

Anthony knew this was not exactly the truth but it didn't hurt to plant a seed if it would help Lieutenant Davy's cause.

As Anthony made ready to leave, Lord Ragland spoke once more. "I wish your lieutenant luck, Gil. I hear Penn is a crack shot. He's won most of the island's shooting competitions."

"Aye, but has he ever faced a man who was shooting back?" Anthony asked in a solemn voice.

***

The two parties met the following morning. A borrowed carriage stopped on the top of a small hill. Sugar cane stalks stood higher than the carriage and rustled in the dawn breeze as Gabe, Lieutenant Baugean, Davy's second, Isreal Livesey, *Peregrine's* surgeon, and Lieutenant Davy arrived.

Benjamin Briggs was Penn's second. He walked over to greet Lieutenant Baugean. In the half light Gabe could see Penn's party consisted of three men, four if you counted the man holding the bag standing by their carriage. He was obviously the Penn's physician. The elderly man, probably Penn's father, was whispering into the younger man's ear. The younger man replied in a somewhat heated manner then turned his back on the older gentleman.

"Let's be about this," he shouted. But that was a false bravado. His voice cracked with an unmistakable tremor.

"Gentlemen!" the elderly man cried. "Can we not call this thing off?"

Lieutenant Davy bowed respectfully to the man and said, "He has but to apologize to the young lady, sir."

"I'll see you in hell first," Penn retorted.

Speaking quietly, barely above a whisper, Briggs said, "We'd best get on with it then." He then opened a case of beautifully matched dueling pistols. "You'll inspect these if you please, sir."

Lieutenant Baugean lifted both pistols, felt the weight, and checked the priming. More shot and powder was available if the gun was not to his satisfaction. Briggs then offered Davy his choice of weapons. After a last plea for reconciliation was declined, Briggs called the two men together.

Davy could feel Penn's back touch his. For all his swagger, Penn's shirt was soaked with sweat. Reaching up with his free hand, Davy quickly felt the front of his shirt. It was dry. *He's scared*, Davy thought to himself, realizing that he was not. He'd faced death too many times to not know it could come at anytime. But he was at peace with it.

"Commence on one," Briggs said, giving instructions. "Take ten steps on my count, turn and fire. Any man firing before the count of ten will be shot down. Is that understood?"

Both men nodded their understanding.

"One, two…"

Davy walked slowly feeling the hard packed road beneath his feet.

"Three, four…"

*Did I put everything in the letter that I should before I gave it to Gabe?*

"Five, Six…"

*That's a cool breeze I feel but it'll get hotter.*

"Seven, eight…"

Davy felt the buzz of the ball pass his ear before he heard the shot from his opponent's pistol. Standing there, Davy realized Penn had turned and fired early. *The coward. Still where was the man that was supposed to shoot him down if such a thing happened?*

"Foul, sir," Baugean cried out. "Foul. That was a cowardly thing to do."

Briggs stood there silent, obviously sickened by his party's actions. After a pause he resumed counting, unable to fulfill his obligation to fire on his childhood chum.

"Nine, ten…you may turn and fire."

Penn stood there shocked, smoking pistol still in his hand. Fear overwhelmed him and his bladder let loose, staining his white pants. Sweat poured from his brow. His hands were shaking. The arm holding the pistol out fell limply to his side.

Davy was disgusted at the sight before him. "You, sir, are a braggart and a coward," he said. "Your actions speak louder than words."

As he raised his pistol and took aim, Penn fell to the ground whimpering. He lay there in a balled up heap. Davy could not bring himself to kill the man so he shot into the air then threw the pistol at Briggs's feet.

In doing so he asked, "Where is your honour, sir? You were to prevent any cowardly foul."

Briggs hung his head and muttered, "You have my deepest apology, sir. If you require more I will stand for you to shoot."

"Apology accepted," Davy hissed as he made his way to his party.

Suddenly there was a scrambling noise behind him. Penn had crawled passed his father and took a pistol from the family carriage and was now aiming at Davy.

"You bastard!" he screamed.

The stillness was shattered by the explosion of two pistols. Penn crumpled and fell face down in the hard dirt. A crimson color was spreading over the back of the white silk shirt, his gun still unfired. Standing behind the fallen man, both Briggs and Penn's father held smoking pistols. They had both fired to prevent another cowardly act.

"Which bullet found its mark?" Davy asked his fellow officers.

"Only God knows," Gabe said. "But I thought Briggs fired an instant after the boy's father."

After a moment Davy spoke again, "Maybe it will spare the old gentleman some grief not knowing which ball took his son's life."

"That would have been my thoughts," Gabe replied.

"Aye," Baugean joined in. "Mine as well."

The surgeon sat quietly, thankful his services were not needed.

## *Chapter Twenty-three*

The days following the duel turned into weeks and suddenly it was Christmas, then New Year's Eve. Parties were given and balls were held that were attended by all of the island's prominent citizens, even the Penn family, though they were adorned in black. An attempt was made to offer his condolences but Penn turned and walked away before Anthony could speak.

Lord Anthony and Lady Deborah had been invited to dine aboard each of the ships in the squadron, starting aboard *Viper* the week before Christmas and finishing aboard the flagship on Christmas day. Gabe, Captain Markham, and Lum joined the ship's musicians and played one joyous song after another.

At the noon meal, the officers of *SeaHorse* and the captains of the other ships joined together to eat. When everyone had been seated, Lord Anthony rose. The group quickly quieted themselves to hear what their admiral had to say. Each one of them expected some sort of Christmas speech or discussion with regard to being away from home, doing one's duty for King and country. What transpired surprised everyone…except Bart and Lady Deborah.

"Gentlemen," Anthony said. "I thank each of you for being here today…for joining Lady Deborah…and my staff for such a joyous occasion. None as special as the celebration of the birth of Christ. It is with understanding the sacrifices of Christ who gave his life as a gift to all mankind that I would like to take the time to honour one among us today. A man who acted without considering the possible consequences to himself…" Anthony paused and gave a small chuckle. "If he had I wouldn't be standing here today."

This brought a chuckle from the group.

"A man who I've…who Bart and I have known for years. A man who has served his King and country most diligently. A man I'm proud to call a friend. You've all guessed who I'm talking about, I'm sure. Our ship's master…George Jepson."

The group started clapping. A few were shouting and whistling. Jep turned red, embarrassed that he was recognized so. When Anthony was able to get the group's attention again, he called Jepson up to the head of the table.

As if on cue, Bart appeared holding a box. Taking the large box from him, Anthony said, "No…no, it's not a year's supply of cards."

This brought hoots and laughter again as the master's ability at whist was well known throughout the squadron.

"George," Anthony continued, using Jepson's first name, "this is but a small token on behalf of Lady Deborah and me."

Taking the box, Jep opened it to find a beautifully tooled leather case. Handing Bart the box, he opened the case to find a gold sextant.

"My Lord…" Jep said, trying to constrain his emotions.

Seeing his friend so, Bart chided, "Well these ain't gold but they's good. Straight from Havana they be." He then handed Jep a box of cigars. Bart then leaned over and whispered, "We's a jug o' good rum chillin in the bilges when the dinner is done."

***

The New Year came and went and now a convoy had arrived. Gabe, Markham, and Ambrose Taylor, of the ship *Alert*, had been chosen to escort the convoy ships to Halifax.

"It'll be damned cold," Markham declared upon hearing the news.

"Aye," *Lizard's* Captain Culzean had replied. "And it's damn glad I am to be staying here." The last convoy still on his mind...*Lizard* had been mauled badly by privateers when they last had escort duty.

It was then that Lieutenant Jem Jackson, captain of *Viper*, and Ferrets Hallett entered the tavern and greeted their fellow ship's captains.

"Did you hear about the new guns being transported to Lord Howe?" Jackson asked. When the officers indicated they hadn't, he continued, "The brig, *Britannia*, has several of them."

"What kind of gun is it?" Markham asked.

"A carronade," Hallett replied. "It's supposed to be hell in close action."

"Have you seen one?" Gabe asked.

"Aye, a squat little monster it is," Jackson exclaimed.

"I'd like to see it," Gabe said, very curious.

"Aye, so would we," the rest chimed in.

Seeing Dagan, Gabe excused himself for a moment and went to him. "Go aboard *SeaHorse* and see if Captain Buck is there if you will. Tell him about the brig with the new guns. I'm sure he'll want to see them himself and it may be he can arrange for us to see one."

"Aye," Dagan replied. "What about His Lordship?"

"I'm headed there now. We, Faith and I, are to have lunch with Gil and Deborah."

"Don't eat to much," Dagan said, patting Gabe's belly. "It looks to me like it's the size of a nine pounder."

Gabe sucked in his stomach and swore, "It's the holidays."

***

Captain Ford of the brig, *Britannia*, was more than willing to play host and lord his knowledge of the new carronade over the gathered naval officers. The admiral's presence did make him a tad nervous however.

"You do me honour," Ford said when Anthony boarded the brig. "No one of such a lofty status has ever stepped foot aboard my humble ship, sir," he exclaimed. "Not even when they were loading the smashers."

"Smashers?" Buck repeated.

"Aye," Ford replied. "That's the nickname that's been given to these little beauties."

"Damned ugly if you ask me," Captain Fletcher from *Intrepid* declared.

"Ugly she may be…but it's a heavy ball she flings I'm thinking," Bart volunteered.

This brought a stare from Fletcher. He was not used to anyone other than an officer speaking without being spoken to. However, Markham spoke up and agreed with Bart, which was further acknowledged by the others. Fuming, Fletcher thought, *Treat him as an equal they do.*

Seeing Fletcher's reaction, Buck thought, *I once had to take a lieutenant aside. Now am I going to have to speak to a captain. Humph,* he thought, *better me than His Lordship. He'd not likely recover if His Lordship was to get involved.*

The laughter broke Buck's reverie. *Likely comparing the gun to someone's personal artillery,* Buck thought.

When the group controlled their laughter, Ford said, "The carronade was developed for the Royal Navy by the Carron Company in Falkirk, Scotland. It was created to serve as a devastating short range weapon that would wreak utter havoc to ships and crews at short distances."

"Who invented it?" Fletcher asked. "Some naval gunner?"

"No," Ford answered. "I was told it was a lieutenant general in the Army. A Robert Melville."

"Humph. It'll never work aboard ship," Fletcher responded after hearing the gun was invented by an Army man, lieutenant general or not.

"I'm not so sure," Anthony said speaking for the first time. "I've heard Howe speak of the guns. He's at least impressed with them enough that he's talked Lord Sandwich into buying several."

When Anthony had finished, Ford continued, "Well, while it was General Melville who invented the gun, it was Mr Charles Gascoigne at the Carron Company what developed and perfected it."

"No doubt," Fletcher said, salvaging a bit of something after everything else he'd said had been challenged.

Cutting his eyes at Fletcher, Ford once more continued. "This baby," he said patting the gun's short barrel, "has a low muzzle velocity and needs only a small crew to work it."

Hallett was puzzled about the significance of the muzzle velocity and asked Ford to explain.

"The lower velocity of a carronade's round shot was created to inflict more damage to a ship's hull, creating many more of the deadly splinters when fired at the enemy vessel. That's where the nickname smasher comes from."

After a pause, Ford started again enjoying his role as schoolmaster. "They've discovered that with the short barrel and short range there's a risk of ejecting burning wadding. This was then thought to add to the benefit as the most likely ship the wadding would land on is the one being fired at."

"How much does it weigh?" Gabe asked.

"Depends," Ford answered. "Carronades were manufactured using standard naval gun calibers including twelve, eighteen, twenty-four, thirty-two, and forty-two pounders. Now the weight of a standard thirty-two pound long gun is about three ton. A carronade of thirty-two pounds would weigh one third or about a ton."

"I don't see any trunnions," Jem Jackson put in, not wanting to be thought dull by not finding something different to inquire about.

"It's mounted on a slide so it doesn't have trunnions," Ford replied. "It also has a turn screw like a field gun instead of quoins (wooden wedges) for elevation."

In summing up his discussion, Ford said, "This gun in close action will be a distinct advantage over our enemies."

"Aye," Bart said. "Till they gets their hands on a few."

Fletcher fumed again but had to agree with the admiral's cox'n.

# PART III

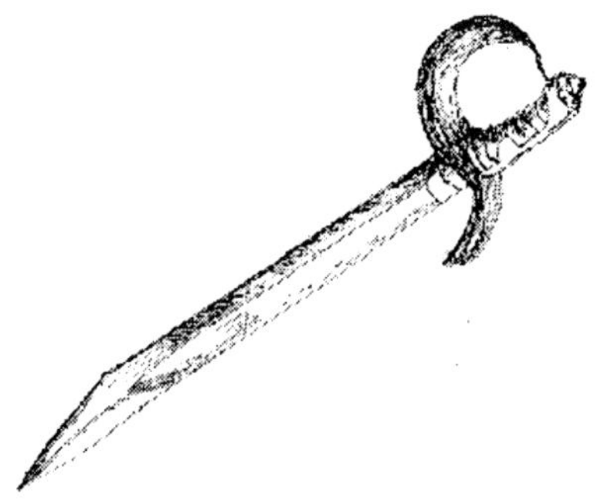

## The Gun Captain

The cap'n yells, "Fire!"
The guns leap as one.
Round after round,
We worked 'um 'till we's numb.
I smells the stench o' powder,
I's blinded by the smoke.
It hurts me chest to breathe,
It makes me cough and choke.

I felt the ship shudder,
They's scored another hit.
A gun be overturned;
The mainmast is split.

Broadside after broadside,
That last un were the worst.
I see the chaplain praying,
I 'urd the bosun curse.

I steals a look about me,
So many mates lay dead.
The thunder from the guns,
Echoes thru me head.

I 'ear the word, "Cease fire."
Yonder ship 'as struck.
I give a sigh and wipes me face,
A victory cheer goes up.

Michael Aye

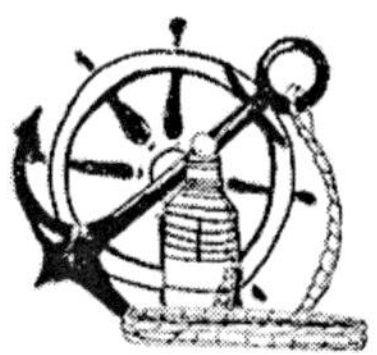

## Chapter Twenty-four

Josiah Nesbit stepped from the pantry and peered at the untouched breakfast on the cabin table. Strewn next to the empty coffee cup were sheets of paper discussing the new gun, the carronade. The captain seemed to be much impressed with the guns. He'd spent a lot of time pouring through the sheets. He'd explained to Sir Victor how they could really be an advantage to a frigate.

Well, Nesbit knew nothing of naval warfare. He was, however, very pleased with his present position…berth. Paco had said it was a berth, not a position. Captain Anthony was an easy taskmaster. Once one got used to all the bells and pipes it seemed to grow on you. He wouldn't care to be a jack tar mind you. No, that was not his sort. However, being a gentleman's gentleman it would be rare indeed to improve on Captain Anthony. *I must remember to thank Dagan*, he thought. He certainly rescued me from the illiterate lout I'd been working for.

Overhead the air was alive with the noise and hustle bustle of a ship getting underway. It all seemed so strange to Nesbit that out of such apparent utter chaos and confusion order actually existed. Paco had said it was because I'm a landsman…meaning I'm the opposite of a seaman. Nesbit had asked and Paco had confirmed.

The miles of cordage, each mast, spar, and sail played a different yet distinctive and important part of the ship's ability to sail and maneuver. He was learning under the polite tutelage of Paco, Dagan, and even the captain at times.

Standing beneath the skylight, Nesbit could hear the unmistakable sound of the fiddle blaring out a shanty. The men are going to raise the anchor so it's time to leave…to get underway would be the seaman's term he thought, trying his best to get a firm hold of the lingo that was so much a part of his new world.

Once back in the pantry, Nesbit shook the coffee pot. Still enough for a last cup and it was not cold. It was surprising how long the hot bricks kept things warm. One of the oddities was you never knew when the captain would be ready to eat…or when he'd be able to finish a meal without being summoned.

Taking the pot and a clean cup, Nesbit headed topside. Seeing his servant, Gabe walked over to meet him. "You must be a mind reader," he said as Nesbit filled the cup.

"It's warm, not hot sir."

"It'll be fine," Gabe replied. As he smelled the coffee, his stomach growled. Smiling, Gabe touched it with his free hand. "I should have eaten this morning."

"Yes sir. One must eat to keep his strength up. There's some sliced beef and some bacon. I could fix it for you, sir."

"Aye, I'd be grateful. The bacon will do I think."

Nodding his understanding, Nesbit rushed below.

It was a bright morning. The hills past Bridgetown looked very green. Gabe glanced toward the flagship. He could not see his brother but there was little doubt he wasn't watching…thinking. They were to escort three fat transports, one of which carried the carronades for Lord Howe. The other two were full of supplies for the troops.

They'd been transported a long way and now they had another two thousand miles to go. *How*, he wondered, *could England expect to maintain such a long supply chain? Half would never reach the destination.*

*Damn all politicians*, he thought for about the hundredth time. *Well, you can bet with all the miles between here and New York they'd be challenged...would he make the trip there and back with his crew intact? Would all the transports make it with the needed supplies?* Questions, questions, questions but rarely the answers.

Standing next to the companionway were Dagan and Paco, both of them watching Gabe. Each with different thoughts.

"He takes it personal," Paco said, "like he's responsible for everyone."

"As his father and brother did and they were both made admiral."

"Aye," Paco said, "if he lives."

"He'll live," Dagan responded. "I'll see to it or die trying."

"As will I, amigo," Paco said, meaning it.

Glancing toward Lieutenant Lavery, Gabe said, "I shall go below and break my fast."

"Aye, Captain."

As he headed below he motioned for Dagan to follow. Nesbit had the bacon, fresh bread, and a pastry waiting when the two made it to the cabin. Gabe had eaten his fill while Dagan snacked on one of Nesbit's mouth-watering pastries. The meal had been washed down by a lemon-lime juice mixture with just enough sugar to remove the tartness.

A knock at the door and the marine sentry announced, "Midshipman Ally, sir."

Standing there with his hat in his hand, the youth was staring at the remaining pastry.

"Well?" Gabe asked.

Ally cleared his throat and reported, "Mr Lavery's respects, sir, and the transports have weighed anchor."

"Very well, I'll go up." Gabe then paused and with a wink at Dagan. He turned back to the boy, patting his stomach. "Mr Ally, I would take it amiss if I returned and found yonder pastry still on the plate."

"Aye, sir," Ally exclaimed, his eyes lighting up.

Later, reporting back on deck, Lieutenant Lavery said, "I was beginning to think about sending the master-at-arms in search of you, young sir."

"Yes, sir."

"Now go report to Lieutenant Davy. I'm sure he's tired of doing your duties."

"Aye, sir," the youth said as he turned to find Lieutenant Davy.

"Mr Ally."

Slowly the boy turned again, "Yes, sir."

"Wipe the crumbs from your mouth."

Overhearing the conversation, Gunnells couldn't help but chuckle. Lieutenant Lavery turned, a stern look on his face, but seeing the master's face he couldn't help but laugh as well.

***

"Breeze is a might brisk this morning," Gunnells spoke, seeing the captain. Taking the hint from the master's comment, Lieutenant Lavery turned.

"Signal from flag, sir. Smooth sailing. We've acknowledged."

"Thank you, Lieutenant. You may get us underway."

"Aye, Captain," Lavery responded. Then turned and cried out, "Hands aloft, loose topsails."

It never ceased to amaze Gabe how quickly the men went about their duties. Sign of a good first lieutenant. He would never admit it was a sign of a good captain.

"Permission to gain the quarterdeck." This was from Sir Victor. He was learning as well. To stride upon the quarterdeck was at the captain's permission only, something he'd previously learned when Dagan had taken him aside after his first breach of etiquette. Looking aloft, Sir Victor watched as the seamen fairly ran up the shrouds and out onto the swaying yards. Never a man for heights, it made him nervous to think he'd have to go aloft. Quickly canvas fell loosely from the yards and a vibration was felt in the deck planking.

"Man the braces," Lieutenant Lavery bellowed out. From forward the cry of anchor's aweigh.

"Free o' the lands," Gunnells volunteered.

Indeed they were, Sir Victor realized as the wind filled the sails and the ships gained speed, quickly outpacing the transports.

"Make signal to the transport," Gabe ordered Lavery, "make haste. No need for them to think we will be easy."

"Aye Captain," Lavery said with a grin. He knew as well as the captain it was best to assert authority from the beginning. Complain they might but comply they must. Especially with the admiral likely watching.

Gabe watched as Barbados and Faith slipped slowly astern. "Until I return," he whispered to himself, "until I return."

"Mr Lavery."

"Aye, sir."

"Once we clear Carlisle Bay, signal *Dasher* and *Alert* to take station to windward."

"Aye, sir."

Turning back to Sir Victor, Gabe said, "A fine morning is it not, sir?"

"Aye, Captain, that it is," Sir Victor replied, feeling somewhat happy to be back at sea with Gabe again.

"Would you join me for dinner tonight?" Gabe asked.

"I'd be pleased, sir. Your servant sets a fine table."

Watching the ships sail off, Faith sat in Governor Ragland's carriage with Lum by her side. When they disappeared over the horizon, she turned to Lum. "Let's go."

Lum paused before climbing aboard the driver's seat. "He'll be all right, Missy. Captain Gabe can take care of hisself. 'Sides he's got Dagan wid him."

"I know," Faith said. "I just don't know what I'd do if something were to happen."

"It won't," Lum replied reassuredly. "It won't because we's 'll pray the Lawd be wid him till he comes back."

"I'll pray," she said. "Every night I'll pray."

## *Chapter Twenty-five*

Guard boat approaching, sir."

Gabe had seen it approaching but his mind was elsewhere. They had made excellent time since weighing anchor in Barbados. The weather had held with warm days until the last day when there was some briskness in the air. "No squalls," Gunnells had said. "Neither privateer nor perversity of the elements. A fine cruise indeed."

Gabe had already sent a midshipman to rouse Sir Victor and let him know they were approaching the anchorage. In the distance Gabe could make out a two-decker with an admiral's flag flying from the mizzenmast. Shifting his gaze back to the guard boat, Gabe could see a lieutenant in the bow instead of a flag to mark where *Peregrine* would anchor. Gabe barked out orders to reduce all sail and heave to rather than proceed to the anchorage. The guard boat was finally alongside and Lieutenant Lee from Admiral Graves's staff came aboard.

"Did you not come in contact with the patrol frigate?" the lieutenant asked, full of self-importance.

"We've seen no ship since leaving Barbados," Gabe snapped back.

"Egads," the lieutenant replied. "A whole convoy has apparently slipped past the patrol ship. Admiral Graves shan't be happy about this. Probably out chasing a prize, I'd think."

Gabe didn't give a damn what the man thought as long as he remembered he was talking to a senior officer and got to the point.

"You were not to know of course," the lieutenant said with an irritated gesture. But seeing Gabe's frown continued, "Well…ahem…you, of course, could not know but the Army is covering the evacuation of the city. Philadelphia will soon fall."

Gabe was shocked. *What would his brother think of this news? What would be his reaction?*

Sir Victor took advantage of the pause and addressed the lieutenant. "Now see here, young sir. I have business with the commander-in-chief. Could you tell me where he might be found?"

Sensing this was an important man, not merely a naval officer, Lieutenant Lee answered in a more differential manner. "Lord Howe and several other senior officers are at Halifax I'm told, sir."

"Very well," Sir Victor answered curtly. "I will require you to take me to see Admiral Graves. There you'll stand by to return me to this vessel if required."

Gabe couldn't help but smile. Sir Victor's orders could not be refused and requiring the young lieutenant to provide transport would save his sailors the effort. As Lee turned to go down to the waiting cutter, Gabe stopped him.

"Tell me Lieutenant, did Admiral Graves issue instructions regarding the transports, or am I to guess?"

"Ah…forgive me, Captain. They are to be escorted to Halifax."

"Thank you," Gabe replied but swore under his breath. He'd found from experience the coast of Nova Scotia was a haven for privateers. Waiting for Sir Victor to return, Gabe signaled for all captains to repair on board.

Passing Gunnells on his way to his cabin, he heard the master tell Lieutenant Lavery, "Knew it was too damn good to be true."

***

Gabe offered the captains a glass of claret as they seated themselves around the cabin's table. He noticed Taylor had on a jacket. It was cool Gabe realized and would be colder where they were going if the privateers didn't heat things up a might.

"So," Ford said, "another leg to the journey."

"So it seems sir," Gabe replied.

Smiling the jovial man said, "Just adds to the cost of transportation."

This brought a chuckle from the rest of the men at the table. A knock at the door and the sentry announced, "Sir Victor."

Sir Victor bowed to Gabe but didn't take a chair. "As a matter of convenience I signed for your sailing orders." Everyone's attention was now on the foreign office agent. "I have not read your orders, of course, but I believe it was Admiral Graves wish that we sail on the tide."

"Yes, well let's not disappoint the admiral. Gentlemen let's return to our ships and pray for continued luck."

Sir Victor stood to the side and let the transport captains file out. As Markham and Taylor approached the cabin entrance Sir Victor said, "A word, please."

Once the cabin was empty, except for the naval officers, Sir Victor began, "Things are bad…worse than we knew. Burgoyne has surrendered at Saratoga. Washington's men have surrounded both Philadelphia and New York. Raiders and privateers are overwhelming our convoys and confounding our every effort."

"I thought we were winning all the battles," Taylor spoke out.

"We are, but you can win pitched battles and lose a war. Our generals still refuse to admit the Colonies' tactics of hit and run warfare will win out. They forget these tactics were perfected during the Seven Year War…or as the Colonies called it, the French and Indian Wars." Sir Victor paused, cleared his throat, and continued. "Admiral Graves has warned us to sail with caution. Several privateers, including the rebel John Paul Jones, are attacking every convoy that comes this way. From here to Nova Scotia according to Admiral Graves is filled with a labyrinth of waterways the enemy uses to its full advantage. Inlets and coves provide the perfect hiding place so that when a convoy passes they dart out and take what they can. They then return where no King's ship would dare."

"Sounds like General Washington has his share of spies," Taylor quipped. Then seeing the look he got from Gabe he added, "No offense intended, sir."

"None taken," Sir Victor replied then continued. "Admiral Graves has entrusted us with dispatches for Lord Howe." To emphasize this, he lifted the leather satchel that filled his hand. The bulging weight at the bottom gave evidence of its significance. All knew it was to be tossed overboard at all cost if it looked like the ship was to be taken.

"Captain Markham and I have first hand knowledge of the capabilities of these…" he paused trying to remember the term he had heard. "These Yankee seaman," Gabe finished. "A fearsome lot who know the sea. I'll expect the worst and not be surprised if we get it."

Feeling the ship rock slightly and hearing the water slap against the hull, Gabe said, "Another drink, then let's be about it. Nesbit."

"Coming, sir. Something a little warmer, perhaps, such as a brandy." Seeing the appreciative look from the officers gathered, Nesbit knew he was right on time with the recommendation.

***

The convoy was on its way by dusk. The temperature was dropping considerably as the sun went down. Lieutenant Davy had the watch. Like the rest who'd sailed this area he was concerned about the privateers. Not apprehensive, just concerned. Unlike a lot of what the master called young snot-nosed lieutenants, he'd been baptized by the fire of enemy cannons. The crew knew this and thereby trusted and respected the young officer.

Since the duel, the respect had turned into something close to hero worship. Their lieutenant had fought a duel without so much as raising a sweat. Regular fire-eater Mr Davy was…firm but fair. Not a flogging in his division. There'd only been two floggings since leaving England. Both were for drunkenness, something the captain couldn't tolerate at sea. "Port is the place for pleasure. Not at sea when your mate's life may depend on you being alert," the captain had said.

Having finished his evening meal, Lieutenant Wiley came on deck. He'd found Lieutenant Davy a wealth of information. Not gossip but information. He'd been surprised that Davy had been with Captain Anthony since they were both midshipmen. It was not unheard of for two officers to be together that long but it wasn't that common either.

The quartermaster turned the ship's glass and the ship's bell rang out four times. Calling to a seaman, Davy ordered him aloft and when the watch aloft gained the deck, he told him to go get a cup of coffee if any was left. "I don't like to keep a lookout aloft for too long if I can help it," Davy said. "After a while they're more concerned with themselves and the cold than what is around them."

"Aye," Wiley agreed. Something he'd learned as a midshipman after being mast headed for skylarking. After a time he'd lost all concern about what was around him and started daydreaming and planning what he'd do when he was allowed to come down.

Through the skylight the sound of laughter could be heard along with the pleasant smell of pipe tobacco.

"Used to have music a lot of nights before Lum decided to stay ashore with the captain's wife," Davy volunteered. "Now Lum can play a tune, be it on a flute, fiddle or this stringed instrument he has. I miss his music," Davy said, remembering the nights he'd fallen asleep listening to Lum's ballads.

"What about Dagan?" Wiley asked. "I've heard different stories but no one is sure what his position is. Course I ain't asked the first lieutenant."

"Dagan is the captain's uncle and his protector. This has to do with their culture. The captain's mother was a gypsy. But while the captain doesn't hide it, I wouldn't mention it none. When we were midshipmen…the captain and me, Dagan was rated as a top man under Lord Anthony. He was a captain then."

Davy then told of Dagan's intervention with the sadistic Lieutenant Witzenfeld and then saving the captain's life when Drakkar fought the *Reaper*. Wiley was mesmerized when he finished.

"Once the captain was given his first ship…a brigantine, *HMS SeaWolf* she were, Dagan went aboard with him and since he's just been...Dagan. But when they's trouble about, Dagan will know fore it happens," Davy almost whispered.

"Mr Davy."

The two lieutenants jumped not expecting anyone at that time of the night to be on the quarterdeck.

"Evening Dagan," Davy replied. "Need some fresh air do you?"

"No," Dagan said. "But something is in the air. I feel it in my bones." He then ducked as he went through the companionway.

"Damme," whispered Wiley.

## *Chapter Twenty-six*

It was seven bells in the first watch. The sky was overcast so that hardly a star shone down. The wind was brisk and Lieutenant Davy pulled his coat a little closer about him. Lieutenant Wiley had gone down to his cot shortly after Dagan had appeared on deck. Davy did not blame Wiley. It had been unnerving for Dagan to show up as he had. However, the conversation had made the watch go by faster.

"Deck thar," the lookout called down, which gave Davy a start. "I seen something, sir."

*Something*, Davy thought. *What the devil does he mean by something?* Then recalling Dagan's words, Davy grabbed a night glass and went aloft. "Where away?" he asked the lookout who moved over to allow room.

"There, sir, just a glimpse…but look there, sir. See."

"No…yes by all that's holy." Miller had picked up a ship's wake where there shouldn't be one.

"You'll get an extra tot and that's no error," Davy exclaimed excitedly as down the backstay he slid. "Mr Hawks."

"Aye sir," the midshipman responded, trying to stifle a yawn.

"My compliments to the captain and I believe we have sighted an enemy ship."

Hawk was suddenly awake as he ran below to inform the captain. Davy then turned to a petty officer, "Go wake the first lieutenant and the master."

"Aye, sir."

Davy started to rouse out all hands but felt the captain would be on deck soon enough to let him make that decision.

"A wolf among the sheep."

Davy turned. *Damme that was fast*, he thought. Then he realized the captain had probably talked with Dagan and therefore slept in his clothes. "Aye, sir, that's my thoughts." He then told of the wake but no actual ship had been sighted.

Gabe started to go aloft then decided not to. Davy had done so and he had every trust in his lieutenant. "Roust out all hands and let's go to quarters…quietly," Gabe ordered. "Hopefully we can turn the surprise around."

"Nine minutes, sir," Lavery said, snapping his watch closed.

Gabe felt like it was closer to twelve but he'd allow the lieutenant his three minutes as the hands had gone to quarters quietly and efficiently out of a dead sleep. Turning to the bosun Gabe ordered, "Send up a flare and repeat it until I order different."

"What direction sir?" Graf asked.

Pointing toward the convoy, Gabe ordered, "That way. Light up the damn sky."

"That'll surprise somebody," Gunnells chuckled as the flare went up.

"I'll bet the privateer's man shat his pants with it," Sir Victor volunteered.

"I didn't realize you had been roused out," Gabe said.

"Not officially," Sir Victor replied. "But it's hard to ignore the sounds of a ship preparing for battle."

This caused Gabe to smile. "Aye, it would wake the dead."

"Maybe not a midshipman though," Dagan threw out.

"Aye," Gabe replied, "not necessarily a mid."

By the time the second flare was sent up, two privateers had been spotted.

"That one's an odd creature," Lavery swore.

Gabe was thinking the same thing when Gunnells spoke up. "An xebec. She is an xebec. Something you usually see in the Mediterranean. Usually, a Spanish or Turkish vessel. They carry large crews and the last one I saw carried thirty-two guns…often eighteen pounders. They are usually pierced for sweeps (long oars) to maneuver in light winds. I'll bet she has a crew of three hundred or more being a privateer."

"You're full of good news," Gabe said to the master sarcastically after hearing his narrative on the xebec.

The flares had alerted the rest of the convoy so it was not unexpected to see the flash of cannons.

"The xebec has fired," Sir Victor swore, the percussion coming after the flash.

"They've fired on Ford's ship sir," the lookout called down. Then followed with, "Two more off to larboard."

*Two more what?* Gabe wondered but couldn't worry. That was where Markham and Taylor were. They'd have to deal with it. For now the xebec demanded his attention. Flashes of gunfire filled the dark. Orange flames leapt out from the cannons and small flashes almost like lightning bugs from the smaller weapons. Another flare went up and Gabe could see the xebec was now alongside the brig, *Britannia*.

"Lieutenant Davy."

"Aye, Captain."

"Soon as you have a target, commence firing. Fire as you bear, don't waste time waiting on a broadside."

"Aye, Captain."

"Mr Lacey."

"Aye, sir," the little midshipman responded, terror in his voice.

"My compliments to the gunner and he is to fire the bow chasers as they bear."

The mid ran off to do as ordered, forgetting to answer Gabe.

"Scared that one," Gunnells remarked.

"You weren't at the age?" Gabe asked.

"Aye…and still am," Gunnells replied.

"Me too," Gabe admitted.

Druett, a master at his trade, let loose with a forward gun. Gabe couldn't tell if he hit anything or not but it would at least let the privateer know they had company. Several flashes leaped from the xebec's side and the waters around *Peregrine* came alive. A couple of balls were heard as they sailed overhead, holes appearing in the sails where the balls had passed through. Several balls churned the waters next to the ship as spray soaked the helmsman.

A dull thud was proof that at least one ball had hit the ship, but where and how much damage was not known. A shudder went through the deck planking as Lieutenant Davy's gun crews were finding their target. The bright flames that flashed out into the dark were blinding. Gabe found it difficult to focus on the enemy ship or judge the distance. A crash and screams forward were further proof that the enemy was giving as good as they got, and from the sound of it Gunnells had been right. They were firing eighteen pounders. They would have to close soon or the superior firepower would take its toll on *Peregrine*.

"Mr Lavery."

"Aye, Captain. We've got to board yonder ship if we stand a chance. See the surgeon and have him supply you with enough white bandages for each man to tie around his head. I don't want to shoot our own men."

The firing continued as crash after crash was now heard along the hull. Cries and screams could be heard as the enemy's huge ball plowed into the ship. Another crash was felt amidships. A cannon was hit just as it was being fired, the ball and wadding going skyward.

"Keep your eyes open for a fire," Gabe ordered the bosun unnecessarily.

Sharpshooters were now firing as the ball thudded into the deck and rails along the quarterdeck.

"Firing blindly," Gunnells hissed. "They're hoping to find a mark."

"They're finding to damn many for my liking," Dagan said, breaking his silence as he looked at a hole in his coat sleeve.

"A cable's length," Gunnells informed Gabe.

The boarders had got down behind the bulwark. Baugean's marines were returning fire from the tops.

"A half cable," Gunnells shouted out.

*Soon,* Gabe thought.

"Hold on tight," Gunnells yelled just before *Peregrine's* hull ground into the xebec.

"Grapnels away," Lavery ordered.

Several loud bangs were heard as the marines fired several swivels loaded with grape into the privateer. Men went down as the balls tore a path like a scythe in a hayfield.

"Boarders aweigh."

Screams, curses, pistol and musket shots rang out in the night. The clang upon clang as metal blades crashed against each other. The yelps as weapons found a victim. The cannons had ceased firing but the occasional muzzle blast still lit up the dark. Dagan had two men attacking him, one with a cutlass, and the other with a boarding pike. Gabe shot each man at point blank range then threw down his pistols and took out his sword. The privateer's men began to retreat but a whistle was heard and more men joined the fight, leaving the captured brig to join their comrades against *Peregrine's* crew.

The fighting was now more a shoving match, with only the front group of people fighting. It was then the marines fired the swivels again, over the heads of the British sailors into the mob of privateers. At that time, shouts of encouragement were heard aft as Lieutenant Wiley had gotten *Peregrine's* gun crews together and flanked the privateers.

Between the fire from the swivels and the flanking maneuver, the privateers began to fall back. Gabe felt someone grab his legs and he fell to the ship's deck. He felt two hands grasp his shoulders and roughly jerk him up. It was the bosun and a petty officer. Looking down, Gabe could see a man trying to crawl, his movements leaving a stain on the deck. Wounded badly, the man struggled once more then died. Friend or foe Gabe wasn't sure but he didn't see the white bandanna.

The struggles continued as Gabe felt a burning sensation along the back of his hand. He lunged out with his blade and felt it grate on a bone then a cry of agony. Touching the burning spot on his hand he felt the wet blood on his fingertips. Not too bad, he hoped. A pistol was fired close by and someone fell into him. Dagan was there and righted the man. It was Sir Victor. Gabe didn't even know that he'd joined the fight. His arm was hanging limply and a dark stain was spreading over his white shirt. *Damme*, Gabe thought, *I can't let the government man get killed.* Seeing Ally, Gabe caught the midshipman's attention and told him to get Sir Victor back aboard *Peregrine* and to the surgeon.

Men were now throwing down their weapons and surrendering. However, with it dark, some continued to fight not knowing their mates had given up. Finally Gabe was able to gain control of his crew.

"Surrender or be cut down," he offered the privateers. The men reluctantly laid down their weapons. One or two at first then the rest quickly followed suit.

Seeing Dagan, Gabe said, "Check below. I don't see the captain."

Once the marines had gathered Gabe called to Lieutenant Lavery, "Take the carpenter and see what damage we have. Mr Graf."

"Aye, sir. Get some lanterns lit, torches if need be. But be careful as they've probably spilled powder on the deck."

"Aye, sir."

"Lieutenant Baugean, you had the swivels at the right time. I thought we were going to be swamped."

"Thank you, Captain, only that wasn't me. It was Mr Davy who directed the fire. I was with Mr Wiley."

"Where's he at now?" Gabe asked, not seeing the lieutenant.

"He's with the surgeon, sir," a seaman volunteered. "A ball creased 'is noggin. He was dizzy and bleeding like a stuck pig so Mr Livesey 'ad 'im taken below."

"Mr Wiley."

"Yes, sir."

"Take the gunner and a couple of men and make sure this ship is secure. Check the hole and see if they are carrying anything of use."

"Aye, sir."

"Mr Hawks."

"Yes, sir."

"Let's go aboard the *Britannia* and see how Captain Ford is."

"Aye, sir," Hawks said timidly.

"Is there something wrong?" Gabe asked the boy.

"I glanced over the side during the fighting, sir…to see if any of the brig's crew was coming to help but they weren't. They were standing looking down at Captain Ford. He'd fallen. I…ah…I think he's dead, sir."

"Damn," Gabe swore. "Well, let's go see how bad the brig is damaged." *Damme*, Gabe thought to himself, *I liked the man. A good seaman he was.*

## *Chapter Twenty-seven*

The Britannia sat low in the water. Her crew was numb from the savage attack by the xebec and, with the loss of their captain, stood around without direction. Seeing one of *Peregrine's* bosun's mates, Gabe ordered him to make a quick inspection of the ship. Within minutes he was back.

"She's got some stove in planking, Captain, right at the waterline. Her holds are filling fast. If we can lighten her up then the pumps should keep her afloat till we's get to Halifax."

Looking across the brig's deck, Gabe made a quick decision. Speaking to the bosun's mate, he ordered, "Go get Mr Graf.

"Aye, Captain."

The bosun returned quickly. "You sent for me, Captain?"

"Yes, Mr Graf. Get a working party together. I want those two carronades swayed up onto *Peregrine*. I'll get the carpenter busy rigging a way to lash them down." Gabe paused and ordered, "If the two guns on deck don't do it, hoist up the easiest two you can get to."

"Aye, Captain."

"Beg you pardon, Captain."

"Yes, Mr Hawks."

"*Dasher* has signaled, sir, one prize taken."

"Very well," Gabe replied. "Signal *Dasher* to close with the *Britannia*."

"Aye, Captain."

"Mr Lavery."

"Here, sir."

"Take possession of the prize while I return to *Peregrine*." Pausing, Gabe looked about him. *So much to do. The dawn was just coming up over the horizon. Would the new day bring better luck? Not for some it wouldn't…the ones being sewed up in their hammocks.*

***

Instead of the usual "Damn, Gabe, have you lost your mind?" Captain Frances Markham willingly agreed to hoist up two of the carronades from *Britannia* onto *Dasher*.

"That along with the two sitting on *Peregrine's* deck will lighten the load on the battered brig by several tons making her seaworthy," Gabe explained, and then continued, "If His Lordship," speaking of Lord Howe, "asks why we did it we can honestly say it was to save the ship. Then if he inquires as to where his little beauties are now, we can apologize for not making it clear in our report and inform His Lordship that they are lashed down good and proper on our ships."

"Along with a sufficient supply of powder and shot," Markham added, raising his eyebrows. Putting the empty glass down on Gabe's cabin table, he looked over to Dagan and said, "Pick up anything useful on the xebec?"

Dagan shook his head, stifled a yawn, and replied, "Nothing worth mentioning."

Gabe knew different. He had seen the two leather bags Dagan had taken from inside his coat pockets.

"A deposit on retirement," Dagan had whispered with a smile. His inspections of prizes taken usually generated a deposit for retirement as Captain Markham knew from years of being together. The penalty for such actions was severe per naval regulations. Dagan's philosophy was what they don't know won't hurt them—besides, they get the ship.

As Dagan made his way topside, Gabe said, "Give a care you larcenous old lout."

Sitting in the pantry, Nesbit was enjoying the last few swallows left in the bottle of hock. Larcenous lout...Dagan...must be another nautical term.

***

The sun was up when Gabe returned on deck. Lieutenant Davy was on the quarterdeck with a bandage around his wound. The sight caused Gabe to look involuntarily at the dressing around his hand. He'd been so busy that once stitched up by the surgeon, he quickly forgot about it. But now...now it was starting to swell and feel stiff.

"The crew has been fed," Davy volunteered, knowing his captain would ask.

Looking about, Gabe could see the men were tired, spent from their battle and continued efforts to get the ship ready. The torn and useless sails were taken down and replaced. The carpenter and his mates were everywhere measuring, sawing, and hammering. The bosun had men aloft replacing a broken spar. New cordage and tackles had to be replaced. The decks had been washed and a group of men were working way with holystones scrubbing the decks to remove the stains that had been a man's lifeblood.

Gabe stared down at the bodies. Shrouded in canvas like mummies, they lay waiting to join countless brothers of the sea who had given the ultimate sacrifice. Twenty were dead; several more were likely to die. There was also another twenty or so that would soon recover and return to duty. *Duty,* Gabe thought. *What an empty, hollow sounding word.* Without speaking, Gabe nodded to Davy, who had the bosun assemble all hands.

Taking his book of prayers from his pocket, Gabe cleared his throat and read the Lord's Prayer. Nobody spoke. Men stood, some with hats in their hands as they honoured lost mates, friends. Gabe could hear one of the midshipmen sniffle. A few coughs were heard and one or two silently wiped tears. After the prayer, Gabe called each name on the list Livesey had given him. As the name was called, two bosun's mates lifted the plank and the body went over the side, weighted down by a shot placed in the canvas. Captain Ford was the last to go. The sound of the bosun's lone pipe filled the air as the corpse splashed over the side to the unknown depths below.

"Lieutenant Davy."

"Aye, sir."

"You may dismiss the hands and have the bosun pipe up spirits. It'll be make and mend today."

"Aye, Captain," Davy replied.

Gabe thought, *It won't hurt if Lord Howe has to wait another day. Not after what they'd been through, it won't.*

***

Heading to his cabin, Gabe saw Sir Victor, his arm in a sling and a bandage on his shoulder. "Will you join me, sir?"

"Thank you, Captain, I believe I will."

Once at the cabin table coffee was poured. Sir Victor shifted in his chair to ease his shoulder. Sensing something was on the man's mind, Gabe sat silent sipping his coffee.

"I killed a man last night," Sir Victor said, breaking the silence. "I've never killed a man before. It didn't dawn on me at the time, but later lying there in my hammock I realized I'd taken a man's life."

Not knowing what to say, Gabe said nothing. Still he remembered the first time for himself. It had been kill or be killed, but that knowledge didn't help when you felt sick on your stomach with a heaviness in your chest.

Sir Victor had been staring into his coffee cup as if looking for answers among the coffee dregs. Finally he looked up at Gabe and asked, "Why are we fighting this damn war?"

## Chapter Twenty-eight

The convoy made it into Halifax without any further incident. The brig, *Britannia*, with the assistance of a master's mate and several of *Peregrine's* crew members limped into the harbour but the pumps were manned two of every four hours. The ship's log, kept meticulously by the master's mate, shored up the need to reduce the weight by removing four of the carronades.

*Britannia's* first officer held his position due more to being Captain Ford's kin than having the seamanship and knowledge for the job. They would have to find a qualified seaman if the ship was to ever return to England.

The salute to Lord Howe had barely been banged out and the cannons secured when *Peregrine's* number and 'captain repair on board' was given. Paco had anticipated the signal and had Gabe's gig and crew ready. Midshipman Ally was brought along to carry the leather satchel filled with letters, dispatches, and Gabe's report. Most of the report was written by Dawkins, Gabe's secretary. The bandaged hand had made it difficult to write.

Once in the gig, Gabe noticed the crew looked freshly scrubbed. All were dressed in white ducks. They were wearing straw hats with *Peregrine* embroidered on a hatband made of blue ribbon. The crew was evidence of the pride the ship's crew now felt. They were, Gabe realized, no longer an unhappy ship.

It was a short pull to the flagship. The sound of pipes greeted Gabe's appearance through the entry port. Standing next to the port was Lord Howe's flag captain and another officer whom Gabe had met before but he hadn't been a captain at the time.

"Captain Anthony, may I introduce you to Captain Nelson?"

"We've met," Gabe replied, shaking Nelson's hand. "I was a lieutenant in command of *HMS SeaWolf* in company with the schooner, *Swan*. The convoy you were escorting had been attacked by privateers and the other escort vessel had been lost!"

"Of course," Nelson exclaimed. "Gabe Anthony and the commander of the *Swan* was Lieutenant Markham."

"Captain Markham now," Gabe said. "'Tis good to see you again, sir."

"What is your date of rank?"

Gabe told Nelson, who grinned and said, "Not but a year after my date."

Gabe first thought the smallish man was trying to establish seniority but quickly changed his mind when Nelson said, "I wish I had time. We'd celebrate our swabs but the admiral has given me orders to sail on the tide."

"Some other time perhaps," Gabe said, extending his hand.

Nelson gave a firm shake then turned to depart but paused. "A prize, I see."

"Aye," Gabe replied. "We were lucky."

"Well yes, God's speed to you, Captain," and then Nelson was gone.

"Not been lucky with prizes, that one," the flag captain said. "A fine officer, however. He'll fly his own flag one day. Probably sooner than later."

*No doubt*, Gabe thought. *He has an air about him…one that makes you forget his smallish size.*

"Well, let's get along. His lordship doesn't like to be kept waiting."

"Yes, sir," Gabe responded and followed behind the flag captain.

Gabe was made comfortable as the admiral read his report, occasionally responding to questions the admiral asked.

"Eighteen pounders were they?" Lord Howe asked once, speaking of the size of the cannons the xebec carried. "The carronades, what did you do with the ones you took off the *Britannia*?"

*Damn,* Gabe thought. *Caught. The bugger doesn't miss a thing.* "They…er…two are aboard the *Peregrine* and another two are on the *Dasher*," Gabe answered.

"Do you think they would have made a difference in your battle with the pirate?" Howe asked.

Gabe was quick to notice the term *pirate.* Not *privateer.* "Yes sir, I do," he answered truthfully. "Captain Ford gave us a great deal of information on the guns before we left Barbados. I was very impressed."

"Would you like to keep them?"

Gabe couldn't control his excitement. "Oh yes sir, My Lord."

"Does *Dasher's* captain feel as enthused about them as you do?"

"Yes, sir."

"Very well, I'll have them signed over to you along with powder and shot."

"Thank you, My Lord."

Howe waved Gabe's thanks away. "I wish my frigate captains felt the way you do," he said.

"Well, in truth I am one of your captains," Gabe said.

"That you are!" Howe exclaimed with a smile. He then stood and walked out on the quarter gallery. "How is Gil doing?" he asked using Lord Anthony's first name.

"Fine, My Lord. He is a father now…a little girl."

"No boy to follow in his father's footsteps."

"Not yet, My Lord."

Howe then gazed toward the xebec. "A queer looking ship…the xebec."

"Aye," Gabe replied. "But she is fast and her guns pack a hell of a wallop."

"Yes, I read your report. I've never figured out where they come up with the design, though I've pondered it on occasion."

Gabe understood Howe's way of thinking, as for the last few days he had pondered the same questions. The ship was a wonderful looking vessel. She was long and sharp in appearance with a high platform that extended aft of the rudder, called an open overhang. It carried three masts but with lateen sails in addition to combinations of square, fore, and aft sails.

"It resembles a galley the way it's pierced for sweeps," Gabe said.

"Aye, that and the prominent beak. She's fast because she is so narrow."

"Yes, she's made to slice through the water."

Howe gave a sigh then turned and made to go back into his cabin. Gabe stood aside to allow him room to pass.

"Do you think Gil could use her?" Howe asked.

*Damn right*, Gabe thought, but replied, "I am sure, sir. As you know our resources are stretched."

"Aye," Howe said, nodding his head as he sat down behind his desk. "The damn spies tell me France will enter the war with the Colonies soon…if they've not already done so. You know how slowly the mails and dispatches are. But tell me, Captain, does that ship…the presence of that ship in these waters mean anything to you?"

Gabe gathered his thoughts before replying and in doing so noticed how tired the admiral looked. "It's of Mediterranean decent, sir. My master says she's not a tartar so he makes her out to be Spanish. We know the Dons render help to the rebels when they can. Therefore, My Lord, I would guess Spain is considering joining France and become an ally to the Americans. This ship is probably a private venture to test the waters, so to speak."

Howe nodded in the affirmative then surprised Gabe slightly when he said, "Your master knows his ships. It's a wise young captain that heeds the master. They usually know. Tell your brother I asked of him and my congratulations on the child."

Gabe, who had seated himself upon returning inside the cabin, now rose. "Thank you, My Lord. I'm sure Gil will be glad to be remembered by you."

Lord Howe then asked a question that surprised Gabe. "When did Gil get promoted to rear admiral?"

"In July, 1775."

"Ahem…well with half those on the list retiring I'd not be surprised to see him promoted to vice admiral soon."

"May I repeat My Lord's words?" Gabe asked.

"Aye, repeat them all you want to. However, my supposition is nothing more."

*I'll bet,* Gabe thought.

As he was leaving Howe called after him, "I'll expect a report on those carronades or I'll take them back."

"I'll report," Gabe replied.

Once topside, the flag captain caught up with Gabe. "Likes you, he does. Rarely ever takes up half that much time with a junior captain." As they neared the gangway the captain said, "Well, be off with you." Patting Gabe on the back, he said, "Have a care, Gabe. Your orders will be sent over quickly I expect. His Lordship plans to sail on the morning tide for England."

Now Gabe understood why His Lordship had been so willing to let the carronades stay aboard *Peregrine* and *Dasher*. It also explained the willingness to let the xebec be sailed back to Barbados for Lord Anthony's use. Generally, an admiral always had an officer he was ready to promote. However, Lord Howe had been on station since 1775 or 1776 so any of his officers that were qualified for command probably were ready to go home with His Lordship.

*How would I have felt?* Gabe wondered. *A ship or home?* Settling himself in the gig Gabe smiled at Paco. "To *Dasher*, Paco, I've a word for Captain Frances Markham."

*With that smile on your face I bet you do*, Paco thought as he ordered the gig to be shoved off.

## *Chapter Twenty-nine*

Sir Victor was hurting when he returned to the ship. His increased activity had caused his shoulder wound to open as evidenced by the growing red stain on the dressing. Livesey, the surgeon, had said the ball had gone completely through, just missing the lung. He had gently probed the wound but found only a small amount of debris. This was removed but a drain was placed in each side to help drain the wound of any suppuration.

"It's good you are wearing a silk shirt. Silk is the least damaging to the tissues in case of a wound," Livesey said as he went about applying a new dressing. Gabe came down to see how Sir Victor was doing, having been told of the man's obvious distress once he returned to the ship. Shunning a bosun's chair had not helped.

"One must put his pride aside," Livesey said, scolding his patient for putting pride ahead of care for the wound and climbing up and through the entry port.

Seeing Gabe, Sir Victor spoke, "A minute of your time please Captain...when this ole mother hen finishes."

Gabe, unable to hide his grin, said, "I'll await you in my cabin."

"Thank you, Captain," Sir Victor replied between grimaces.

As he walked out the door, Livesey called after Gabe. "Captain, it would be good if you were able to convince our foreign affairs agent that should he fail to take care of his malady now, he will certainly pay for it later."

Gabe nodded his answer and made his way back to his cabin where he informed Nesbit he'd soon have a visitor and some strong refreshment might be in order. After a second thought he amended his statement. A strong refreshment for our visitor, that is.

"Sir Victor?" Dagan asked. He had been sitting at the cabin table when Gabe entered.

"Aye," Gabe replied.

After a moment Dagan said, "The French are in it now. I feel it."

"Maybe so," Gabe answered, knowing it was a high probability.

Sir Victor was soon announced by the marine sentry. Nesbit had mixed one of his special drinks…a concoction of rum, lime juice, and sugar.

"Careful sir," he said as he sat the drink before Sir Victor, who immediately took a heavy slug of the tasty liquid. "It packs a punch, sir."

Taking a deep breath, Sir Victor swore. "Damme, but I feel that down to me toes."

"A rum punch it is, sir," Nesbit said.

"Where do I start?" Sir Victor said, his head now feeling the effects of the alcohol on an empty stomach. After a pause, he asked, "What day is this…day of the month that is."

"February the tenth," Dagan answered.

"Well, gentlemen, unless there has been a change of heart I would think we are now at war with France." Not waiting for any questions, he continued, "In early December the French foreign minister was quoted as saying the King was ready to recognize the independence of the United States. He is…er…was to sign a commercial treaty and contingent defensive alliance. The information was to go out to all of France's holdings so that upon February the sixth, 1778, all the French commanders, both ashore and at sea, would know and react."

"Aye, I see where this forewarned knowledge would put the French at a great advantage over our ships," Gabe said. "We pass a French ship one day and pass honours. The next day they fire a broadside on our same unsuspecting ship. Lord Howe is leaving for England. Is he aware of this? He didn't mention it when I went aboard the flagship."

"He is now," Sir Victor answered. "I stopped there before returning here. He is sending dispatches to the fleet at Philadelphia and New York. Admiral Graves will see that dispatches will be sent from there southward."

"Does His Lordship not know they're preparing to evacuate Philadelphia?"

"Aye, but he's sending reinforcements from Halifax and New York to shore up our defences. After the failed attempt on Nova Scotia and Canada, Lord Howe feels the troops are needed more at Philadelphia."

"A little late I'd say," Dagan commented.

"Aye," Gabe agreed.

"I don't disagree," Sir Victor said. "However, the reinforcements may stall the American advance until more help arrives."

"Or…the French," Gabe said.

"Yes, there's that," Sir Victor admitted. "Spain will take advantage of the alliance…that's something you can bet on."

"I agree," Gabe answered. "But they have very few holdings…West Florida, Havana, and Puerto Rico. So what are the Dons hoping to gain?"

"Gibraltar or possibly even England. We could be invaded with little to defend ourselves," Sir Victor replied tersely, thinking of his homeland. "Since the Seven Year

War (French and Indian War) most of our fleet has been laid up. We are nowhere as near as strong as we were. And what we have is stretched so thin it wouldn't take much to break us. I almost forgot," Sir Victor said, reaching into his bag. He pulled out several papers. One was obviously the sailing orders, but the other two?

*Well, he'd find out later*, Gabe thought as he opened the sailing orders. "We are to depart immediately," he said.

"I thought as much," Sir Victor responded. "They are busy as bees getting the flagship ready to put to sea. Shall we notify the others?" he asked, meaning the commanders of the other ships.

"There will be time for that later," Gabe said in an obvious hurry to get underway.

*Aye*, Dagan thought to himself. *Sir Victor should have given Gabe the sailing orders upon coming aboard. His not doing so could put Gabe in a bad light with the commander-in-chief for taking his own sweet time complying with orders.*

Going on deck, Gabe was about to call for Lavery when he recalled he was aboard the xebec with a prize crew. Wiley would now have to fill in for the first lieutenant. *Well, it's time I see his seamanship*, Gabe thought. *I just wish it wasn't under the eye of Lord Howe.* He briefly thought of taking the ship out himself then remembered his brother letting a junior lieutenant take *Drakkar* out of harbour under Admiral Graves watchful eye. What was it he had said to Buck when questioned? "No time like the present for him to learn." What more pressure can be upon him than the admiral's eye? Well, Lieutenant Anthony had poured sweat but got the ship underway with only a couple of helpful whispers from the master.

"Mr Wiley."

"Aye, Captain."

"You are now acting first lieutenant. Which of the midshipmen do you wish to promote to acting third lieutenant or do you have a master's mate in mind?"

"Hawks is the senior, sir."

"Very well," Gabe replied. "You may inform Mr Hawks he may temporarily move his gear into your cabin and you into the first lieutenant's cabin." Wiley's eyes lit up with these orders.

"However," Gabe added, "let's delay that until the first watch. For now, have a signal sent to our other ships to prepare to get underway. Upon that you may prepare *Peregrine* to set sail."

"Aye, Captain," Wiley replied, still excited. "Ah…Captain."

"Yes, Lieutenant Wiley."

"Thank you, sir. For now and back in Portsmouth."

"You are more than welcome," Gabe replied. "Now don't make me think I was amiss in my judgment by ramming the flag ship. I'm sure His Lordship would have us on the beach the rest of our lives."

Standing to the side, Gunnells chuckled to himself. Ramming the flagship indeed. I doubt the captain would let us get even close to such a thing but it would help Wiley's anxiety by the captain making light of the situation.

***

Wiley did fine, and without the convoy ships slowing down progress, the convoy escorts along with their prize quickly set sail. Once over the horizon, Gabe ordered the group to heave to and captains repair on board. It was a surprised group that met in Gabe's cabin.

He discussed his meeting with Lord Howe and the news about the French.

"You can bet things will get hot now," Markham said. And like Gabe, he felt like it would only be a matter of time before the Dons joined in.

As the men were departing for their ships, Lavery said, "I hear you've moved into my cabin, Wiley."

"Aye, and I hope to stay there."

"So do I," Lavery responded, enjoying his first taste of command, yet knowing it would be temporary. The xebec would be considered a fifth rate, which required the rank of captain. Therefore, he'd not be in command long. However, Lord Anthony would surely vacate one of the smaller ship's commanders to take command of the prize. This would create an opening. The only other lieutenant senior to him would be *SeaHorse's* First Lieutenant Lamb. He was senior but was he ready? Well, he'd do everything he could to show he was ready and that was no error.

## Chapter Thirty

The voyage back to Barbados was not hampered by slow merchant ships that had to be continuously coerced to keep station or to make more sail. This allowed the group to clip along at eight knots, a speed that would take less than half the time to reach port. Sir Victor sat next to Dagan and watched as he carved on a small piece of whalebone.

"What are you doing?" Sir Victor asked as he adjusted his sling and sat down by Dagan.

"I'm carving a likeness of *Peregrine* on this bone."

"Do you do that for every ship?" Sir Victor asked.

"No, sometimes I make a model out of balsam wood or make a carving from a good piece of oak wood. I do have one or the other from every ship Gabe and I have been on."

"What will you do with them?" Sir Victor asked, shifting around some more trying to find a comfortable position for the wounded shoulder.

"Most likely give them to Gabe or his son at some point," Dagan replied, feeling heaviness in his chest at the thought of the child Faith had just lost.

"What kind of bone is that?" the curious Sir Victor asked, very amazed at Dagan's craftsmanship.

"It's a whalebone, actually part of its jaw."

Then before Sir Victor could ask Dagan added, "I traded a jug of rum for it back in Portsmouth." He paused in his carving and pulled out his pipe. He packed it full of tobacco from a small round tin, then lit it.

Enjoying the aroma of the fresh-lit pipe, Sir Victor leaned back against the taffrail and closed his eyes for a moment, dozing. The shrill sound of the bosun's pipe brought him up with a jerk.

Chuckling, Dagan said, "They've just piped make and mend."

Seeing the puzzled look, Dagan took a breath, put down his carving knife and piece of whalebone. He reached for the pipe dangling between his teeth, and packed the tobacco with his finger. Then after taking a puff he explained, "Wind, weather, and the enemy permitting, Thursday afternoons and most Sunday afternoons are considered make and mend."

The part about the enemy permitting struck home as it made Sir Victor recall an event that had actually happened once while he had been aboard *Peregrine*.

"Make and mend," Dagan continued, "gives the crew time to take care of personal needs." Seeing he still did not comprehend, Dagan said, "Thursday afternoons is traditionally the day and time men are given to fix torn clothing. Them that can throw a fancy stitch or knows how to embroidery will fancy up their shirts or trousers. Some will embroider the name of the ship on a ribbon and sew it on their hats. A man that can read and write will read letters or write them for those who can't, thereby picking up a shilling or two or an extra tot of rum. Some ships serve punishment every Thursday and pipe 'make and mend' afterwards. Gabe rarely flogs a man so most punishment is given the morning after an offense is made."

"I see," Sir Victor responded. "I've been amazed there hasn't been a flogging or two during my time on the ship. I've seen it many a time aboard other ships."

"Not those under Lord Anthony you ain't. He feels that flogging means that a ship's officer has failed. Not every time, of course, but most of the time."

"Do you agree?" Sir Victor asked.

"Look about you," Dagan replied. "See how everybody goes about their duties with rarely a fuss."

When he nodded, Dagan continued, "Well, you should have seen her before Gabe took command."

"I see," Sir Victor said, but Dagan doubted he did. It would be tough for any landsman to fully understand the hell life could be aboard a ship with a flogging captain.

Siding up to Dagan so as to not be overheard, Sir Victor asked, "When do the men bathe?"

"Bathe?" Dagan repeated feigning shock. "Why would they bathe? They're at sea."

Seeing Sir Victor's eyes grow big, Dagan laughed and said, "Friday is usually the day but Gabe will allow the crew to rig a pump and wash twice a week…in salt water mind you, not fresh water. There's never enough of that. There's only a few of the men who has soap. That's why Gabe allows a twice a week washing. Otherwise, there's some that can get rank."

"Aye," Sir Victor said. "I've run across a couple. That's why I asked."

"Well, if he gets too rank you can bet a man's mates will see he gets scrubbed. Bart tells a story of a bosun's mate who came aboard the first ship Lord Anthony commanded. Said a gull was sitting on a piling and when the man passed it to walk up the gangway the bird keeled over dead. Them days, Lord Anthony welcomed every new crew member, petty officer, and above. When His Lordship walked up to shake the man's hand, the stench was so bad His Lordship had to turn away gagging, tears coming from his eyes. The man took a step forward, thinking the captain had suddenly taken ill. The closer he got the more Lord Anthony backed up still gagging until finally he held out his hand for the man to stay where he was at. Captain Buck, he was a lieutenant then, saw the commotion and thought the man was attacking the captain. He ran towards the two but slid to a stop when he got close and shouted, 'Damme, man have you shat yourself?' Bart then walked up and swore it was so bad the flies dropped dead when they got close. Lord Anthony ordered a screen be put up so as not to embarrass the man. Then he had his servant bring a new bar of soap, which he slid across the deck under the screen and had the man wash from head to toe with a crew pumping up seawater from a deck pump. He then had the fellow empty his ditty bag and had the man wash all his belongings. I think Gabe took to twice a week washings after hearing Bart's story."

"I believe I would as well," Sir Victor said, not quite sure whether to believe the tale or not.

After a bit Dagan said, "Saturdays is when the ship washes clothes for inspection on Sunday. After divisions, that is the men and the ship has been inspected, Gabe usually reads a few passages from the Bible. Often someone will request a certain scripture. They like stories about David but don't care too much about Moses beyond him parting the sea."

"Wandering around in the desert doesn't seem to strike a chord, does it?" Sir Victor said, understanding the men's feelings.

"Once a month Gabe reads the Articles of War. Most of the men, even those who can't read or write, can recite them. They've heard them so much. Gabe once had a contest with Lieutenant Davy being the judge. Members of the crew could stand and recite an article. The man reciting the most articles with the fewest mistakes won a guinea. One time the sod who won went ashore with a working party, slipped away, got drunk, and was punished for drunkenness on duty. When Gabe asked if he had anything to say the poor man answered, 'Nay, Captain. It was knowing the articles that won the contest for me. Only I should have spent the guinea on a doxy and not the drink.' Gabe agreed with the man."

"Did he flog him?" Sir Victor interrupted.

"No, just took his grog issue for a week but promised a flogging if it happened again."

"I recall the captain eating in the wardroom last Sunday," Sir Victor said. "Does he usually do that? I thought he was the one to invite the officers to dine with him."

"It's a tradition that the captain be invited to the wardroom on Sundays. But it's an invitation only type thing. I've heard of captains that were never invited and some who were that wouldn't attend. His Lordship…Gabe and Admiral Anthony's father…told it was a good time to get to know the men who may be needed to take the captain's place suddenly. A time to build confidence and kind of an unofficial time to speak of certain matters. It's the first lieutenant's place to make sure questions and merriment stay within bounds. If a man gets as we term it, in his cups, it's his fellow officers' duty to get him to his cabin. I've not heard of that happening very often."

Dagan realized he'd been talking so long he'd thereby neglected his pipe and it had gone out. He ducked down, cupped his pipe, and lit it again.

Sir Victor watched as he lit the pipe with such practiced ease. *A very knowledgeable man, this Dagan*, he thought. *A man of mystery if you believed some of the tales told about him. Yet a man who held the respect of everyone from the admiral down to the midshipmen. Will I ever gain such loyalty? No, it's rare a spy gains friendships, let along the respect and loyalty the Anthonys, the Dagans, and the Barts of the world enjoy. That's why I like Captain Anthony*, Sir Victor realized. *He has been open, honest, and at least willing to see the needs of my kind. Well, if he ever needs a friend I will be there*, Sir Victor thought to himself. *I'll be there.*

From forward, the fiddler struck up a tune and several men burst into a song. Turning to Dagan, Sir Victor was about to ask, "What's that?" But Dagan answered the question before it escaped his lips. "It's time for the grog issue. The tune is 'Nancy Dawson,' another of our traditions. When a sailor hears the tune he knows it's time for the grog."

"I see," Sir Victor said as the men lined up and cups seemed to appear out of nowhere. *I'll bet that's where they get the saying, "He's in his cups,"* he thought. Hearing his stomach growl he realized he was hungry. Looking at his watch, he saw it was still some hours to dinner. *I think I'll walk about a bit*, he decided. *Maybe I'll happen in on the captain and he'll invite me to a glass. If not maybe I can get into the grog line.*

## Chapter Thirty-one

Land ho!" The shout came down from the mainmast lookout just as the ship's bell rang six bells in the forenoon watch.

"A perfect landing, Captain. I see it's not yet noon so your prediction of by noon is right on."

"Thank you, sir," Gabe answered Sir Victor. "But we are still a good eight leagues or so before we make it to Carlisle Bay."

"How far is a league?" Sir Victor asked, trying to gain as much nautical knowledge as possible.

"Most define a league as three and one eighth miles. However, my father always said there's no use splitting hairs so most ship commanders will round it off to three miles equal a league."

Doing the quick math, Sir Victor said, "That's twenty-four miles. You can see that far at sea?"

"Not from the deck but from the mainmast lookout post," Gabe answered. "I suspect the lookout has sighted Needham's Point."

"Well, it's still a perfect landing you've made," Sir Victor said.

"Most of the credit for that goes to the master, Mr Gunnells. He's the one that lays the course. I just tell him where I want to go."

"I think you are just being modest, Captain, but I'll take your word for it," Sir Victor said, dropping the subject.

***

Lieutenant Wiley was on the quarterdeck when Lieutenant Davy came to relieve him. Davy noticed how Wiley seemed to hang around while the forenoon was relieved and the afternoon watch was set. They were almost to Carlisle Bay so things would be happening quickly in order to get the ship ready to enter port, fire the salute, and drop anchor.

As Wiley seemed to hesitate to speak, Davy asked, "Something on your mind?"

"Well…yes. How long do you think it will be before we see any prize money?"

"Long enough I wouldn't hold my breath waiting on it."

"Oh."

"Is this your first prize?" Davy asked.

"Yes," Wiley admitted sheepishly.

"Well, it'll come but not soon. Could be a year, could be longer. The captain will see you gets your share though. So don't worry about it."

"I won't," Wiley replied. He then said, "One more thing. Do you think Lavery will get to keep the xebec?"

Davy looked at his fellow lieutenant in dismay. He almost asked, "In what Navy have you been in all these years?" But he refrained from doing so. Wiley might have been senior in regards to time in service but he had almost no experience. He had constantly pumped Davy for information since weighing anchor in Portsmouth. He had seemed reluctant to talk with Lavery, but why? He was a good sort, he never shirked his duties, and he seemed to care. As an officer he had improved significantly since starting this commission. *Well he might be senior*, Davy thought, *but he's got enough sense to know who his sea daddy was. He's got the first lieutenant's job on his mind,* Davy suddenly realized.

"Mr Lavery is the second senior lieutenant under Lord Anthony, who is not in command of a vessel," Davy explained. "Lieutenant Lamb is senior but I don't know much about him. The xebec's the size of a frigate, which is a captain's command. I would expect either *Lizard's* captain to get her or maybe *Alert's* Taylor. It might be a four-way switch...Culzean to the xebec, Taylor to *Lizard*, Jackson to *Alert*, then possibly Lavery to *Viper*. However, if any of that happens you'll be the new first lieutenant. Or...His Lordship could throw a new officer into the mix and all this calculating will be for naught. Do like I do, sit back and let His Lordship figure it out. That way you don't wind up with indigestion."

"I guess you're right," Wiley said.

Glancing over to see Gunnells eyeing him, Davy realized he'd cut it close. "Mr Ally."

"Yes, sir. My compliments to the captain and we are entering Carlisle Bay."

"Aye, sir."

"Mr Gaff."

"Here, sir," his look saying I've been here while you've been gabbing.

Davy swallowed, and then ordered, "Call all hands. Reduce sails for entering the harbour."

Gaff's reply was in the form of a shrill blast from his bosun's pipe.

"Cutting it close are we?"

"Sorry Captain."

"That's all right, Davy. But I concur with your recommendations of leaving the decisions to your betters. That way you won't have indigestion."

This caused Davy to swallow twice before he could speak. "Yes sir, Captain."

As Gabe turned away to speak with the master, Davy thought, *Damme the skylight is open. The captain heard every word from his cabin. That won't do me or Wiley any good…damme.*

***

Gabe with Sir Victor in tow reported to the flagship immediately upon dropping anchor. "I trust I can leave the ship in capable hands," Gabe said to his two lieutenants. "Should something arise that will limit your attention to duty please inform the master so he can assume the watch."

"Aye, Captain," the two said in unison.

Bart was at the entry port and fell in beside Gabe after Buck had welcomed him aboard. Hazard escorted Sir Victor to the wardroom for a glass, which was Lord Anthony's way of seeing Gabe and being brought up to date in a precise yet timely manner.

"Damn, Gabe," Bart swore as they crossed the coaming and went down the companionway. "Be they a ship on the ocean what you don't consider taking?"

"Aye," Gabe replied, glad to see his brother's burly cox'n. "There was one but it smelled like a whore's drawers so I thought you'd already taken her."

"Impish, that's what ye be, talking to old Bart that way."

The marine sentry came to attention and opened the door to the admiral's cabin, allowing Gabe and Bart to pass.

"Gabe, how good to see you!" Anthony exclaimed. "It seems Dagan's lady luck is still with you."

"Aye, sir. It was hellish hot for a while but we had better gunners."

After Gabe finished his narrative, Buck, who'd made his way down, said, "So you got a prize and the smashers too. Have you practiced with them yet?"

"No sir," Gabe admitted. "The carpenter said we'd have to make some modifications to *Peregrine* before we chance a test firing."

"How about the prize, Gabe? Does she need a lot of repair?"

"She's seaworthy but I wouldn't doubt she'd need time at the dockyard in Antigua before I'd take her into battle. Druett says her guns were as mixed a lot as her crew so you may consider rearming her. I'd try to keep those eighteen pounders if possible. They cause a hellish lot of damage."

Thinking aloud, Buck said, "Who do we put on her?" This caused a chuckle from Gabe.

"Pray tell what's humoured you?" Anthony asked.

"That's been on my second lieutenant's mind as well."

"Surely he can't think it would be him?" Buck asked.

"No sir, he's just trying to figure a way to get Lavery promoted so he can become the first lieutenant."

"Well, at least he's enthusiastic about it," Buck said after hearing Gabe's tale. "I can't get Lamb to decide if he's to shat or go blind without asking."

"Well, first things first," Anthony said. "We've kept our foreign affairs agent cooling his heels long enough. Bart."

"Aye, I'll go collect the spy." As Bart left, Gabe told of Sir Victor boarding the xebec and getting wounded.

"Not afraid is he?" Buck said.

"Nay, there's no run in the man. He has also tried very hard to learn and understand shipboard life. The men have taken to him. He even shared a wet with them."

"Grog, Sir Victor?"

"Aye, Captain Buck, and it grows on you I might add." The sentry had failed to announce Sir Victor, who had walked in as his name was mentioned.

*Something to discuss with Bart later. He'd remedy that*, Anthony thought to himself.

## *Chapter Thirty-two*

The dawn was breaking over the horizon. A reddish cloud hung over the Caribbean Sea. Looking out the bedroom window of Lord Ragland's house, Anthony could hear his wife's gentle breathing and rustle of bed linens as she rolled over. *Peaceful...peaceful here inside the comfort of the house, but what about out there? What lies in wait just over the horizon? Red sky in the morning, sailor's warning.* Anthony couldn't help but think of the old sailor's quote.

Where was *Intrepid* and *Ferret*? They should have been back a week ago. Two gray gulls could be seen as the sun rose, flapping their wings, then hovering a moment before gliding on the early morning breeze. Down at the harbour, the daily routine would be in full swing. He could picture Captain Buck, his sea hat jammed down over his eyes against the glare of the sun and glitter it caused reflecting off the long line of swells of the incoming tide.

Gabe, on the other hand, would be hatless. His long unruly hair would be tied in a queue at the nape of his neck with a simple black ribbon. Buck would have on his uniform whereas Gabe was apt to have on sailor's slops, black sea boots, and a white shirt. He may have a scarf, one that Faith had given him, knotted about his neck. Thinking of Faith caused Anthony to feel a touch of sorrow. While he and Deborah had shared last night together, Gabe had had to return to the ship last evening. The squadron would weigh anchor this morning. Anthony felt the need to be at sea. When Gabe and Sir Victor returned with the news in regards to the French signing a treaty with the Colonies, Anthony knew it would only be a matter of time before he had to face them.

He didn't want it to be while he was at anchor in Carlisle Bay. He had dispatched *Viper* to Antigua with the news. She should have been back yesterday. But a squall, perverse winds, anything could have held up the ship for a day. What worried him was *Intrepid*. The weight of her metal would be missed if they came up on a French fleet, especially if it was Admiral Jacques de Guimond's eighty-gun *Tourville*. *La Tigre* had been fifty guns, as had *La Vipere*. As it stood now, the odds were definitely in the Frenchman's favour. Gabe and Markham had worked hard and were finally satisfied with the carronades. They had been placed forward in each ship so as to not interfere with shrouds and other riggings and to make sure the wadding cleared the ship's rail.

"I wish I had two more for the quarterdeck," Gabe said. "I'm tempted to relocate the two up forward." But after so much had been done to locate them where they were, he didn't have the heart to move them.

Druett had been skeptical at first due to the short range of the weapon but after a little practice he seemed impressed with the smashers.

"Gil." Deborah was awake. "It's not time yet, is it?"

Turning to his wife, he shook his head. "No, not yet."

"Then come back to bed."

Looking once more out the window, he said, "I couldn't sleep."

"Who said anything about sleeping?" This caught his attention. Deborah had sat up with the covers about her neck. When her husband turned back, she dropped them. "Am I as enticing as those old ships?" she asked.

"Much more enticing madam…much more." For the moment his other worries were completely forgotten.

On board *HMS SeaHorse*, George Jepson looked at the red sky, "Squalls, Captain."

"Aye," Buck replied with a shiver.

The island trader, *Anna*, dropped anchor in Carlisle Bay within an hour of Lord Anthony's arrival on board his flagship. Unlike a naval vessel, the little schooner dropped anchor within a pistol shot of the towering man o' war. The captain of the schooner picked up a speaking trumpet and hailed the flagship. In the man's broken English, he stated that he had three wounded sailors and could they send a doctor over.

Anthony felt a sinking feeling in the pit of his stomach, sure his fears had been realized. Buck had called for the surgeon, who was getting into the captain's gig.

"I have decided to go over myself, sir," Buck informed Anthony.

"Thank you, Rupert," Anthony said, laying a hand on his friend's shoulder. Buck had known how important it was to get the information fast and correctly.

Bart, standing next to Anthony, whispered, "Maybe they're not ours, sir." But deep in his heart he knew otherwise.

Buck returned before the hourglass turned. He was accompanied by the schooner's captain, a smallish man who said he was from Trinidad. He was sailing home from Guadeloupe when as the sun went down he thought he heard the distant rumblings of thunder. However, it didn't take long for him to realize it was cannon fire. He got close enough that he could see the orange flames from the cannons just as it got dark. Not wanting to be mistaken as the enemy to either of the ships, he decided to heave to till dawn.

"How long ago was this?" Anthony asked.

"Two nights ago, señor," the little captain replied. "I waited until the sun was high before I made sail. I wanted to make sure there were no ships that would take my little *Anna*. She is all I have."

*A smart move*, Anthony thought.

"Soon as we set sail we began to see…how do you say it…pieces of ship?"

"Debris," Buck said.

"Si. There was debris everywhere. We reduced sail to see if we could find anything we could use." The man paused, a little embarrassed by his admission of being a scavenger.

"That's all right," Anthony said, wanting the man to continue.

"I soon see bodies floating. Some mangled by battles, others by the sharks." The man quickly made the sign of the cross. "It was terrible, señor." The man paused again as he recalled the floating carnage. "I soon see two men hanging onto a floating section of a mast and then one holding onto a hatch cover. They were in a bad way. One of the men kept saying, 'The French, it was the French.' I knew then I could not go to Martinique so I decided to come here."

"What about St. Lucia?" Buck asked.

"It was too close to Martinique so I didn't want to chance it."

"Neither would I," Anthony replied.

"I hope *Viper* hasn't run up with the frogs," Buck said. "I told him to stand far enough out that he should miss the French patrols."

After questioning the man further regarding his having sighted any French ships and getting negative replies, Anthony thanked the man. He had Hazard to fetch a small bag of gold coins to reward the man for his actions. Hazard escorted the man topside and had him rowed back to his ship.

When the man was gone from the cabin and out of earshot, Buck spoke. "That reward was probably more than he makes in a year."

"It was well worth it," Anthony answered. "Let him know we British are a thankful lot. You never know when he may be of some help in the future." He then called for Bart.

"Aye."

"Call my barge so we can go ashore. I need to make Lord Ragland aware of the situation. Rupert, I should be back in an hour. Have all captains, first lieutenants, and masters repair on board by that time. See if you can round up Sir Victor and let him know. I'm sure he needs to be apprised of the situation also."

"I'm sure he's on board *Peregrine*," Buck said with a smile.

"He and Gabe have gotten that close?" Anthony asked.

"More like him and Gabe's new cabin servant."

"Yes, that Nesbit has a talent." Bart had just returned to escort Anthony to his waiting barge and overheard the conversation. "Maybe we could sit ole Silas on the beach and steals Nesbit."

This brought a chuckle to the group but not from everyone within hearing. Silas had been in the pantry and overheard Bart's remarks. "Put me on the beach would 'e. We's a-see who's on the beach. It'll be a cold day in torment for Bart gets another snack. A cold day and that's no error."

***

Lord Ragland accompanied Anthony back to the flagship for the officer's call. To Anthony's relief, *Viper* had entered the bay and would be anchoring soon. One of the survivors picked up by the little island trader was Lieutenant Hallett, captain of *Ferret*. Against doctor's orders, he'd left the hospital on Barbados and reported to the flagship. Understanding his need, Buck had personally welcomed him aboard like a returning hero. The officers were all seated at Anthony's table with the first lieutenants and masters standing against the bulkhead. The group got quiet as Anthony made his way to the head of the table.

"*Viper* has just dropped anchor," he told the group, "so we'll wait a few minutes for Jackson. In the meantime let's enjoy a glass of claret."

As the glasses were being filled, Anthony looked at his officers. *We are so few*...he thought...*so few*.

***

Once Lieutenant Jackson had joined the group, Anthony asked Hallett to tell of their action with the French.

"It was just at dusk," the wounded officer said. "We had sighted the sails but thought nothing of it as we didn't know the French had joined with the Colonies. The lead ship was the eighty-gun *Tourville*, which was sailing in formation with several smaller ships. Two of fifty guns each, I'd say, along with a heavy frigate, probably a forty-four, and a corvette of twenty-two. Captain Fletcher fired a salute to the French flag. Then quick as you please...almost like that was a planned signal, the French broke formation. The flagship sailed down *Intrepid's* larboard side while the two fiftys broke to starboard. The gun ports were opened and Captain Fletcher never had a chance. It being a calm sea, upper and lower deck guns were used. Round after round was poured into *Intrepid*. By the time the ships were past, there was nothing left. Nobody could have survived. There was no call for surrender. It was the most vicious attack I'd ever seen. I tried to put *Ferret* about but the heavy frigate fired on us, sending balls up our arse just as we come about. One second I was standing on a hatch, my glass in my hand, the next I was flying through the air."

"Who, besides yourself, survived?" Markham asked.

"My master, Nate Hayes, and the bosun, Abe Pogoda."

"How bad are they?" Gabe asked.

"Knocked about mostly. I think they will be back to duty soon. No others survived." Taking a breath and wiping the tears that filled his eyes Hallett tried to gain control of his emotions. "Several survived the blast but then at dark the sharks came. Scream after scream filled the air. Once I felt one brush my leg but I was able to pull myself up on the hatch cover. It was a frenzy. The water churned as the devils tore my men apart. I prayed to God that if they come after me let it be quick. I don't know how long it lasted but it seemed like an hour or so before the screams went away."

When Hallett finished his narrative, he grabbed his glass and downed the contents, feeling the warm liquid go down. The men at the table were silent, each thankful they'd not been put through the ordeal. After a moment, Anthony stood and raised his glass.

"To fallen comrades...and death to the French."

## *Chapter Thirty-three*

The loss of *Intrepid* was a tremendous blow to the squadron's firepower. Therefore, the xebec had to be pressed into service.

"Who do we put in command?" Anthony asked Buck. "Every situation I come up with weakens us somewhere else. We'll have to strip *Viper* and *Alert* then take a few from the frigates to finish out the crew."

"That's the only way possible," Buck said, agreeing with Anthony.

"I'll put Culzean aboard as captain."

Nodding his agreement, Buck added, "He has a cool head and the man's no coward. Where will you assign Taylor and Jackson?"

After thinking a bit, Anthony said, "I'll let Jackson stay aboard *Viper* with a dozen hands, just enough to sail her. He will be ordered to not engage in battle. If we fail it's his job to report to Lord Ragland. As for Taylor, he can go with Culzean to the xebec."

Overhead the ship's bells could be heard. It was six bells in the afternoon watch, one hour till the first dog-watch.

"Do you still intend to weigh anchor on the evening tide?"

"I think so," Anthony replied. How he longed to say no and postpone leaving until dawn, spending what might be his last night on earth with his wife and daughter.

Reading his thoughts, Buck said, "You'll see her in a few days, sir. I feel certain."

"Thank you, Rupert. That was kind, old friend." However, inwardly Anthony thought, *I wish I was as certain*.

The men were transferred and were just settling in when Captain Richard Culzean was piped aboard. He didn't read himself in knowing this was a temporary command. He just hoped it wasn't too temporary. Making his way through the ship, Culzean heard the unmistakable giggle. Seeing the bosun, Culzean called to him. "Get the women ashore. All of them."

"Aye Captain. I already made one sweep but a second wouldn't be amiss."

Hearing a shout, Culzean grinned. "Caught in the act I'll bet. Well, the trollops would rather face a little awkwardness than a French cannonball."

***

The sky was overcast with fast moving clouds. Bart walked in the admiral's cabin and saw him looking out the stern windows.

"Jep says the clouds are heavy with a promise of rain."

Anthony did not speak and Bart, knowing his moods, didn't press it. It seemed to have been easier when His Lordship had been a captain. Then he had the workings of the ship to keep him busy…his mind occupied, but now it was stay out of the way and worry. Getting a cup of coffee from Silas, Bart made a motion toward Anthony. Silas understood immediately. He took the cup back, poured a quarter of it into another cup, and then refilled the cup with brandy. He added a spoon of mixed cinnamon and sugar then handed the cup back to Bart. He ambled toward Anthony, sneaking a quick taste before offering the cup to Anthony.

As Anthony turned, Bart could see the old meerschaum pipe in his hand. The pipe had been Anthony's father's, Lord James Anthony. Taking the cup in one hand, Anthony put the pipe in his coat pocket.

Taking a drink of the coffee, Anthony looked at Bart and said, "Tell me, Bart, how many Barbados plantation owners are going to lose their holdings after playing cards with you and Jepson?"

"Well, they's a few what owes us but none to the point of losing they land. Course that boy what dueled with Davy owed a few guineas but we didn't ask his father for it."

"I'm glad you didn't." Anthony was about to ask another question when he and Bart heard the noise.

Thinking of Jep's prediction of rain, Bart said, "Thunder." He instantly knew he was wrong.

"Gunfire," he and Anthony said at the same time. Rushing on deck, Anthony found Buck on the quarterdeck.

"We've spotted a sail fine on the weather bow, My Lord. It appears she's being chased."

"Deck thar. Ships in sight behind the lone ship, sir. I make out six sail of the line."

"Damme," Buck pounded the rail, "six to four." Then seeing one of the helmsmen eye him, Buck turned to Lord Anthony, "Not much of a bargain for the French would you say, sir?"

"Why no, Captain Buck. I thought we were in for a battle there for a moment." This brought a chuckle from those within hearing distance. "Captain Buck, general signal to our ships to prepare for battle!"

The signal flags were quickly run up *SeaHorse's* yards. Buck then called to his first lieutenant. "Mr Lamb."

"Aye, Captain."

"Beat to quarters and clear for action."

"Aye, Captain."

The rattle of drums filled the air as men poured from the hatchways and rushed to their stations. Anthony braced himself and looked at the ship being chased by the French.

"Mr Buck."

"Aye, My Lord."

"There's every chance that we can snatch yonder prize right out of the frog's clutches."

"Wouldn't that disappoint them," Buck said with a laugh. "What a pity."

Anthony smiled to himself when Lamb reported to Buck. "Cleared for action, sir, all hands at their stations." Eight minutes flat.

"Damme," declared Buck. "It seems our jack tars are in the mood for a little frog stew."

Standing at his station beside the big double wheel, Jepson smiled. "Aye, they are eager. They've got revenge on their minds after what the French did to their mates on *Intrepid* and *Ferret*." Chomping on the remains of an unlit cigar, Jepson recalled the last days of the Seven Year War. There had been carnage aplenty. Well, some of these lads hot for revenge will find there's a price to pay…a high price for some who wouldn't live to see the sunset.

Bart appeared on deck with Anthony's sword belt and a brace of pistols. "I let the belt out a mile. I noticed it was a bit snug the last time you wore it."

"You mangy cur," Anthony exclaimed. "I'm surprised you can even make it through the damn hatch."

"I just follow yew," Bart replied. "If yews make it through, I's can."

Those close by hid a smile. The gentle bickering between Bart and Anthony was well known.

"Pray, Captain Buck, tell me what you find so humourous."

"Bart got the last word in again, My Lord."

"The rascal did at that. I'll see him on the beach yet, Captain. Mark my word."

"Aye," Buck replied, trying not to smile. *About the time you haul down your flag*, he thought to himself.

A flapping noise from above made Buck look up. It was Anthony's flag. It flapped briskly from the mizzen. Hopefully it won't be hauled down too soon.

"Rupert."

"Aye, My Lord."

"I believe we have time for a quick walk and speak to the men." Another of Anthony's traditions. A moment with the men before the metal started flying—to let them know he cared.

With Bart trailing, the trio made their way down to the deck below. Speaking to the men, Anthony said, "After we've showed these frogs what for, I think we'll have spirits and a double tot for all hands. I'm sure they'll work up a thirst."

"Huzza...Huzza for His Lordship!" the hands cheered. Once the cheering died down, Anthony cleared his throat and continued.

"And if the purser complains, he'll get a dozen." This brought more cheers.

As Anthony moved along, a gray-bearded, grizzled gun captain rose up, a dirty handkerchief already tied about his ears. "Don't you worry none, Admiral." Patting the breech of his cannon with his gnarled, rheumatoid hand, he continued, "We'll give 'em a good dost of what they gave the poor buggers on *Intrepid* and *Ferret*, we will. Old Betsy and me, twenty-four pounds atta time."

Johns, the third lieutenant, stood grinning at the gun captain's comments. "We'll all give them a taste of British metal, My Lord."

"I know you will," Anthony replied. "I can't wait to see how they act from the reception you lads plan."

Another cheer went up as Anthony and Buck went back up to the upper deck, ducking the low beams as they did so. *It'll be hell down here*, Anthony thought, *utter hell.*

Pausing before the last step, Anthony stooped down and shouted, "Death to the French, give them hell men!" Another cheer.

"They're ready!" Buck exclaimed.

"As I am," Anthony replied. The walk along the upper deck was much the same. Shaking Lieutenant Neal's hand, Anthony made his way back to the quarterdeck. Hazard was there with his hand resting on the handle of his sword. His empty sleeve was pinned up and he had a determined look on his face. Anthony had come to not only like but also to rely more and more on this young man. "Have a care today, Everette."

"Aye, My Lord, and you as well."

"I'll take my leave now, sir," Buck spoke to his admiral in a business like tone. It was time.

"Take care, Rupert."

"Aye sir," Buck replied, and then went to do his duties.

Taking a glass, Anthony could now clearly see the approaching vessels. They were in a ragged formation. Jepson could be heard speaking to Buck.

"They have the wind gage, sir."

Anthony thought of the battle plan he'd laid out not twenty-four hours ago. It was his feeling that while the French were excellent sailors, they showed little imagination when it came to battle. What they had done to *Intrepid* was what he planned to do in return. He hoped they'd never expect the maneuver in a fleet to fleet battle. Upon his signal, *Peregrine* and the xebec would break to larboard while *SeaHorse* and *Dasher* would pass to starboard. This would put the enemy at a disadvantage, as the French crew would have to be split or face an all-out onslaught without any return fire.

The xebec with its heavier cannons should have led the charge to larboard but with the makeshift crew and Culzean's lack of experience, it fell to Gabe to lead and the xebec to follow. Thinking of Gabe, Anthony wondered would Faith ever forgive him if something happened to his brother. Would he...could he forgive himself?

Both he and Gabe understood the dangers of their chosen profession. Gabe had turned into a good seaman, a good captain. *Our father would have been proud*, he thought, *as I am.*

Clearing his mind, Anthony called to the signal midshipman, "General signal. Form line of battle." This would be read and expected by the French Admiral. The next would not. The signal would be a simple one. He would dip his flag and the ships would split lines. Waiting—that was the hard part.

"Well, they gave up on the chase," Buck said, breaking Anthony's reverie.

"I would think so. The French admiral probably thinks he'll have bigger fish to fry."

"Aye, but while he has the advantage in weight and men, we have something they don't," Buck declared.

"And what is that, Captain?"

"You, My Lord."

"That was well said, Rupert. I thank you."

The sound of a cannon firing rumbled across the water. There was no sign of where the ball landed.

"Anxious, that un," Bart volunteered.

"Aye."

The French had shortened sail but Anthony held off. He wanted the French Admiral de Guimond to think they intended to charge down in tight formation. Anthony looked at the oncoming ships. Another bow chaser on the leading French ship roared.

"Not long now, Captain Buck."

"Aye, sir."

"You may load the cannons, double shot and a measure of grape if you will."

"Aye, My Lord."

## *Chapter Thirty-four*

The protective tampions had been removed and the gun loaded as the admiral had ordered.

"General signal," Anthony ordered. "Shorten sail."

"Aye, sir."

Anthony felt the gentle breeze make his hair flutter. The gap was very close now. *May God keep us*, Anthony prayed silently. Barely a hundred yards now separated *SeaHorse* from the lead French ship, which continued to fire her forward guns, smoke billowing out and drifted aft. *That's good,* Anthony thought. *It will momentarily blind the French admiral.* When the smoke clears, we will have completed our maneuver. Anthony let the French fire the forward guns once more then shouted, "Quick now. Dip the flag."

The signal was instantly given and Gabe, who had been waiting, shouted, "Now, Mr Gunnells!"

*Peregrine* veered to larboard with the xebec following in her wake. The forward guns on *SeaHorse* were now firing at the French double-decker. Then they were broadside to broadside.

"Fire as you bear!" Buck shouted. "Fire as you bear!"

The cry was taken up by Lieutenants Johns and Neal. The cannons roared from both decks, causing *SeaHorse* to shudder and vibrate through the planking. As flames of hell belched forth, the cannons hurled themselves inboard against the tackles. The crews coughed and choked as acrid smoke filled the deck. Neal could be heard shouting encouragement as the gun captains cursed. The Frenchman was firing at *SeaHorse*, the flames flashing through the smoke as ball after ball pounded against *SeaHorse's* hull at a distance of seventy yards or so.

Gabe opened fire to larboard with the xebec following. The two ships had poured complete broadsides into the Frenchman without having returned fire.

"I can't believe it!" Lavery shouted, now back in his first lieutenant's role.

"Aye," Gabe replied. "But the next ship will be ready."

The big fifty-gun ship was now firing its forward guns. Again *SeaHorse* and *Dasher* raked the French to starboard as *Peregrine* and the xebec fired into their targets to larboard. The French returned the fire but with less efficiency. The broadsides were ragged with only one broadside to two of Anthony's ships. Nevertheless, the balls were finding their marks as the heavier eighteen-pound ball outweighed the British twelve pounders.

Druett had personally taken charge of the carronades and they were evening up the odds at the close range. They had just come to bear on the third French ship, which was the second of fifty guns. The smasher fired and a moment later a thunderous explosion was heard as the ship seemed to buck in the middle and flames shot skyward. Was it the smasher or a combination of being raked by both *SeaHorse* and *Peregrine*? Regardless, the ship was no longer a threat as it broke in half with both ends sinking quickly.

The French frigate tried to avoid ramming the destroyed French ship by veering to starboard. This sudden move cost her the wind. Several things happened. The frigate behind the ship rammed into the stalled frigate amidships.

Gunnells yelled, "She's in stays!" as *Peregrine* sailed past the unprotected stern and *SeaHorse* the bow. Again each ship was firing gun after gun into both frigates with the second only returning a ragged volley. Seeing the result of the ships ahead of her, the corvette quickly came about. The French flagship *Tourville*, however, had quickly come about and was firing into the stern of the xebec and *Dasher*. Markham quickly veered to larboard to lessen the French ship's ability to bear. Culzean was not as quick to do so. Suddenly the ship's wheel spun out of control.

"We've lost our rudder, sir!" the helmsman shouted.

This news was delivered only seconds before the stern was lifted as more of the French twenty-four pound ball crashed into the ship. Deadly debris filled the air and men were impaled with sharp splinters. The *Tourville* was vicious in its onslaught. Another broadside was poured into the xebec, bringing down the mainmast and the mizzen. Cannons were overturned and screams filled the air as the entire rail was blasted away.

*SeaHorse* had come about and now the two flagships were coming together. The *Tourville* fired once more as it passed *Dasher*, who had changed tack and increased the distance between her and the mighty French eighty gunner. Markham was everywhere encouraging his men as ball after ball ploughed into *Dasher's* hull and rail, reaping its toll in human carnage. One of *Tourville*'s balls smashed into the mizzenmast.

"Look out, look out!" a bosun's mate screamed as stays and shrouds were snapped as the mast fell. The weight of the mast caused *Dasher* to list, and as the downed sails hit the water, the ship slewed to starboard and came to a halt. Markham quickly sent axe men forward to chop away the riggings and cast the mast over the side. Pausing to look, he saw the hulls of the two flagships grind together. Past that he could make out Gabe's *Peregrine* trading broadsides with the French frigate.

She had broken loose from her sister ship that remained still in the water. As Markham watched, the corvette was now closing and firing at Gabe's stern.

"Hurry," Markham shouted. The corvette's snapping could change the tide. It had to be stopped now.

On board *SeaHorse*, Anthony did not like the direction the battle was taking. The xebec was out of action, *Dasher* at least temporarily out of action, and *Peregrine* fighting two ships. The French's remaining fifty-gun ship was following in her admiral's wake.

Touching Buck's arm to get his attention, Anthony shouted to be heard. "We have to keep the French from hemming us in!" Buck nodded his understanding and spoke to Jepson, who stood astride a dead helmsman, helping with the wheel until another helmsman arrived and the body moved.

As Buck turned, he collided with a seaman who fell to the deck, his face a bloody pulp. On board *Dasher*, the downed mast was finally cast over the side and the ship began to pick up speed.

"Sir, look sir," one of Markham's men called. On board the xebec Culzean was waving and shouting, "Give us a tow. We've rigged a rudder and we've several of the cannons still workable!"

That would certainly help, Markham decided, and a grapple was quickly tossed with the end of the rope tied to a larger rope or hawser. "Tie it off quickly!" Markham bellowed. They didn't have time to spare. Culzean had his men quickly tie the five-inch cable securely to the capstan and was ready when the slack ran out and the line became taut. *Dasher* slowed as she felt the added weight of the xebec but quickly picked up speed.

The two flagships were now grappled together and the other fifty-gun ship was maneuvering to come up on *Sea-*

*Horse's* other side. Markham ordered the forward guns to fire.

"Let's give her something else to think about!" he shouted to his gunner. The mastless xebec followed in *Dasher's* wake. The French fifty now turned its attention to *Dasher. I hope the cable doesn't part,* Markham thought. The ships were now almost abreast.

"Fire, fire as you bear!" Markham yelled and felt his ship shudder as her guns fired. The smasher again proved its worth as it spewed a double load of grape at the French sailor. Culzean now had the xebec's guns firing its heavy ball into the Frenchman.

A cheer went up as smoke then flames shot up the French ship. Watching, Markham saw flames leap up the mast and the sails were quickly engulfed in fire. Men were already jumping overboard. Grabbing his speaking trumpet, Markham hailed Culzean.

"Cast off your tow and grapple the French flagship as we pass." Culzean nodded his understanding. "Hold on, Gabe," Markham said to himself. "Hold on, old friend."

On board the two flagships, the battle was now hand to hand. Cutlasses and axes flashed through the air as each ship's boarders tried to cut through the nets to get to their opponents. Finally the nets sagged then fell loose. A bearded French sailor hurled curses at the British only to be shot down. The marines were in the fighting tops and with both swivels and muskets were marking down the French boarders. Thanks to the marines overhead, the British boarders gained *Tourville's* deck first.

Anthony had just made his way on the enemy deck when a screaming sailor ran at him with a boarding pike. A heavy bosun's mate stepped in from the side and, slashing down with his cutlass, severed the man's arm at the elbow. Anthony was soon attacked by another. He parried the man's blow but the heavy sword sent a shock up his arm.

Bart was there and shot the man in the chest. The bullet at point blank range lifted the man as he fell backward. A French marine then lunged at Bart with a bayonet, ripping his shirt and blood started to flow. Anthony swung his blade down with all his might across the man's neck. This all but severed the man's head and blood pumped from the man's arteries as he fell lifeless to the deck.

All about the battle raged amidst the cries and curses that filled the air. Pistol shots rang out as steel blades darkened with blood. A French lieutenant charged with a group of men following. Bart shot the man with his last pistol then turned to meet his next foe but slipped on the bloody deck. The hatchet face man attacking Bart was quickly surprised to find Anthony's sword impaled in his chest. The man shrieked as he realized he was done for. Trying to pull his blade free, Anthony had to put his foot on the man's chest and give a great heave that lifted the dead man off the deck.

Seeing the opportunity to kill an admiral, another Frenchman charged. Anthony looked up, still trying to dislodge his blade. He knew he was dead. He watched as spittle came from between the gaps of rotten teeth. Then, like a shadow, a figure whirled between Anthony and the charging Frenchman. The crash of steel upon steel was echoed by the screams of pain when Jepson ducked under the charging man's swing, parried his next blow, and then drove his cutlass through the man's stomach and out his back. No sooner was the first assailant dispatched with when another threw a belaying pin at Jepson. A grazing blow caused pain to shoot through his ear as it swelled and turned blood red. Jep turned to face his new assailant, swinging his blade in pain and anger. The blade found its mark and the rogue dropped instantly to the deck in a heap.

The man's death seemed to punctuate the British victory. As the survivors from the xebec swarmed over the

*Tourville's* side, the French quickly found themselves in a helpless position. Cheers went up as the French threw down their weapons. Looking about him, Anthony could see the enemy deck was strewn with lifeless forms...men who'd given their last. The lingering smell of gunpowder was mixed with the coppery stench of blood.

Both sides had hacked and slashed bravely at one another. It was Culzean and his men who had quickly changed the tide. Looking about, Anthony saw Jepson was lending a hand to help Bart from the blood soaked and stained deck. A sigh of relief escaped Anthony.

Watching, Anthony realized the man had saved his life...a second time. He had waded into the Frenchman with reckless abandon. His only thought was to save his admiral. *I can't let this go without reward*, Anthony thought. Yet in his heart he knew Jepson would say he was only doing his duty. Well not this time, Anthony promised himself.

## *Epilogue*

The French prisoners were disarmed and secured. The carpenter had reported to Captain Buck that *SeaHorse* had been holed and there were places that the planking was staved in but she was seaworthy.

"Well that's more than we can say for the *Tourville*. She was in a bad way. Her bilges were already filled as she was settling fast. We'll never get her to port," the carpenter declared.

"What a victory, My Lord!" Buck exclaimed. "Six against four, out gunned, out manned and still you were victorious. I can't wait to see the gazette."

"Aye, a victory but at what cost? The butcher bill is high already."

"Aye, I know," Buck answered sadly.

Culzean had fallen as the xebec's people had boarded the *Tourville*. On board *SeaHorse*, Lamb was one of those who had fallen.

"I wonder if it was best for him," Buck said. "He knew he'd never make captain. He should have joined the merchant service where he'd have eventually made master."

"Aye," Anthony said. "He did love the sea."

The French admiral had been killed almost at the onset. He'd never suspected Anthony would split his line. The French flag captain had refused to lower the admiral's flag, thinking it would discourage the others. However, when the guns fell silent, Devereux had fallen as well. In fact only one lieutenant aboard the French flagship had survived. All the other officers were dead.

Bart had been lucky. The bayonet had hit his belt buckle and glanced up, only nicking his abdomen. Only two stitches by the surgeon were all needed to close the wound.

"You could have lost a couple of inches and never missed it," Jepson had sworn.

"Well, somebody got the last word on Bart," Buck said.

"Aye," Anthony admitted. "But Bart's in his cups. I wouldn't bet against him if he was sober."

The wound must have been painful for Bart to have drunk so much, Buck knew.

"Gabe and Markham did well," Lieutenant Hazard volunteered.

With Markham's arrival, the frigate surrendered as did the corvette. A prize crew went aboard the first frigate but it was already sinking. Having been raked by each of the ships in Anthony's squadron, the frigate had been doomed from the onset.

"Her captain should never have turned," Markham said.

"I know," Gabe replied. "Yet to see a ship explode right in front of your bow might make you react without thinking."

"You're right, of course," Markham agreed. "But the move cost the fellow his ship and his life. Maybe it was God's will."

"I would like to think that," Gabe said, responding to Markham's remark. "But do you think the Almighty takes sides? We can't all be on the right side in his eyes."

"Aye," Markham said. "I try to not think about it."

***

By the time Anthony's squadron limped into Carlisle Bay, the word of their return quickly spread through Bridgetown. Lord Ragland was at the waterfront to meet the ships. Faith and Lady Deborah rode along in his carriage. The concern and tension on the women's faces were evident as they waited, each hoping and praying their man was safe. Lum had tried to be encouraging but he, above the others, knew first hand the dangers of a battle at sea. He also prayed.

As the ships tacked and were anchored, the sight of Anthony's flag flying let Deborah know he was at least alive. Lord Ragland was looking through a glass when he spoke to Faith, "I see Gabe, madam. He's standing on the quarterdeck. Here. Take a look."

However, tears of relief filled Faith's eyes so that she couldn't focus. "Oh, blast the thing," she hissed.

It took awhile to have the wounded off-loaded and taken to the hospital at Bridgetown. Finally, the admiral's barge was seen as Anthony was rowed ashore. He greeted his wife and assured Faith that Gabe was well and would be along directly. He then shook hands with Lord Ragland, whose knowing eyes were quick to realize this had been a costly battle. He also noted the two prizes as well as what was left of the xebec being brought in under a tow. She was little more than a hulk but the hull was still intact.

Gabe was soon ashore and Faith ran to him, smothering his face with kisses. As the group gathered together, Lord Ragland spoke to Anthony.

"Go home and be with your family. We'll talk on the morrow. In fact," he said speaking a bit louder, "we'll have a victory celebration at the governor's house."

***

The days following the battle with the French were easy. The victory celebration was attended by all of the island's social elite. The officers under Anthony's command were treated like conquering heroes. *As they should be*, Anthony thought, *but the jack tars deserved just as much praise.* He had mentioned this to Lord Ragland during one of their many conversations.

Lord Ragland surprisingly held a party for all the sailors in Anthony's squadron. Great bonfires were built and pigs were cooked over an open spit. Several of the local island dishes were available, plus varieties of dessert…and, of course, rum.

Anthony had each ship's captain address his crew and while he wanted everyone to have a good time, he wanted to make sure they knew anyone drunk or disorderly would answer to the admiral. The party went off without incident. Lord Ragland even had food carried to the watch aboard each ship.

Repairs on the ships were completed with the exception of the xebec, which was sailed under jury-mast to Antigua for the dockyard to decide upon repairs or salvage. Lord Anthony had written his dispatches and sent them to the admiralty on the mail packet with requests for personnel and ship replacements. He promoted Ambrose Taylor to captain, placed him on *Lizard* and gave Hayward Hallett the *Alert.* He had considered promoting him to captain and giving him the captured corvette. But in the end, he felt Hallett needed more time on a smaller ship.

He then called in his flag lieutenant, Everette Hazard. He had more than enough time as a lieutenant and he had commanded merchant ships before the war. So he seemed the right choice. He had mentioned it to Gabe, who felt he was the right choice also, one armed or not. Calling Hazard to his cabin, he offered the lieutenant a glass of hock and asked him did he still think of commanding a ship.

"Of course, My Lord. But with my lost wing I have accepted the fact that it would be improbable."

"Not if you want it," Anthony said.

Hazard sat there, almost in a daze, not sure he had heard right. "Are you offering me a command, sir?"

"No," Anthony smiled. "A promotion and a command. The corvette we captured...she's yours if you want it."

"But what about you, My Lord? Who will be your flag lieutenant?"

"My secretary can fill in until we find someone."

"Thank you, sir. I...I don't know what to say but thank you."

Smiling, Anthony shook Hazard's hand. "Before you get her ready for sea you may be cursing me," Anthony joked.

"Oh no, sir, never."

"Everette!"

"Yes, My Lord."

"The prize court has quickly ruled the ship a legitimate prize and I've agreed to buy her in for the Navy. However, this requires admiralty approval."

"I understand sir."

"Good. They usually approve my recommendations but if they don't, yours could be a temporary command."

"I understand, My Lord."

Later that day, Buck dined with Lord Anthony. "I think it's time we set up an examination board for lieutenant," Buck said while munching on a piece of cheese. "Do you have any recommendations, sir?"

"No," Anthony replied. "You as senior captain can convene the board and set up a date. You can have it ashore or aboard the flagship. Do you have a certain mid that needs to be made?"

"Aye," Buck said smiling. "I'm going to have two of *SeaHorse*'s mids take the exam."

"Have you asked the master if he would like to sit?" Anthony questioned Buck.

"Not directly," Buck replied. "But when it comes up in conversation, he usually doesn't voice a desire."

"It would be hard to be a master one day and a junior lieutenant the next," Anthony said, as much to himself as to Buck.

"Any word on the frigate?" Buck asked, meaning had it been evaluated by the prize court.

"Not yet, but I don't think it will be much longer," Anthony said. "Surely you're not thinking of the frigate for the master?"

"Oh no," Buck answered. "I was thinking of writing my prize agent." This got a chuckle from Anthony.

***

The following week, a mail packet pulled into Barbados. There were several documents from the admiralty that Anthony put to the side for his secretary LeMatt to sift through. Looking at the personal mail, he saw the usual from his sister, his banker, and solicitors. However, today there was one from Admiral Lord Howe. Anthony read the letter, set it down, and then re-read the letter.

"Bart! Where the devil is Bart?"

Silas ran out of the pantry. "Is there something wrong, My Lord?"

"No. Go get Bart and ask the flag captain to see me at his convenience."

"Aye," Silas said, and then scooted out the cabin. Bart made his way into the cabin, quickly followed by Captain Buck.

"Silas."

"Yes, My Lord."

"Pour us all a glass and pour one for yourself."

Excited, Silas hurried to get four glasses and a bottle of hock that had recently been opened.

When the glasses were filled, Anthony said, "A toast to Lord Howe."

Not understanding what the toast was about, the men toasted the admiral as requested. Once the glasses were placed on the cabin table, Anthony gave the letter to Buck.

"Damme, My Lord, just damme. Bart!"

"Sir."

"Your admiral has been promoted. He is now vice admiral."

For once, Bart didn't know what to say. Suddenly the marine sentry knocked at the door and announced, "Admiral's secretary, sir."

LeMatt rushed into the cabin with papers in his hand. "My Lord, it's wonderful news. You've been promoted." This brought a laugh from the group, leaving LeMatt thinking, *This is funny*.

***

News of the promotion quickly spread throughout the squadron. Lord Ragland held another party in honour of the promotion.

"It seems like all we are doing lately is partying," Deborah said. Still, no one was as happy as she for her husband's success. It was getting close to the time she and Faith would be going back to Antigua. She had gotten used to his presence most evenings but knew to stay longer would prove an imposition. Lord Ragland's sister would be coming soon, so the space would be needed. *Damn this war*, she thought. But she knew their time together would always be subject to the needs of the Navy, until…until.

She constantly prayed the Lord would protect him from harm. Having Macayla and Faith close to her helped with the loneliness. She had drawn very close to the girl. It was almost like a mother and daughter relationship.

***

Gabe was on board the flagship, talking to his brother. Dagan and Bart were having a wet while Gabe was telling

Anthony he had received a letter from Sir Victor. "His...ah...agents have informed him of a large French fleet, under the command of French Admiral Comte d'Estaing, sailing for America in April with twelve ships of the line and five frigates. It was not known exactly where he intends to land."

"This along with the politician's ineptitude will cost us the war," Anthony said angrily. "Mark my word, Gabe, it's the beginning of the end."

Gabe didn't respond as the sentry had announced the midshipman of the watch. *However*, Gabe thought, *it was a losing war from the start.*

"Ahem...well let's go topside."

"Sir."

"Didn't you hear the messenger?" Anthony asked, but continued before Gabe could answer. "Buck has requested my presence topside."

Once on deck, a smiling Buck handed Anthony his glass. "I thought you'd want to see this, sir."

Taking the glass Anthony looked, focused the glass, and then looked again. "Look at your old first lieutenant," Anthony said, handing the glass to Gabe.

"Lord," Gabe said. "He didn't take long."

Captain Hazard was returning to Carlisle Bay after being on patrol. Under his lee was a small ship with the British flag over a Colonies flag. A prize...his first patrol and he's already taken a prize, lucky sod.

***

The marine sentry knocked and announced, "The master, sir."

Jepson entered the cabin, "You sent for me, sir?"

"Aye," Anthony replied. "Have a seat. Would you care for a glass?" Then without waiting, he called for Silas to bring two glasses of Sangria. "Something cool," Anthony said by way of explaining his choice.

When Silas had brought the glasses and left, Anthony said, "George, you are one of the best seamen I know. You are a natural leader."

Somewhat embarrassed, Jepson tried to deny it but Anthony raised his hand to quiet any denials.

"It's rare for a man who started on the lower deck to be commissioned," he said. "However, those that have are usually successful. Some have even made admiral. I can understand your reluctance to sit for the lieutenant's exam with a bunch of snot-nosed midshipmen. I don't blame you. I wouldn't want to think of you as a thirty-six-year-old junior lieutenant. That's not what I'm offering. What I'm offering is a commission and a command. Yonder sits as fine a brig as you've seen. She was built before the war by the Americans, and then converted to be used as a privateer. Much as Gabe's first command, she's sleek, fast, and carries fourteen six pounders and two four pounders in the forecastle. She's even pierced for sweeps. That's what I'm offering. I owe you that and so much more. What say you?"

Jepson sat there deep in thought. Anthony watched as he blinked his cold blue eyes and ran his hand through his salt and pepper hair. After a moment, Jepson spoke in his usual quiet manner, "I'll take her, sir."

# *Appendix*
# *Historical Notes*

In June, 1777, British Lieutenant General Burgoyne left Quebec with over ten thousand men, followed by some sixteen hundred regular and provincial troops and Indians. After a victory at Fort Ticonderoga (American Brigadier Arthur St. Clair withdrew in the face of overwhelming odds) Burgoyne pushed south, all the while being harried and hampered by ambushes, blocked roads and rebuilding bridges so that the Army became much fatigued and went at least two days (July 9 and 10) without provisions. With supplies still low, the British Army gave a general order warning troops to "be cautious of expending their ammunition in case of action." They were to avoid firing on a retreating enemy. On September 13 and 14, Burgoyne's army crossed the Hudson River near Saratoga. On September 19, American Major General Benedict Arnold smashed into Burgoyne's troop columns with three thousand men. The battle lasted till dark with the British suffering more than six hundred killed and the Americans half that. British Lieutenant Digby wrote that "the clash of cannon and musketry never ceased till darkness...when they [the Americans] retired to their camp leaving us masters of the field but it was a dear bought victory."

Burgoyne decided to "dig in" with his army after he received word from British Lieutenant General Clinton in New York promising he'd push up the Hudson River with three thousand troops. After seizing several forts, Clinton was finally able to send two thousand men and supplies to Burgoyne. However, the Americans had all but cut off British communications. On October 7, Burgoyne decided to attack the American positions at Bemis Heights but was repulsed. It was then discovered Clinton's detachment had been turned away. On October 8, Burgoyne decided to fall back to his former defensive position, only to discover that his retreat had been cut off by American General Gates.

Outnumbered two to one and out of supplies, Burgoyne surrendered six thousand men to the Americans on October 17, 1777. The surrender shattered British prestige the world over. The tidings reached Europe on December 2, 1777, and on December 16, the French foreign minister informed the commissioners of Congress that the King was ready to recognize the independence of the United States, and to make with them a commercial treaty and contingent defensive alliance.

The treaty between the United States and France was signed on February 6, 1778. In April 1778, Comte d'Estaing sailed with a fleet of superior warships to join the Americans. In September 1778, the French turned their attention to the West Indies.

## BARBADOS

The West Indies was very important during the American War for Independence. The main two islands were Antigua and Barbados. Barbados was the most windward of the West Indies islands and was felt by the Navy to give it a tactical advantage. A small naval hospital was built there and it was used as a stores base. When an enemy ship was captured, "the prize" could be adjudicated by the Vice Admiralty Court located at Bridgetown. Barbados gained its wealth during the seventeenth and eighteenth centuries from its sugarcane plantations and the export of rum and molasses. The fields were worked by African slaves until slavery was abolished in the British Empire in 1834.

Bridgetown is located at the southwestern end of the island. It was named for a small bridge that crossed over a stream. This is where all government offices are located. Carlisle Bay is where most ships anchored with boats ferrying people and supplies to the wharfs.

## CARRONADES

While doing research for this book, I read *The Arming and Fitting of English Ships of War 1600-1815* by Brian Lavery. In real life, the naval board proposed these "smashers" be fitted out in ships in July 1779. Therefore, my installment of the smasher was almost a year prior. Lavery discussed the carronade only enough to create a desire within me to know more—thanks for the Internet. The discussion between Captain Ford and the officers under Lord Anthony's command is as accurate an account as I could give of the carronades.

# *Age of Sail Glossary*

**aft:** toward the stern (rear) of the ship.
**ahead:** in a forward direction.
**aloft:** above the deck of the ship.
**barque** (bark): a three-masted vessel with the foremast and mainmast square-rigged and the mizzenmast fore-and-aft rigged.
**belay:** to make a rope fast to a belaying pin, cleat, or other such device. Also used as a general command to stop or cancel; e.g., "Belay that last order!"
**belaying pin:** a wooden pin, later made of metal, generally about twenty inches in length to which lines were made fast, or "belayed." They were arranged in pin rails along the inside of the bulwark and in fife rails around the masts.
**binnacle:** a large wooden box, just forward of the helm, housing the compass, half-hourglass for timing the watches, and candles to light the compass at night.
**boatswain's chair:** a wooden seat with a rope sling attached. Used for hoisting men aloft or over the side for work.
**bosun:** also boatswain, a crew member responsible for keeping the hull, rigging and sails in repair.
**bow chaser:** a cannon situated near the bow to fire as directly forward as possible.
**bowsprit:** a large piece of timber that stands out from the bow of a ship.
**breeching:** rope used to secure a cannon to the side of a ship and prevent it from recoiling too far.
**brig:** a two-masted vessel, square rigged on both masts.
**bulwarks:** the sides of a ship above the upper deck.
**bumboat:** privately owned boat used to carry out to anchored vessels vegetables, liquor, and other items for sale.
**burgoo:** mixture of coarse oatmeal and water: porridge.

**cable**: (a) a thick rope, (b) a measure of distance-1/10 of a sea mile, 100 fathoms (200 yards approximately).
**canister:** musket ball size iron shot encased in a cylindrical metal cast. When fired from a cannon, the case breaks apart, releasing the enclosed shot, not unlike firing buckshot from a shotgun shell.
**cat-o'-nine tails:** a whip made from knotted ropes, used to punish crewmen—what was meant by being "flogged."
**chase:** a ship being pursued.
**coxswain (cox'n):** pronounced cox-un—means the person in charge of the captain's personal boat.
**cutter:** a sailboat with one mast, a mainsail and two headsails.
**dogwatch:** the watches from four to six, and from six to eight, in the evening.
**fathom:** unit of measurement equal to six feet.
**flotsam:** debris floating on the water surface.
**forecastle:** pronounced fo'c'sle. The forward part of the upper deck, forward of the foremast, in some vessels raised above the upper deck. Also, the space enclosed by this deck.
**founder:** used to describe a ship that is having difficulty remaining afloat.
**frigate:** a fast three-masted fully rigged ship carrying anywhere from twenty to forty-eight guns.
**full and by:** a nautical term meaning "proceed under full sail."
**furl:** to lower a sail.
**futtock shrouds**: short, heavy pieces of standing rigging connected on one end to the topmast shrouds at the outer edge of the top and on the other to the lower shrouds, designed to bear the pressure on the topmast shrouds. Often used by sailors to go aloft.
**gaff:** a spar or pole extending diagonally upward from the after side of a mast and supporting a fore-and-aft sail.
**galley:** the kitchen area of a ship.

**glass**: shipboard name for the barometer, a sand-glass used for measuring time, or a telescope.

**grapeshot:** a cluster of round, iron shot, generally nine in all, and wrapped in canvas. Upon firing, the grapeshot would spread out for a shotgun effect. Used against men and light hulls.

**grating:** hatch cover composed of perpendicular, interlocking wood pieces, much like a heavy wood screen. It allowed light and air below while still providing cover for the hatch. Gratings were covered with tarpaulins in rough or wet weather.

**grog:** British naval seaman received a portion of liquor every day. In 1740, Admiral Edward Vernon ordered the rum to be diluted with water. Vernon's nickname was Old Grogram, and the beverage was given the name grog in their disdain for Vernon.

**gunwale:** pronounced gun-el. The upper edge of a ship's side.

**halyard:** a line used to hoist a sail or spar. The tightness of the halyard can affect sail shape.

**handsomely:** slowly, gradually.

**hardtack:** ship's biscuit.

**haul:** pulling on a line.

**hawse**: the bows of a ship where the hawse-holes are cut for the anchor cables to pass through. The space between the stem of a vessel at anchor and the anchors or a little beyond.

**heave to:** arranging the sails in such a manner as to stop the forward motion of the ship.

**heel:** the tilt of a ship/boat to one side; a ship normally heels in the wind.

**helm:** the wheel of a ship or the tiller of a boat.

**holystone:** a block of sandstone used to scour the wooden decks of a ship.

**idler:** the name of those members of a ship's crew that did not stand night watch because of their work, such as a cook or carpenters.

**jetty:** a manmade structure projecting from the shore.
**jib:** a triangular sail attached to the headstay.
**John Company:** nickname for the Honourable East India Company.
**jolly boat:** a small workboat.
**jonathan:** British nickname for an American.
**keel:** a flat surface (fin) built into the bottom of the ship to reduce the leeway caused by the wind pushing against the side of the ship.
**ketch:** a sailboat with two masts. The shorter mizzenmast is aft of the main, but forward of the rudder post.
**knot:** one knot equals one nautical mile per hour. This rate is equivalent to approximately 1.15 statute miles per hour.
**larboard:** the left or port side of a ship when facing the bow.
**lee:** the direction toward which the wind is blowing. The direction sheltered from the wind.
**leeward:** pronounced loo-ard—means downwind.
**Letter of Marque:** a commission issued by the government authorizing seizure of enemy property.
**luff:** the order to the steersman to put the helm towards the lee side of the ship, in order to sail nearer to the wind.
**mainmast:** the tallest (possibly only) mast on a ship.
**mast:** any vertical pole on the ship that sails are attached to.
**mizzenmast:** a smaller aft mast.
**moor:** to attach a ship to a mooring, dock, post, anchor.
**nautical mile:** one minute of latitude, approximately 6076 feet—about 1/8 longer than the statute mile of 5280 feet.
**pitch:** (1) a fore and aft rocking motion of a boat. (2) a material used to seal cracks in wooden planks.
**privateer:** a captain with a Letter of Marque, which allows a captain to plunder any ship of a given enemy nation. A privateer was *supposed* to be above being tried for piracy.
**prize:** an enemy vessel captured at sea by a warship or privateer. Technically these ships belonged to the crown, but after review by the Admiralty court and condemnation, they were sold and the prize money shared.

**powder monkey:** young boy (usually) who carried cartridges of gunpowder from the filling room up to the guns during battle.

**quadrant:** instrument used to take the altitude of the sun or other celestial bodies in order to determine the latitude of a place. Forerunner to the modern sextant.

**quarterdeck:** a term applied to the afterpart of the upper deck. The area is generally reserved for officers.

**quarter gallery:** a small, enclosed balcony with windows located on either side of the great cabin aft and projecting out slightly from the side of the ship. Traditionally contained the head, or toilet, for use by those occupying the great cabin.

**rake:** a measurement of the top of the mast's tilt toward the bow or stern.

**rate:** Ships were rated from first to sixth rates based on their size and armament:

First rate: line of battle 100 or more guns on 3 gun decks
Second rate: line of battle 90 to 98 guns on 3 gun decks
Third rate: line of battle 80, 74 or 64 guns on 2 gun decks
Fourth rate: below the line 50 guns on 1 or 2 gun decks
Fifth rate: frigates 32 to 44 guns on 1 gun deck
Sixth rate: frigates 20 to 28 guns on 1 gun deck

**ratline:** pronounced rat-lin. Small lines tied between the shrouds, horizontal to the deck, forming a sort of rope ladder on which the men can climb aloft.

**reef:** to reduce the area of sail. This helps prevent too much sail from being in use when the wind gets stronger (a storm or gale).

**roll:** a side-to-side motion of the ship, usually caused by waves.

**schooner:** a North American (colonial) vessel with two masts the same size.

**scuppers:** Drain holes on deck, in the toe rail, or in bulwarks that allows water to run into the sea..

**scuttle:** any small, generally covered hatchway through a ship's deck.
**sextant:** a navigational instrument used to determine the vertical position of an object such as the sun, moon or stars.
**ship's bell:** the progress of the watch was signaled by the ship's bells:

| | | | |
|---|---|---|---|
| 1 bell | ½ hour | 5 bells | 2 ½ hours |
| 2 bells | 1 hour | 6 bells | 3 hours |
| 3 bells | 1 ½ hours | 7 bells | 3 ½ hours |
| 4 bells | 2 hours | 8 bells | 4 hours |

**ship's day:** the ship's day at sea began at noon; the twenty-four day is divided into watches measured by a four-hour sandglass.

12:00 p.m. to 4:00 p.m. - Afternoon watch

4:00 p.m. to 8:00 p.m. – Dog watch is broken into 2 separate sections called the first and last dog watch. This allows men on watch to eat their evening meal.

8:00 p.m. to 12:00 a.m. – First watch

12:00 a.m. to 4:00 a.m. – Middle watch

4:00 a.m. to 8:00 a.m. – Morning watch

8:00 a.m. to 12:00 p.m. – Forenoon watch

**shoal:** shallow.
**shrouds:** heavy ropes leading from a masthead aft and down to support the mast when the wind is from abeam or farther aft.
**skiff:** a small boat.
**skylark:** to frolic or play, especially up in the rigging.
**skylight**: a glazed window frame, usually in pairs set at an angle in the deck to give light and ventilation to the compartment below.
**slew**: to turn around on its own axis; to swing around.
**spar:** any lumber/pole used in rigging sails on a ship.
**starboard:** the right side of a ship or boat when facing the bow.
**stern:** the aft part of a boat or ship.

**stern chasers:** cannons directed aft to fire on a pursuing vessel.
**tack:** to turn a ship about from one tack to another, by bringing her head to the wind.
**taffrail:** the upper part of the ship's stern, usually an ornament with carved work or bolding.
**thwart:** seat or bench in a boat on which the rowers sit.
**topgallant:** the mast above the topmast, also sometimes the yard and sail set on it.
**transom:** the stern cross-section/panel forming the after end of a ship's hull.
**veer:** a shifting of the wind direction.
**waister:** landsman or unskilled seaman who worked in the waist of the ship.
**wear:** to turn the vessel from one tack to another by turning the stern through the wind.
**weigh:** to raise, as in to weigh anchor.
**windward:** the side or direction from which the wind is blowing.
**yard:** a spar attached to the mast and used to hoist sails.
**yardarm:** the end of a yard.
**yawl:** a two-masted sailboat/fishing boat with the shorter mizzenmast placed aft of the rudder post. Similar to a ketch.
**zephyr:** a gentle breeze. The west wind.

LaVergne, TN USA
27 May 2010
184219LV00001B/8/P